What the
horses heard

REBECCA GETHIN

INDEPENDENT INNOVATIVE INTERNATIONAL

Published by Cinnamon Press, Meirion House, Tanygrisiau, Blaenau Ffestiniog, Gwynedd LL41 3SU
www.cinnamonpress.com

Acknowledgements

The initial inspiration for this book came from Richard Jefferies (1848-1887), whose vision of a changing world led me to this story. Grateful thanks to Daphne Williamson for her meticulous editing; to the staff at the Imperial War Museum, the Friends' House Library, the Army Medical Museum; to my friends in RABS for all their good advice in the first draft; to Ros Knight; to Elly Nobbs; and to my husband, Chris, who has supported me throughout, as always. I am also indebted to the late Professor Richard Holmes for his initial encouragement. Heartfelt thanks to Jan Jones for permitting me to use the beautiful painting on the cover by her partner, Anthony Amos. And last, but by no means least, to Jan Fortune who believed in this book from the start.

'...the silence of the fields. If a breeze rustled the boughs, if a greenfinch called, if the cart-mare in the meadow shook herself, making the earth and air tremble by her with the convulsion of her mighty muscles, these were not sounds, they were the silence itself.'

extract from *Meadow Thoughts*, 1884,
Richard Jefferies

PART ONE

1

The sound of boots tramping along the passage grew louder. The flap of the peephole shot open and a thin beam of gaslight pierced the gloom. An eye as bright as anthracite regarded him for a second. The flap snapped shut, the boot steps clomped away.

He was standing in nothing but his underpants. He swallowed repeatedly, with his tongue tense against his dry palate, his gullet in spasm, unable to stop himself gagging on the sickening stench. His nostrils burned with it. After a few minutes his throat relaxed a little. Some handholds of sound came to him. He deciphered a hacking cough, a moan, odd yells as if from a mad house. He made out other noises, but divining their meanings was like having to learn a new language in a hurry – was that the cocking of a mainspring or a key clicking in a lock, a cough or a cell door shutting, gunfire or boots running down a staircase?

A dimness punctured by a slanting ray of light from a small, high window. A bare plank and one blanket. No chair or table, no pen, paper, book. Not even any water. As his eyes adapted to the gloom he saw the source of his nausea: a bucket, full of putrid liquid, faeces slimed on the rim. The floor was not something he'd choose to stand on with bare feet. They had taken away his clothes but had not yet given him the prison uniform he had been expecting. He wrapped the blanket round him to keep out the penetrating damp-cold, and sat on the plank, trembling at the thought of the night. When the peephole rattled again a voice barked, 'No bed, no blanket till lights-out'.

What lights? Minutes ticked by. Maybe hours. He didn't know. He thought he was forgotten, that he was

7

being left to die there without food or water. He clasped his arms, held his knees to try and keep warm. He sneezed over and over again. Hard to think with that suffocating smell. Some time later, the hatchway snapped open and a hunk of old bread and a cup of water were pushed through.

The cold became stupefying. Would he fall asleep if he leaned against the wall? The door was flung wide: a warder strode in and threw a uniform on the planks. A soldier's uniform. He longed to put it on, or even to get underneath it. But he knew that if he succumbed he would be transformed into the soldier he was refusing to be. So he turned his back on it and left it lying.

He whistled birds' songs in the way that he and his brother used to: blackbird's morning clarion, robin and thrush. He knew them by heart. He only had to imagine the bird, and the song was with him. He remembered Leo finding a little pile of faeces that had been deposited in a scuffed-out hole in the ground. Badger's, most likely. It had caught his eye because it glinted like sapphires in the sun. They knelt down and dissected the heap with a stick and found it chockfull of bright blue beetle wing casings, their tiny indigestible antlers, legs and mandibles. Leo discovered that when they put their ears close to it they could hear insects boring their way into and through the glistening shit.

Outside, someone banged on the cell door and shouted, 'Shut your mouth, Five-six-two.'

After three more nights he had completed Punishment No.1 – the penalty for refusing to obey an order. He was handed his prison uniform and was allowed to clean out his cell. While he was slopping out, a gob of spit landed on his cheek and his bucket was shoved so the contents spilt down his trouser leg. In the latrine two men pushed him so that he stepped into foul-smelling sewage.

The rule was silence, not that he had anyone to talk with. Stifling the urge to ask questions meant that he was always in the wrong. The strain of not-speaking stung his throat, and the questions he couldn't ask bored their way into his mind, repeating themselves as if they held him in thrall.

On another day in the wash-house two stark naked men dodged in front of him as if he was standing in their way and, when he stepped aside, one lunged towards him and pulled up his arms behind him. 'Pro-German bastard, you!' hissed the other, sinking a fist deep into his belly. His breath belched out of him and pain flashed through his ribs. As he fell forward his arms were yanked higher and he heard his shoulder bones crunch.

He woke some time later on the plank in his cell. His chest hurt with every intake of breath and the thin daylight hurt his eyes. His head blasted with pain. Footsteps walked past the door, came back again. The wooden flap over the grille in the door rattled and opened. 'You awake, Five-six-two?'

'Yes.'

'Can you get up?'

'I don't know.' He'd rather not try. Couldn't he carry on lying still?

'Get up, Private. Walk about a bit. Show me you can walk.'

His feet stretched toward the ground and a pain leaped in his stomach. He pulled himself into a sitting position and gasped, 'I'm not a Private.' Both his shoulders seemed to be coming away from his body. His spine was all crooked and the pain of the effort made his head swim.

'Stand up, Five-six-two. Get a move on.'

He stood up, trembling all over. The key jangled in the lock and the door opened. Air rushed in as a warder stood blocking the doorway – his buttons glinting, his eyes hidden beneath his cap, his voice sounding like a ratchet.

'That'll teach you something. You'd do better to change tack than think you can slouch off here. This is what it's like.'

'If you say so.'

'I'm telling you so. I'd give you a kicking in the ribs myself if I could.'

'My mind won't change.'

'Maybe it'll be changed for you.'

'They'll have to kill me first.'

'Big words,' the door slammed shut, the key turned. Footsteps thudded away down the stone passage.

Later that night he was woken by tapping. He tried to stay asleep but the metallic clanking wouldn't stop. A regular tap-tap as if someone was hitting a piece of pipe with a nail or a spoon. He thought the water pipes must be frozen and were becoming blocked. The noise wouldn't leave him alone. He pulled down his blanket and tried to look at the wall. The darkness was like being shut in a drawer. Listening to the tapping he realised another prisoner was deliberately making the noise. A shout almost came from his lips. The tapping was the rhythm of the first bars of Beethoven's Fifth Symphony. Just hearing it made him dizzy with gratitude. He climbed gingerly out of the bed and fumbled around for his wooden spoon. When his fingers closed on it, he groped his way to the end of the bed and felt up and down the wall for the pipe. He hit the pipes three times and waited. Three taps came back. He beat out a faster rhythm and when the same rhythm came back he muttered, 'Oh, Hell Fire.' He felt like a thirsty man given a sip to drink. He started beating out *Pack up your troubles in your old kit bag*, smiling in the darkness as he tapped. It was a song that applied to the conchies as much as to the soldiers out there, he reckoned.

Over time, he noticed that other prisoners on long sentences almost forgot their own language, could scarcely remember even their name, becoming a cog in the prison's engine house that was grinding people to pulp. If he tried to address one of these men, they looked away as if he were not there. It did not take very long, he found, for speaking to become almost a physical pain in the jaw. The space inside the mouth was like another cell to be kept locked. Every so often, under his blanket he would murmur, 'Orion, Orion … Orion,' just to hear the sound of his own name.

He learned to notice little signals, as with understanding horses. Leo had taught him well when they were young. Even where there was no speech, Leo had known how communication passed between people.

At first, he kept his eyes averted, not wishing to precipitate another assault. It was surprising how much he could see when he wasn't focussing directly. He began to read the expressions of shoulders, the questions in hand gestures, the affirmation of a glance, the vowels and consonants of gait. He began to work out who was a conscientious objector and who a criminal. And at night the rhythms of life-giving communication were tapped from cell to cell like murmurs of insurrection.

During the night his brother seemed to draw close. As he drifted towards sleep his brother materialised: he could feel his warmth beside him. He said, 'I thought you were dead,' and Leo answered, 'I came to see how you're getting on.' The voice would move around the cell and he would struggle to rise and touch his brother, take hold of his arm, but his body would not be prised from lying prone on the plank. When he woke, he found himself standing alone in the cell, having to remind himself that Leo could not have been there, nor was he anywhere.

At other times, his sister, Cass, seemed to be speaking to him: he couldn't catch what she said, but he saw her curling hair catch the light, her eyes searching his, her habit of telling him exactly what she thought. And he saw how angry she was and guessed what it was she was waiting to say.

2

There was a rattling in her ear… it accelerated and grew louder… with a start, it came back to her – the rat-a-tat of guns somewhere not far away – mortar fire. Cass did not want to open her eyes… the coloured Verey Lights in the dark behind her closed lids flared – red, green, yellow, red again. She crept deeper into the bedding. Her feet were rigid with cramp and the cold pain spread up through her legs and into her hips. Should she waggle her feet or keep still? Might she be about to wet herself?

She witnessed such scenes every night: corpses slumped on the road, hooves twisted round at impossible angles, bloated bellies decomposing where the horses had fallen in the traces… was it blood staining the liquid mud on the road? She curled herself into a ball and felt the nails of one hand dig deep into the back of the other and it made her shout out. Stupid! When she heard it she bit her lip… were there other people about? Was that tapping sound footsteps?

A rhythmic thumping in her ears… breathing-in made something sharp catch in her throat. When the booming sound faded she peeped out and saw white clouds through the barred window, raindrops sliding down the glass. A thin curtain wafted. She could hear voices in the blankets, an incessant babble.

A lady with a white cap tied in a ribbon under her chin pulled back the blanket and was unlocking her hands. There was a red cross printed across her bleached pinny. But the more she hauled, the tighter grew the lock of Cass's hands. 'You need to stop this. Do you hear me? Stop this noise now. No one can sleep. It's time for your tablets. Oh, you're scratching yourself. And, drat you, you

silly bitch, look at the blood on my nice clean sheets.'
The sinews in the woman's neck started to pulsate.

Cass grasped the woman's hard hand and the
sensation of someone else's warmth flooded through her.
She felt the tough skin of her palm, smelt the hand
cream she'd rubbed into her hands. The smell of it made
her feel so tender she started to weep. She seemed to
have no skin between herself and the outside world. No
protection.

'There now, you must've been having a bad dream
again. Swallow this and I'll call Doctor to take another
look at you.'

Her tongue had swollen and although her mouth
opened she could not think what she wanted to say… no,
not the doctor, but how to stop him? His eyes were too
kind and he kept repeating that he understood what she
meant to say. She let out a whimper. How pathetic! Her
head shook from side to side. Her hands began to claw at
themselves again but the nurse now held them apart in a
vice-like grip.

Cass drifted off. Leo's face appeared briefly out of the
jumble behind her eyelids, his fading expression
beseeching her. Orion, her other brother, was there
sometimes, too, trying his damnedest to translate what
Leo couldn't articulate. And she could clearly hear the
voices of the men who had sunk under the mud.

Her sleep sprang open. She didn't recognise anything
around her… the ceiling was too far away and seemed a
strange colour. It had patches of light and dark like damp
or mould. The colour of the air was unfamiliar. She heard
little whining sounds. In her mouth was a smouldering
taste.

The rest of her body would not wake up. Her arms
and legs felt so heavy she wanted to sleep again. She
thought she must be awake but why would her limbs not

move when she asked them? Would she ever be able to move at will again? Was she trapped? Or was she perhaps dreaming about an old dream? But she couldn't remember any dreams and usually they felt so real she was astonished to wake out of them and find they hadn't happened. Somewhere in her dreams her missing brothers seemed to be waiting for her: in the distance or round a corner they would be talking and larking with one another but she couldn't reach them. Without them, she did not feel at home in her own sleep.

And this place wasn't home. Was she back in France? She couldn't remember. How did she get here? Perhaps it would all come back to her in a minute.

A voice jabbed her in the ribs, 'Cassandra, time to wake up!' *Cassandra?* What a cheek – she had always hated being called Cassandra. No one ever called her by that name. Far too familiar. Her name was Miss Forrester. She opened her mouth to say as much but her tongue was too fat to move. She looked round for the speaker. The woman standing beside her bed had eyes the colour of bluebells and looked as if they could see right through you. She wore a long white pinny and one of those tall white caps was fastened on her head.

So, I'm in a hospital, she thought. Has it something to do with my limbs? Have I been in an accident and have lost them and am only imagining they are still attached to me? She knew that missing limbs could hurt as much as if they were injured.

A moan emerged from her throat, and her legs tried to move sideways, but the sheet was tightly bound and only her toes wriggled. But she could feel the sheet: it wasn't her legs that were missing. Drawing her arms into her sides, she felt the rough fabric of the nightie she was wearing. It wasn't her own.

'No more slug-a-bed,' said Nurse Bluebell, 'time to get up, have breakfast, then Exercise.' When she spoke, the letter S was emphasised as if she said it more often than other people. It was irritating like a wasp buzzing round your head, trying to sting you.

In the dining room there was a long table crowded with disgusting women in ugly clothes. They didn't appear to have combed their hair. The table was crowded and there were no spare chairs. They all seemed very intent on their food. But one of them lifted her head and smiled and moved over on her chair as if to let Cass share half of it.

When she perched herself beside her, the woman's face stayed creased into a smiling shape and when Cass asked 'Where is this place?' the woman shook her head and said she didn't know. 'How long have you been here?' and her neighbour shook her head again and smiled into her tea cup as if looking for an answer in the brown liquid.

Cass realised she would have to fetch herself some breakfast. She poured out some insipid tea into a greenish teacup with a crack in the rim, and took the last slice of burnt toast and some dried-looking bacon. When she turned round she couldn't remember where she was meant to be sitting. The chair she thought she was using seemed to have been taken. There wasn't any space left at the table now and no one noticed her plight. If she left her food while she went in search of a chair she guessed someone would eat what was on her plate. She felt helpless standing there with food in her hand and nowhere to sit. Going to the doorway, she looked along the passage, and seeing a chair there she plonked herself down on it.

The bacon broke into pieces in her mouth. The tea was merely not-cold. Another nurse with a tall white cap walked toward her and Cass was about to tell her about the toast being burnt and the state of the bacon and the tea but the nurse wouldn't let her speak and said, 'You can't sit there, my girl. You must join the others. Mix in, you know. You're not to hide yourself away like this. You know very well it's not permitted.'

Cass felt tears well under her eyelids. Stupid tears. 'When can I go home?'

'You can't go home, not today or tomorrow. Maybe next week, I expect. It's up to Doctor.'

They always said Next Week but it never arrived. Whatever was due to happen Next Week was never going to happen.

'Now get back in the dining room and don't try this hiding-away malarkey tomorrow or you'll have to be punished again. Lady Muck!'

'Punished? But… but there was no space.'

'Nonsense. You can always push along.'

'There was nowhere to sit.'

'The chairs are to be shared.'

'But the people there are all funny in the head, aren't they?'

'We don't talk about people like that. I've told you before.'

'But why am I here? Why am I here?'

'How many times have I told you? You need rest. After your breakdown you need peace and quiet; you need to be looked after. We are looking after you. Mark my words.'

If I could only make a telephone call home Sarah would arrange for someone to fetch me home, Cass thought. I'm sure she would. And what about Father and Mama? How are they managing without me? But they must have agreed for me to be sent here for the rest. I don't know where I might find a telephone to ask Father why I am here.

'Could you possibly show me to a telephone? I've only just arrived, you see, and I don't know where things are.'

'There isn't a telephone. I keep telling you that. You

can only make telephone calls if they move you downstairs.'

'What's downstairs? Where is it? Can't I go there now?'

'Not till Doctor says so, as I said yesterday. Now, time to join your friends.'

'No, that can't be true – I don't know any of these people.'

'Yes, you do. They're your friends in the Day Room and with you all the time,' said Nurse Keep-on-telling-you.

'I don't know their names. I haven't been introduced.'

'We keep telling you, sweetie. And you keep forgetting.'

'I'm very sorry but I've never met any of them before. I can't have. I've only just arrived. They are not friends.'

'You've been here for months, my dear. You've been having Shocks and it makes you forget things. That and the paraldehyde.'

'Shocks! I have been having shocks – you're telling me. Every day is a shock.'

'Quite. That's why you have to have them.'

She did not recall the journey here. Nor her arrival. She remembered other things like a place she thought of as home, what she had done in the War. Now she wondered if she was only imagining things that had happened. Perhaps they were right. She was telling fibs, making up stories to get attention.

The word *home* squeezed her heart. She had to take deep breaths. She must work out how she might get to the island – the island of their childhood, in the middle of the river where she had first swum in the peat brown water. Once she was there, no one would find her, except for her brothers. But how to find her way there, that was the question that itched in every pore of her skin.

3

Leo was sitting in the dog cart next to his father as it trundled towards their home. His brother was behind him – Orion's back, touching his own, felt like an extension of himself. Cass sat beside Orion. With every jolt their bodies bumped against each other.

Gazing beyond the pony's swaying rump, Leo scanned the tall reeds in the bog beside the track, and the hillside where rocks glistened in the soft rain. Sometimes the rocks reminded him of bent figures picking over the ground and other times they were hunched like grazing sheep.

This spot was how he imagined the Valley of Death to be – with the faint smell of decay in the air, the scratching of thorn trees and the rattling of dry spikes of gorse. His breath came a little faster. Inside his laced-up boots he felt a twinge in his toes, which grew into a shudder that crept up through the sinews in his legs and over his knees and into his torso. Gripping the wooden seat, he shuffled a little closer to the bulk of the body sitting next to him. On looking down he was comforted by his father's polished boots planted firmly on the floor of the cart.

Down the steep slope the brake applied to the wheels made a whirring sound, and the seat vibrated through his spine. The pony's ears scissored, on the alert. Drops of rain plopped more heavily on his cap, spattered the pony's slicked rump like buckshot; its skin quivered as the silver lines of rain broke upon it, trickling in small rivulets off its haunches.

Just then, Orion leaned out and pointed towards the spot where some traveller had been lured into the depths

of the quaking ground by the winking light of a Will o'
the Wisp as it retreated through the reeds. In Leo's eyes,
the ghostly glimmer came and went, always a little bit
further away as the traveller stepped from tussock to
tussock until, surrounded by water, he could not find his
way back to firm ground. Then, Cass began to recount a
story she'd been told by Dickon, the village farrier, of
how a fire in the thatch had once destroyed one of the
buildings, now a riddle of stones on the ground. Leo
imagined the crackle of flames and the smell of smoke,
the family's terror in the dark… he cried out, burying his
face in his hands.

'That's enough, you two,' growled their father.

'Look back there,' Orion said, 'by the willow tree: isn't
that a figure sinking into the marsh?' In the wind that
tousled the pony's mane Leo did indeed catch the sound
of someone yelling for help. He was sure he'd heard the
neighing of a horse together with the calls of a man
floundering in the sucking bog. He'd been warned that
struggling makes a man sink further and faster into the
mire. He tugged at his father's sleeve.

The track forded a fast-running stream that cut its way
through the spongey bog. The running water sounded
like ponies' shoeless hooves patting on a road. The dog
cart bumped through the ford and drew to a halt.

'It's nothing, son. Nothing. Just an old story.'

'But still, if it's an old story it did happen. That man
was stuck out there in the bog.'

'Maybe, but not now, old chap. It's just a local legend.'

'I'm awfully sorry for the man – and his horse. No
one heard them, no one helped, did they?'

Their father snapped, 'You two, you'll learn to stop
larking about with your brother.' He jerked his thumb.
'Go on, you can walk from here. A man doesn't play
tricks on people. And you, Cass, can walk, too. There's
nothing to laugh about.'

'But... I... I... didn't mean...' Leo began and faltered.

'The walk will do them good. They're over-excited. Let them cool off.'

The boy twisted round and called back to his brother and sister, 'I'm sorry. I didn't want you to get into...'

'No need for you to be sorry about anything,' said his father.

In that place – almost treeless apart from the odd thorn – Orion and Cass found material to tease Leo into believing anything. Curlew and lapwing often called from the reeds, sounding like the cries of lost children. Sometimes, close to the water's edge, snipe zipped off from under a horse's feet, startling it. In winter the valley was colder and stayed whiter than anywhere else. A ruined building near the ford lay collapsed in the bowl of the surrounding hills and frost lingered inside. This landscape was peppered with stories: they knew them because they were part of the place.

His father breathed out heavily and said, 'They don't hear what you hear, old chap.'

As the cart turned between two gateposts, the pony broke into a trot. Leo always supposed it could not get away from this place quickly enough. But maybe the pony just felt excited to be almost home or because, after the stony track, the turf felt springy under hoof. The cart lurched and tilted on the uneven ground as the pony gathered speed. His father's body swayed against him.

'Does a horse hear what I'm thinking?' he asked, studying the pony's swivelling ears.

'What makes you ask that?' said his father.

'The ears... the way they look at me... it's like they know...'

'I can't answer that, son. You understand more about that kind of thing.'

After a while, the track climbed uphill and their pace

21

slowed again. 'Here,' said his father, handing his son the reins, 'you take over.' Leo grasped them, running his thumbs over their slippery wetness, feeling their thickened edges. The pony's ears flicked as it sensed the change-over down the length of the leather reins and into its mouth. His father folded his arms. The two did not speak: one because he preferred not to, and the other because he knew this.

4

Cass would have preferred being a brother. As she walked home with Orion she wished once again she had been born one or other of them and was not a sister. She did what she could to make herself more like them. She stepped into their mannerisms, practised their tones of voice, slipped her arms into their gestures.

At hay-making time she pitched hay on to the wagon as hard as they did and if they slid down the stack she did the same, even though the drop below made her throat tighten. They could climb a tree and shake the branches but she could not easily reach some of the footholds and had to give up. When frog spawn filled the pools in the bog they picked it up in their hands to feel the jelly and dared her to do it too. But she hated its stickiness and how it slid between her fingers. The balls of jelly were like eyes and this thought made her drop the spawn on the grass.

Leo, the older and quieter one, had dark skin and his mane of brown hair would never lie flat. Orion was taller, though he was younger, and his flaxen hair was less unruly, his skin freckled. On first meeting them, people might not recognise them as brothers. But when you looked, their brown eyes seemed so alike they could have been one person looking out of two faces, two heads. Even their voices sounded similar and when Leo didn't speak Orion sometimes spoke for him.

The boys slept in one large room together and Cass slept by herself. At night, from her bed next to the adjoining wall, she heard the trickle of their talking together but couldn't make out what was said. When their parents had shut the drawing room door she sometimes slipped out of her room to get into bed with one or other of them. Sometimes they fell quiet, Orion reading from a book on birds' nests and eggs, Leo using his black mechanical pencil with its little scarlet tassel to sketch in a notebook the outlines of the moths that were drawn to the light in their window and bumped against the pane. He would not open it and let them in, knowing it would kill them. He knew some of their names: the ghost, the elephant hawk moth, the white ermine, the fox. He crosshatched the veins and shading of their wing patterns, lightly crayoned in soft browns, oranges, a pale cream. The window where they crawled acted like a magnifying glass and their faces looked prehistoric. Cass was a little afraid of their tiny legs and their moving jaws and was glad they stayed on the other side of the window so their powdery wings would not flap in her face.

One night the moon looked like a candled egg with a chick growing inside it. The light shone through the window and covered the beds. She was reading from *The Violet Fairy Book* by Andrew Lang which her father had given her for her birthday. The story was called 'The Girl who Pretended to be a Boy', about a princess who disguises herself as a boy in order to save her father's kingdom from a war. She is helped by two talking horses, one of which is a magician and the other is his younger brother called Sunlight. They advise her how to get through many trials and quests and, by the end, she finds she has become the hero. Cass grew so tired her eyes could not stay open and she fell asleep in Orion's bed, against the warmth of his back.

In the morning she awoke in her own bed, and didn't remember how she had got there.

The river nearby ran like a forest creature between trees. On a shoal of stones her two brothers stripped off and waded in, flopping into the deeper water on the bend.

Cricket, the golden Labrador, ran down to the water's edge to slip in too, swimming round and round in circles, then getting out and shaking his wet fur in little sparks of lightning. The sunlit spray turned mauve.

Cass sat on a rock to watch them as she couldn't yet stay afloat. She was rather afraid of the black water with its undercurrents. Little spasms of energy blipped on the surface as if something she couldn't see stirred below. The current coiled slowly back on itself beneath some exposed tree roots. From her vantage point she spotted the flash of light on the scales of a fish curling its tail, fins barely moving to keep itself still. The eye in its wrinkled socket was like an adder's. She visualised other fish that hid among the boulders below, imagined their speckled skin and undershot jaws full of little teeth, and knew she didn't want one brushing up against her leg if she were to get in their water. The boys' pale, freckled skin turned pink, then whitened with the cold. She wondered why she had not grown a willie too.

'I'll teach you how to swim. Come on in,' called Leo. But she shook her head.

'You'd love it. Don't be such a cissy, Cassy,' yelled Orion, smacking the water with his palms.

She wondered if the nub between her legs might start to lengthen and grow into a willie too and when that happened she'd join them in the pool, swim like them. Meanwhile, she needed to be patient for she was the youngest and only a girl.

Cass watched her brothers. They were performing duck dives and their white stick-thin legs protruded from the water. Cricket was lying on the warm rock, panting. His eyes followed the boys' movements.

Determined to teach herself, she wandered upstream to a favourite place where there was a large island with trees. Where the river bank curved the current slowed and you could see through to the bottom with its copper and amber pebbles. Sandy silt squeezed between Cass's toes. Almost transparent minnows hovered and darted at the edge.

At first, she imagined her skin might be dyed the peat colour of the water but when she put her hand in the river the water slid down her arm and left no mark. She took off her clothes and left them on a rock. She kept on her undergarments, tucking her petticoat into her knickers, but when she kneeled in the water her petticoat ballooned so she stood up and pulled it off, wringing it out and draping it on an overhanging branch.

She didn't mind being alone. She waded out and whatever fear she once had seemed to leave through her fingertips. No need to churn up the water, or put up with being splashed in the eyes. She loved to see her own shadow moving under her body and the ripples her arms sent ahead of her. She liked the feel of water leaning against her flanks, its resistance to her feet and hands, the way it turned to mercury between her fingers. She found herself swimming through a wood, the elm trees shimmering as she moved through their reflections. A nimbus of midges broke open as if making a path ahead of her. No one around. Only bright blue-green damselflies and, upriver, a pair of wagtails on a stone. A passing breeze rustled in the leaves and wrinkled their reflections.

In autumn, silhouettes of hares – some crouched, others upright and alert like sentinels – could be seen on the woodland edge as they waited for twilight to swoop into monochrome when it would be safe to come out into the open and graze.

She knew to keep her arms still, elbows tucked well in, so she thrust her hands in her pockets. Her toes alert inside her shoes, she crept through the grass waving in the warm air. She avoided plantain leaves because they squeak if trodden on, and angled her feet so that grass would not rustle against her ankles as she pushed through. A blaze of butterflies rose in front of her: small blues, orange-tipped, skippers and fritillaries.

She knew to look for the hares in the field called Short Fuzzes. Her eyes sifted through the stalks and leaves of plants and grasses until she spotted a twitch of grey and saffron ears, the blink of an eye, before the whiplash and thump of feet as a hare leaped from its form on the ground and jumped away, running from her in a zig-zag. She placed her fingertips in the depression it had left and felt a residue of warmth.

'What I most want to do when I'm older,' said Leo, chewing on a grass stem as they sat on a stone bench in the Quaker Burial Ground on the edge of the village, 'is to go to Africa and see birds of paradise, and lions. Elephants too.'

'I want to go to the desert and ride camels and live in a tent,' said Orion.

Cass said nothing as she was wondering how to divide her time between the two of them in such distant places so far apart. The people lying under the earth who were called Friends seemed to be waiting for her answer: Susanna, Hepzibah, Samuel. Orion nudged her, 'And you, Cassie, what do you want to do most? Perhaps you could dress yourself up as a boy and come with us? But being a girl you'll have to get married one day and have children, I suppose.'

'No,' she was stung by his assumption, 'I shall stay near the island. If I travel anywhere I'm going to sail to the Hooghly River on a ship named…'

'To the whatty river? Where's that?' laughed Leo.

'The Hooghly River. But I won't die after a short illness.' Not like Captain Kingcome's wife in the church: she visualised the plaque on the wall where the *esses* looked like *effs*, making it sound as though in the olden dayf they all used to lifp.

She jumped up and ran out of the Burial Ground, leaving her brothers with the Friends, shocked that their lives together here might one day come to an end. She couldn't live a life anywhere else. She marched along the lane, elderflower heads so thick and frothy the trees waved like palanquins, and she looked over the gate at the farm horses in their field, named Goose Park, and saw they were both lying down on the grass in the warm sunshine, their legs stretched out as if they were dead. She saw Swan's tail twitch. She went over to the grey mare and bent down to stroke her head, whispering in her ear. Then she crawled round and snuggled up against her bulging stomach, laying her head on the dip in her shoulder. Swan twitched a fore leg, lifting her head as if in annoyance at a fly and then dropped it back on the ground and dozed off.

The boys had followed her into the field. Orion, half way across the field, called, 'How did you do that?' and Cass said 'Try it. Swan will let you if you ask her, but first you must whisper in her ear and scratch her neck.'

Orion crouched like a hare and waggled Swan's ears, then gave her a good scratching in the sweet spot under the mane so that her top lip wrinkled with pleasure. Orion whispered something Cass couldn't hear and then crawled between Swan's stretched-out legs, beside Cass, who moved her head onto the horse's gravid belly.

Leo, who could talk to horses so they heard, looked into young Punch's ear and thought him the story of Achilles' immortal horses, Xanthus and Balius, who had wept when Achilles' friend was killed in battle. At first, Punch stretched and seemed inclined to get up but, after a minute of scrabbling and nonchalant scratching of his coat with his teeth, accepted Leo lying against his belly.

From the copse a chaffinch and a thrush were singing

and bees were purring among the dandelions. Swan's digestive juices burbled inside her stomach – or was it the foal slurping and growing in her womb? Sometimes her skin quivered when a fly touched her. None of them moved for a long time, until the sound of Sarah's voice calling them home rang out across the valley, audible even over the birdsong and the sound of stomach-churning.

5

For weeks Leo had been asking when the foal would be born. 'Swan knows her job,' his father replied, 'Don't worry. She'll take care of everything.'

One morning the answer was different, 'Oh, it'll be next week... Tuesday, I reckon.'

Leo determined he would have to keep watch. The weather was exceptionally windy and wet and the nights were dark as the inside of a pocket. He knew that a foal born in such weather might chill, sicken and die, and, even though Fernley, the stable manager – their father referred to him as 'my right-hand man' – assured him Swan would hold on to the foal till the weather was right, Leo wanted to be certain it was not born into a storm. In the small hours he rose, put on his boots and went out to the field in his pyjamas and, by the light of his hurricane lamp, saw that the mare was grazing in the field, her rump to the wind.

The following night when he looked out of the bedroom window it was obvious the weather had changed, for the trees were no longer thrashing about. By the light of the half moon he could see Swan grazing. The Plough arced above the field, and the grass looked almost frosted with a grey light. He went back to bed and hardly slept, listening to the dark. At the first glimmer of dawn, he went outside to see the mare pawing the ground, her sides heaving.

He knocked on the window of the stable cottage and Fernley soon tumbled through the door. Leo held the lantern high as they watched over the mare, the darkness thinning, the grass turning from grey to mauve. The foal's front legs and head emerged in a shower of water. It lay on the ground struggling for a few seconds, until the mare bit a hole in the silvery casing to let it peep out and shake its head as it took its first breath. It struggled to its feet, swaying on long legs, as the birdsong of dawn began to tune up with all its vague, colourless shapes – the white birth-skin like a fork of lightning slewed across the grass.

Afterwards, the mare turned to a corner of the field and her black foal clamped himself to her flank, knowing her through scent and the mother-whicker. The stars were fading as Leo deciphered the small star on the foal's face and saw that his knees were huge and knobbly. The mother walked the foal purposefully up and down beside the fence for a while and they swished through the wet grass. Leo was startled by how the foal's feet looked feathery and soft, and thought they must be deformed. Alarmed, he asked Fernley, who said, 'Think about it. If fully formed, a foal's hooves would damage the inside of the mare, so they stay spongey. By this time tomorrow all the soft pieces will be walked off.'

Later, at breakfast, his father said, 'I'll let you choose the name, son. Your first foaling.'

Leo looked up at his father and at first made no reply. After a long pause he said, 'I'd like him to be called The Plough.'

'The Plough? Are you sure?'

'Yes,' said Leo.

'Right, so be it… as long as this doesn't make you think he belongs to you,' and he shook Leo's hand and gave him a nod.

Leo was aware you could never lie to a horse. He thought they could tune into the pictures in your mind. When his sister fell off and her foot was caught in the stirrup of the side saddle so that the startled pony trotted off, dragging her along the ground, he knew that to give chase would only make Blackie break into a gallop, so he willed him to stop. And he came to a halt as if of his own accord, snorting and frothing at the mouth. When Leo reached Cass, she was dazed and bruised and her arm was bleeding. Her shoulder seemed crooked but, tearful and trembling as she was, he got her back on the pony and rode home beside her.

To Leo, home was the smell and feel of a horse. Any horse. He mounted one as if he assumed he and it belonged to one another. He only went inside a house to its furniture and walls, to its expectations and protocols, because the sleeping and feeding that took place there were necessary for him to get on with his world of outdoors.

Leo had learned a lot of what he knew about horses from Fernley, who with his dark, curly hair and olive skin obviously had gypsy blood in him – so people said. He managed the stable yard and made sure the farm lad kept the heavy horses in good fettle for the tasks of ploughing and drilling seed, and drawing loads through the year – logs in the winter, hay in the summer. Swan was the brood mare and in between foaling and brooding she carried out her work with the youngster running at foot beside her. Fernley said this was an important part of their education, learning from the dam.

The Pepperton schoolroom formed the nucleus of the indoor world Leo had to endure. The children's governess, Miss Sowden, was a wizened hawthorn twig of a woman with a Roman nose and heavy brogue shoes. She also tutored the Harton Manor boys, Yvo and Alexander Westwood, before they went to Eton. Leo was unwilling to learn his letters because he thought that words were inert, that they did not snort, or fart or poop. But when he divined that words contain their own vital spirits he looked for the sounds of the animals and birds he saw imprinted on the page like a series of spells. He reasoned that individual letters were the shaping of sounds: every mark on the page making its own note, a hoof beat, a calling owl, a dog's whimper. And to him words carried particular smells: wet dog, burnt toast, horse piss. Miss Sowden complained to his mother, 'That boy's behaviour – the way he avoids me – is sheer insolence and should be severely punished. He has no interest in learning to read or write. None whatsoever'.

His mother said that she did not think he was being deliberately difficult, but she had to admit to herself that he didn't try very hard when she taught the children French. His German was no better. Yvo and Alexander, who came to her for lessons at Pepperton, at least made an effort. Cass spoke so fluently it would have been hard for anyone to keep up.

'And that's not all,' continued Miss Sowden, 'I don't know what's to become of him. If I ask him to read out loud he stumbles over simple words he ought to know. He'll never survive at boarding school. They will make mincemeat of him.'

Boarding school! It had never occurred to him that he'd be going away to school. Was that their plan for him? He didn't want to live at a school like Yvo and Alexander Westwood. He'd have to run away and hide himself in the woods. He'd manage on his own somehow. Miss Sowden's outburst made him feel as though the ground in front of him was turned to mush: this quaking, trembling earth sodden with other people's expectations of him. And now this thunderstorm of boarding school as well.

But when he heard this, Father smiled his upside-down smile. 'He'll get by on what he does best. He doesn't need to go to school to learn about horses, so he's going to get along fine. He'll be worth his salt.'

Leo licked his fingertip and dipped it in the salt cellar with its blue glass liner. White grains clung to the skin: he dabbed them on his tongue and the salt taste spread through his mouth reaching into the furthest corners of his palate. The saltiness seemed to hide between his teeth and came out in little whooshes when he ran his tongue over his gums. The wetness of his mouth made the salt sing.

6

Orion watched a white elephant the size of a mountain elongate into a crocodile, become wispy and fray into horses with flying manes. The ground smelt damp and the heather was fading. Hawthorns were laden with berries, and redwings fossicked the hedges where leaves were turning pale gold and crinkly.

It was a shooting day. As soon as the first frosts threatened, Edward occasionally let out the lower fields of Pepperton Farm for a spot of shooting. The boys were allowed to take part along with the Westwood brothers and Frank Lethbridge. Orion was home from school where he had become a crack shot. Leo generally missed his aim and preferred to join the village boys who carried sticks to beat the ground and flush the game into the air. Rabbits and hares ran first and from the muzzles of the twelve-bores popped cylinders of flame, clouds of choking white smoke and then a sharp retort. The air was filled with the smell of rotting eggs. Out of this smoke leaped the gundogs competing to collect up the bodies and bring them in.

Not until the beaters came close would snipe be disturbed. Being the colour of dead leaves they were invisible until they cried 'Tseep, Tseep', sounding like tearing cloth, as they sprang from the leaf litter, their wings whirring. Pheasants were an easier target, lifting their bulk with a startled call and a heavy wing-beat when flushed from the undergrowth. That moment was when the guns started their banging and pheasants rained down, thumping on the ground. A few of the low-flying woodcock managed to escape with their zig-zag flight that only a skilled shot could follow. Moorhens scuttled across the standing water left in the hollows by the recent heavy rains, giving a gunman plenty of time to take aim.

After the bouts of shooting, the gunmen reloaded while Fernley counted the birds and flung them in baskets. Blood dripped on the ground. Feathers rolled around in the breeze.

Orion found himself feeling queasy; tears ached behind his eyes. This was an entirely new feeling. Why did they want to shoot these beautiful creatures, their wings the colour of the autumn ground? Some of the corpses were still warm, brown and tawny feathers already drifting, eyes shining like beads and heads lolling. Birds that were wounded dragged themselves away to hide among the reeds but the dogs found them and the picker-up would break their necks. But what if he didn't find them? These birds would be left to die slowly and painfully of their wounds. The other guns looked smug-satisfied with their bags, lighting up cigarettes as if aiming a gun and pulling a trigger had been hard work.

They were beating the edge of the woodland. Above them the hillsides were blond with dry grass stems. Mist was creeping along in the river valley below. Orion's shot was spent first so he lowered his gun. He peered through the smoke. He saw that Leo had wandered ahead of the line of beaters and was looking at something over a wall. What the blazes was his brother playing at now? Why couldn't he just do the job he'd been given? At that moment, a snipe catapulted into the air from near Leo's feet. One of the twelve-bores swung in its direction with a bright gleam and fired.

Leo cried out and fell to the ground with a skull-shattering crack. Orion ran up to him and saw his face was peppered with shot, his neck lolled. He shouted, 'Bloody idiot, you've killed him!' as they gathered round Leo's limp body.

Someone called, 'Is there a doctor here?' but Orion

knew already that no one could save his brother with his eye bleeding and half his scalp torn away, blood pumping from the back of his head where it had hit a rock. He recognised death when he saw it.

Edward picked up his body and carried him across the fields and up the garden path. He kicked open the door and shouted out, 'Adeline, come quickly. There's been an accident – call the doctor, will you?' He put Leo on the silk chaise longue. Orion ran into the kitchen to find Sarah, who was ironing sheets. He remembered the sting of starch in his nostrils, the wail his mother uttered as she saw her son's crumpled body where Edward had laid him, his blood spreading across the yellow silk.

After that, Orion didn't remember anything – perhaps he passed out – because he woke in his bed, knowing something terrible had happened and couldn't think what it was. The world had changed colour and meaning and he recognised nothing. Light came through the curtains and he turned his head to look at his brother's empty bed. He got up and pulled the covers back. No one had slept in there so he got in and smelt Leo's body on the pillow and down the bed. He closed his eyes and felt surrounded by him.

Orion fell asleep again – or else dreamed that he did – and didn't know whether it was his brother or himself who was dreaming. In his sleep he heard the door latch rattle and someone stepped through the doorway and came towards him, putting a hand on his head. He woke with a jolt to find his mother sitting beside him, the weight and warmth of her hand on his forehead. She said something Orion didn't understand because the language was incomprehensible to him and he tried to reply, 'm dnt nw hw m nm'. She muttered something else and vanished from the room.

She came back some time later with a blanket and a hot brick which she put at Orion's feet, undoing the bedding at the bottom of the bed and tucking it in again. Then she slipped off her shoes and lay down beside Orion, putting her arms round him, drawing him close to the warmth of her body. She spoke quietly in that incomprehensible language and stroked his head. The fragrance of her scent, the slight and familiar smell of her made his body come to life and he slowly began to realise that he, Orion, was not Leo and that he would never be Leo, because Leo was lying downstairs with blood on his face and a ruined head, like the snipe the gunmen shot and threw on a heap. And he sobbed into her shoulder, soaking her blouse, and he could not stop the howls that came from deep under his ribs. His mother continued to hold him, saying nothing at all.

He felt limp after a while as if he was empty. He could see Cass through a watery blur as she lay squeezed in beside Mama on her other side. Her eyes were closed but her face looked shrunken and wet.

When he awoke again he roused himself and went downstairs to find his father sitting by the window in the living room. He felt uncomfortable and embarrassed. Because Edward stayed motionless with a terrible expression of sadness on his face, Orion thought perhaps he was regretting it was Leo that was shot and not himself, and that was why he would not speak. Perhaps it was because he blamed him, Orion, for not taking proper care of his brother.

Over the course of the next few days, Father did not speak to anyone, not even to Cass, not even to their mother. The shock sent him to a place from where Orion thought he might never return.

He was often expecting his brother to appear at the door, to be waiting for him in the stables. Once he thought he heard Leo's steps on the stairs, jumping two at a time. Another time, he distinctly heard his brother shouting for him – 'Orion!' He looked up and almost called out, 'Yes, what do you want now?'

At the funeral Swan pulled the cart carrying the coffin. Orion held Swan's bridle and the brasses on the harness shone in the sunshine. He had read in *The Iliad* how Achilles' immortal horses wept for the death of Patroclus. He didn't know a mortal horse could also weep. Walking beside her, only he could see how her tears had stained the bright fur hidden beneath her dangling forelock.

In the church he automatically left the space to his right for Leo between himself and his father, the eldest son's place. He could not bring himself to shift across to stand in the gap. He was imagining that after the service he or his brother could start a fight, like the last time when they had punched each other as hard as they could, knocking each other off their feet and rolling around on the floor, fists clenched and feet kicking, gasping for breath with an anger they both felt, so that when it drained from their bodies they had looked at each other and wondered in amazement what all that had been about.

Through the hymns, Orion could not stop himself trembling. As if from somewhere deep inside, his whole body was quivering. Even when he folded his arms and squeezed himself there was no controlling the vibration. Mama wept and wiped her nose with her hanky. Cass looked as startled as if she had only just heard the news.

Standing at the graveside he had the sensation that the right side of his body made an agreement with the body in the coffin, that he, Orion, would never again use a gun, that he would not shoot at birds or animals as long as he lived. The left-hand side of his body promised to ensure that this would never happen, that if ever the right needed reminding the left would be sure to do so. And as he thought all this he felt a little golden spark light up in him and the feeling stayed with him until they began to throw earth on the coffin.

He could not bear the sound of the soil landing on the lid and he ran from the crowd. He ran through the village and along the lane back home to Pepperton, where he went upstairs and into the bedroom, throwing himself onto Leo's bed. But by then the smell of him had gone, because Sarah had asked the maid to take away the sheets. And then Orion knew it was Leo who was in the coffin, with the earth being dropped from above and thudding on the wood, and it grew in him that the right-hand side of himself wanted to take down one of his father's guns and shoot the chap who had killed his brother. And he bit the pillow and howled out loud.

PART TWO

7

For months Cass kept thinking she saw Leo. He seemed to turn up at odd moments and sometimes she thought she saw him leaving by the front door or she sensed that he was about to enter the sitting room. The squeaky door handle would turn and she looked up expecting to see him but it would be Sarah or the maid. Cass was attending a girls' school in Ashamstead by then and on her way to and fro she occasionally caught sight of him on the street: someone who walked like him, or someone with a cap like his. When Orion went back to his boarding school the house fell quieter still, Mama seldom speaking but often weeping over the smallest mention of war. Father was usually behind a newspaper or listening with his ear close to the wireless.

Cass remembered something Leo said once: that the words we speak try to link us together. He'd said if I tell you how it is for me and you tell me how it is for you we might connect... but often we don't, because words aren't really accurate enough, are they? But we have more than words. And he told her how he had stopped her runaway pony.

Cass had learned from Leo how never to pressure a horse, to back away when any hesitation showed in eyes or ears. If the muzzle tightened, or the nostrils changed shape, or the eyebrows wrinkled, it would be best to move back a whole step, pause, move forward a half step and watch the reaction. The grey mare stretched her neck towards her, whiffled into her proffered hand. Sometimes when the mare snorted she would throw up her head and trot away, tail lashing. But when Cass turned her back as if she did not care, the mare returned, nudging her in the small of her back. Cass decided to call her Silver.

So Cass spent her time with Silver and talked to her in the stable or while out riding. Her father had said he wouldn't sell the grey mare on. Not till Cass had outgrown her, anyway. The filly had arrived at Pepperton in a batch of gypsy-bred youngsters he had bought at market to break and train and sell on at a good profit. The animal was nervous, and had never been handled by humans except roughly, and she snorted with fear through her petal-thin nostrils.

One day Cass led Silver out into the meadow behind the stables, and climbed onto the top rail of the fence in order to mount her for the first time. She hitched up her skirt and eased her leg over the saddle to sit astride, talking quietly the while. With her legs against the horse's flanks she felt a connection with the horse she'd never known before. She felt as if she and the horse were a new kind of being, together but separate, able to read each other's minds just as Leo had said.

Without gathering the reins, she squeezed her forward with a slight pressure of her legs, and the horse's ears turned right round as if to listen to her intentions. Like wind through grass, tremor after tremor ran through the fur over the shoulder and across the flanks. The heat of the horse came through her stockings down the insides of her legs.

The horse startled sideways and Cass felt a jolt, found herself hitting the ground with a thump. Her head was spinning but she held on to the reins. She got up, limped over to the railings, coaxing the mare with her voice. She knew she had to get back on, so she climbed the fence and slipped herself back into the saddle, digging her feet into the stirrups, gripping with her toes. The mare took a few steps and snorted. The next buck was bigger, but this time Cass was ready for it. The horse must understand your thoughts from the feeling of your body on its back. Could it also detect how you felt?

If I had been using the side-saddle I'd never have stayed on, she thought: from now on I shall always ride like a boy. She was determined. Never mind that Mama complained that it would set tongues wagging. Cass borrowed some breeches from Leo's drawer, tucked them into her riding boots and rode bareback. When her mother found out about this she said Cass would have to stop riding altogether, and kept her inside for a whole day. 'It could damage your internal organs... make you unmarriageable. Some people consider it scandalous for a young lady to be seen sitting astride like a peg out on the hunting field, and I won't have it.'

The matter was resolved when one of Colonel Westwood's guests had an accident while riding to hounds. Her mount tripped at a high bank and landed on her. Because she was stuck in the side-saddle she was not thrown clear over its head, and the weight of the horse broke her pelvis. When the doctors said her legs would be paralysed for the rest of her life, Father bought a cross-saddle for Silver and ordered a young lady's riding outfit with breeches and boots from the local outfitter in Ashamstead.

One day Cass lost her way home in the fog on the moors. She could see no further than a few paces. The path went on and on, becoming much longer and steeper than she remembered. Trees loomed up in front. She heard water trickling somewhere and knew she was near a marsh. A swirl of panic ran through her as she realised she had no idea where they were. So she let go of the reins to give the horse her head. Silver walked out a little faster and Cass hoped she wouldn't try crossing the bog. Encased in this unfamiliar world, her thoughts seized on another thing that Leo had once said: that we can never see what others see, that we can't get inside each other's skulls and look out through their eyes; that you yourself are always somebody else to other people; that you always make a difference to someone wherever you are. And she thought of how she had always been the younger sister and how much of a difference that made to everyone else. And a strange sensation came over her, of looking at herself from the outside, and what she saw was a girl riding a horse through thick fog near a marsh and she felt afraid for that girl's future.

After a while they came to a rise and she looked down across a valley where the fog was beginning to thin and, with relief, saw a house with some farm buildings. She thought she would go down there and ask the way home. But she didn't recognise the farm. And it took her a while to work out that the house with its courtyard and outbuildings which she was looking at was her own Pepperton.

Days later, a motor car bumped to a halt outside their front door and Edward ran down the steps of the garden terrace, calling 'Good morning,' as a soldier-driver held open the back door and stood to attention for an officer to step out. Cass recognised Major Sykes, the local hunt-master, wearing military uniform.

'I'd like to see everything you've got, Edward. Everything.' Major Sykes had a carrying voice. The last word was an order. But the ducks on the pond were making a great racket, quacking as Cricket, tongue lolling, bounded through a gap in the hedge to meet the visitors. Unperturbed, a blackbird was flustering through the hawthorn twigs to tweak off early berries.

'We've brought them all in so you can have a browse at your will,' her father was saying. 'They've been in the yard at least an hour, as you requested. You'll want the nags trotted up, I expect. Fernley will be in the yard to help. And if you need to see them under saddle, that can be fixed in a jiffy. Orion's away at school, but Cass is here to give a hand.'

'I'm afraid Orion may feel in need of a decent horse by the time we've finished here.'

'What are you looking for, exactly?'

'You name it, we need it. Cavalry horses of 15.1 hands or more; Mounted Infantry on 14.2 plus, and pack ponies; Field Artillery wants horses of 15 hands or more; and draught horses for transport wagons and suchlike.'

One corporal was already running his hand down a horse's legs, checking for any lumps. All morning the Major stood watching horses being trotted up and down the yard. Then he ordered each one to be saddled up, and he rode them himself. The driver was completing forms, writing on labels. He kept licking his pencil and, as Cass watched what he was doing, his face turned scarlet.

At the end of the morning, the Major said, 'Edward, your horses are top-notch – good strong quarters, good action, fine fettle – practically cleared you out, my dear chap. Only left you a pony and a few youngsters we won't be needing yet.

'You need these forms so you get paid. The prices are fixed. My men here have made a list of the horses already: they need to affix labels to their headstalls to know the class I've purchased them for and where they'll be going. You must bring them to Ashamstead station to the Conducting Officer this time next week. You get paid for that, too. You'll have to have their hind shoes removed for the journey at your own expense.'

'Come up to the house, then. I'll fix you all a drink while we check the documents.'

Major Sykes said to Cass, 'And don't worry about your grey mare, young lady. I expect she'll be back with you shortly. Think of it as a loan, if you like. Soon as our men have given the Hun the thrashing they deserve they'll turn for home with their tails between their legs. We'll chase them all the way back to Germany and then we can all start hunting again.'

'Edward, one more thing — your farm horses.'

'The farm horses? But we need those!'

'You won't be left without. Anyway, you'll be able to buy a steam tractor now with your profits.'

Fernley, carrying three headstalls, went out to the field where the draught horses were grazing. Cass brought Swan into the yard, the mare's dark eyes hidden beneath her long forelock tinged darker grey by weather, the feathers on her legs spilling over her hooves. Fernley brought the steady Punch, whose jet-black mane would not lie on one side of his neck, and The Plough, just broken to the wagon and whose hooves made sparks fly like infant stars as he jostled and jogged.

Perhaps the horses sensed the waiting inspector standing with his clipboard in the yard where they only seldom came, because they all became fidgety. Mr Sykes walked round each one and asked them to be trotted up and back again while he observed their soundness. He pushed aside the long hairs and ran his hand up their legs, picked up their feet and asked their age as he opened their mouths to look at their serrated and grass-stained teeth, the molars at the back with the dark centres.

'We could really do with them all but we'll just take those two,' he said, indicating Punch and The Plough, 'They make a team, same height, same weight. If they go together, they'll stick together. The youngster will settle down in time, I expect. That'll leave you the old mare.'

8

Soon after the anniversary of Leo's death Swan was heard calling for the other two horses at intervals through the following nights and her pitiful neighing went on for weeks. Eat a bit, neigh a bit, eat a bit, neigh a bit – it went on like that. And Orion's imagination rushed to Punch and The Plough and he felt his heart beat faster at the thought of what they might be having to do – pulling heavy guns, or loads of victuals, or equipment. They hadn't chosen to join up.

His sister saved sugar from the table for Swan and kissed her velvet nose while Orion groomed her or brushed mud off her feathery legs. 'They'll be back soon: I've heard Father telling Fernley,' he said to Cass.

'Yes, one day, they'll be back home again in the yard. The newspapers say so. Silver will whinny when she sees us. I hope you can understand what we say, Swan darling.'

Outside the Ashamstead butcher's shop, hares dangled by their necks, their eyes bulbous. Next to them, Blind Wilf stood to attention, selling matches. His wrinkled lids were glued shut. A medal dangled on his frayed jacket. Orion bought matches, dropping an extra copper in his tray, and at the sound Wilf saluted.

In the bull ring, an officer in his finery was shouting orders to some recruits in khaki. Military music whirred out of a gramophone that had been brought out from someone's parlour for the occasion. The wood was highly polished and a jaunty brass semi-quaver was applied to the front. A grave-looking soldier stood beside it, winding it up whenever the music decelerated.

A long queue of men in their work clothes waited to

give their names and addresses to a colour sergeant at the desk. A poster with the words *It's your duty lad* was attached to the front of the desk and a brick held it firm.

The crowd was cheering the young soldiers. A woman Orion recognised was standing in front of him, and when she turned round she nodded. 'Patriotism,' she said, 'is a manly emotion. Give my regards to your mother, Orion… isn't it?'

It was not the first time he'd felt a qualm – a young woman had once laughingly stuffed a white fowl's malodorous bum fluff in his jacket pocket as she and her friend passed him in the street. When he drew it out he nearly ran after them to yell, 'But I'm not bloody old enough.'

Old Mrs Benson from the village, whose job it was to pluck birds for the shooters, now handed him a white tail-feather and said, 'I'm giving you this, lad, because plenty others will do the same and call you a chicken. It's high time you enlisted before you shame your parents.'

On fine spring evenings their father would lean over the gate and smoke his pipe, watching Swan. Let loose in the field, the horse knelt, lay down, and rolled over to rub the sweat off her back and shoulders. She dropped her head to graze but then stretched her neck up as a whinny burbled from her lips, grass blades dropping from between her teeth.

'Will they be looking after them all right, do you suppose?'

'It wouldn't be in their interests to ill-treat them.'

'Will they put them out to graze at night?'

'I doubt it, son. Let's just hope they're home soon and then Swan won't need to work so hard. But if it carries on you may well be joining them yourself.'

'No need to worry about that, Papa. They won't get me away from here.'

'You ought to enlist before Conscription or they'll stick you in a regiment with men with no experience and no guts. If you want to join up, your mother and I... we won't stand in your way. Fernley's too old to enlist and he'll stay.'

'My country is here. When I finish school I'm going to drive and maintain the new Pepperton tractor.'

'Let's see what the winter brings. See what happens when it happens. You're not eighteen yet awhile.'

9

Before the war, Frank Lethbridge had been a part of the landscape of hills and ditches, gunshot and game. On the hunting field he was said to have a good nose and Colonel Westwood called him 'a cracking young thruster'.

Cass first noticed Frank as a human being on two legs while in Ashamstead. At first she didn't recognise him, not on horseback and without his hunting hat. He was wearing a tailored coat and a trilby. She was surprised to find such a man interested in reading and, what's more, in the Public Lending Library. He was so engrossed, flicking through a reference book at the time, that he took no notice of her, except to move forward, touch his hat, and mumble an apology when she edged behind him.

She noticed him again in the village hall at the last cricket tea of the season. He was Ashamstead's second bat. As Orion also played for the village during his summer holidays, Cass helped Sarah with the after-match ritual. While she was tipping out the last of the tea from a large brown teapot, the lid fell with a clatter and hot drips scalded her hand. She grabbed a cold cloth to apply to her skin, and out of the corner of her eye noticed a flame-haired man with blue eyes beside her. He asked if he could give her a hand with the heavy teapot. When Sarah hoisted the tray of teacups away he asked, 'I say, Miss Forrester, can you recommend any top-hole books for me to read?'

At the hunt ball that September he asked her to dance. The fact that they danced more than just the once together would have been noticed by some of the sparkling dowagers. But Cass Forrester was too young for all that just yet. And quite a little hoyden! Didn't she ride astride? She'd have to grow up before a young man would give her a second look.

They used to pass each other weekly on the hunting field: he hunted almost every day of the week and ran at least three thoroughbred horses of his own to cope with his busy hunting regime. Frank was always keen, and out in front of the field. His polished boots were so high in the leg and so sinuous they could only have come from a top-notch bootmaker in London. So smart they were, they made him look as if he would put his horse at anything, with his blazing hair hidden inside his velvet hat.

But two of his horses were requisitioned, and one stayed only because Frank was about to join the cavalry and would need a mount of his own. When posters with Kitchener's pointing finger appeared, Frank told Cass: 'I say, if the war isn't over soon I'll be joining up myself, for the old school's sake. They say the more of us chums that get together and take on the Germans right now the sooner all the chaps can come home.'

He'd been rated as 'excellent' in the school's Officer Training Corps. He would be off to an officer training depot as soon as he'd ordered his junior cavalry officer's uniform from the military tailor Craven and Sons near Bond Street.

On his last six-day leave before embarkation, he seemed fuller in the figure, so that the uniform fitted snugly. He grimaced, 'Hope I don't make a chump of myself out there'.

On the final day he took her hand as if it were porcelain that might be crushed if squeezed. 'I say, Cassandra, it would be terrific if you wrote to me. You could tell me what you are reading and sometimes send me the books. A lot more fun than reading the Cavalry Officer's Manual. We could then become engaged, make it official on my next leave. What do you say, old girl?'

When she nodded she thought he would seal it with a kiss. Isn't that what was meant to happen? But he remained standing – almost to attention. It gave her a queer feeling – that perhaps he didn't mean what he said. She should be kissed at this moment. Was she not kissable? She tried to keep her lips in the shape of a smile. Thinking about it, later, it really did feel rather insulting – that a man should as good as ask you to marry him, but then not avail himself of the chance to kiss you.

She was determined that however long it took she would wait for him, and meanwhile she'd knit him socks and write him love letters and send him poems by that handsome poet Rupert Brooke that everyone was reading:

We have built a house that is not for Time's throwing.
We have gained a peace unshaken by pain for ever.
War knows no power. Safe shall be my going...

In his perfectly cut breeches and shining top boots Frank seemed like Brooke himself, the epitome of a brave man fighting to protect those of us left behind, she thought. When he held her hand her skin brushed against the fabric of his uniform, and she found herself wondering what it would be like to put it on herself.

'Just suppose,' she mused, 'after we are married, I were to come to the Front with you?' He blinked at her. Her thoughts were racing like a fox before the hounds. She was calculating – how would anyone know I was an imposter? I could go and find the horses and dodge the gunfire somehow, couldn't I? I could wrap a bandage round my very small bosom which no one would notice anyway. Having a wee standing up might be difficult, but men don't watch each other – or do they? If they found out I wasn't a man they'd give me something useful to do, not send me home to knit dratted socks. Life at home without the horses was perfectly awful.

He flung his head back and laughed, his gullet pink and wet, 'And what will they do when the Germans land at Dover and you smart girls on cross-saddles aren't there to frighten them off? Oh, Cassie – that's what I like about you, you have such comic ideas.'

The word stung her. She hadn't intended sounding comical. She had meant what she said, but it was obvious she could never pass herself off as a soldier, even standing beside him, unless she had the training. She wouldn't know how to drill on parade or how to clean a gun or fix a bayonet. And first she'd have to pass a medical and didn't they have to strip off for that? The idea went to ground, leaving only its scent. She had meant it because she wanted to show him that she was worried about him and wanted to make sure he would be safe. That didn't strike her as funny.

She cycled to the station to wave him off. Frank wasn't permitted to say where he was going. His parents were quite blithe and seemed oblivious to any dangers he might be facing. Mr Lethbridge in his bowler hat and expensive coat muttered something about being a credit to his regiment and his family. Apparently the Huns had bayoneted Belgian babies, he said. 'Give them hell, old chap, hound them back to Berlin!'

The local clergyman was shaking the many hands stretched to him from the windows as if the act of touching him would bring them salvation. He was reminding them to trust in the Good Lord.

She turned her face to Frank as he stood on the step, hoping he would now bend down and kiss her in front of his parents, the seething mob of men. For a second she really thought he might not. He didn't seem to know what to do with his hat. But he swept it from his head at last and she felt his lips on her cheek, his dampish soft moustache, and she smiled back at him that she was aware she had been kissed, that it was acceptable. He grabbed her hand and she sensed more feeling in the privacy of that squeeze than in the quick peck.

After the train had vanished she walked away from the smell of heat and steaming grief: it made her giddy and she thought she might faint. The potential embarrassment of fainting in front of his stiff-necked parents made her walk faster. By the time they caught up with her she had composed herself. Mr Lethbridge's face was red, his waxed moustache looked dishevelled. She shook their hands.

'Give my regards to your parents. We must invite them over for bridge one evening,' said Mr Lethbridge. Mrs Lethbridge was scrutinising Cass's face as if she were a schoolmistress looking for someone to blame.

10

Orion was up betimes. Knowing which floorboards creaked, he took pains to avoid them.

His sister's voice caught him up, 'Where are you off to, dressed like that?'

'Got an appointment.' He did not stop to face her. Wasn't it obvious to her he was trying to be quiet?

'They're not going to let you stay behind, you know.'

'No, they mightn't.' He strode away from the snag of her voice.

Her feet thumped down the stairs as she followed him, 'Why don't you just run away?' Orion drew a deep breath. My sister isn't light on her feet, or on anything else, he thought.

'Cass, this isn't a game, you know,' he turned on her, out of earshot of the rest of the house.

She stood in front of him and pulled at each of his sleeves. 'Your suit doesn't exactly fit you.' She flicked at a stray thread dangling from a button on the coat, twizzled it round the button and said, 'You know, brother dear, if you go out smelling of horse they'll think you just want to stay home for the hunting.'

'I wish you might try and believe in me, even just now and then,' he said as he took a piece of pie from the larder. 'See you later,' he hurried back down the passage and out of the front door.

He wanted to arrive at the court in good time. He knew he would need to calm himself before facing the members of the tribunal. Using Leo's mechanical pencil, he'd written out what it was he wanted to say and whispered it, pacing up and down his bedroom until he thought he knew it well enough. He was determined not to read it out because he wanted it to come spontaneously – from his heart. They'd hear it then.

He rode his bicycle over the moor to the station and propped it behind the station-master's house. On the train as he ate the slice of pie he drew out the letter he'd received and read it again.

If you do not avail yourself of the opportunity of being heard or, if having been heard, the Central Tribunal are not satisfied you have a conscientious objection on religious or moral grounds, the Central Tribunal are informed that you will remain under the control of the military authorities.

What was that going to mean for him? What after all could they do to him?

When he stepped onto the platform he walked through a fog of steam, and hoped it wouldn't rain smuts on his face. Outside, the streets smelled of horse dung and exhaust fumes. A preacher on a soap-box, who was haranguing a small crowd in the High Street, looked like a prophet from the Bible. Orion turned a corner into the narrows beside the court and a beggar called to him.

He walked up the steps and pulled open a heavy wooden door. Several chaps had taken the few seats around the hall. Others, with nowhere to sit, leaned against the walls. Like himself, most were dressed in suits, but some wore overalls as though they had just popped over from work. Until that moment, he had had no idea so many other men thought like him. The papers carried sneering articles about conchies and socialists as if they were homosexuals or deviant in some way.

He wondered if the tribunals were running late for some reason or if everyone else had arrived early. Anticipation filled the air like cigarette smoke and choked him. He swallowed the bile that rose to the back of his throat. The sting of it aggravated his thirst.

'You have to report in. To that man at the desk,' said a voice. Orion went across and showed his appointment letter to the clerk, who said, 'Your name will be called.'

There was a spare bit of wall to lean against and nearby was a man of about his own age who had a seat. At first he seemed familiar for some reason until Orion realised it was because he resembled Leo – the same dark brown eyes, the way he blinked. Orion asked him, 'Are all these people applying for exemption?'

'Yes, of course. But judging by the faces of those coming out nobody is having much luck.' His accent wasn't local.

His neighbour leaned across, 'You'd be better off failing a medical than trying to persuade this lot even if you are a Quaker or a Methodist.'

'But I'm not either. Are you?'

'Yes, I am a Quaker.'

'I don't know too much about Quakers. I know they call themselves Friends and have meetings, not services, that they sit in silence.'

'We oppose all war and try to avoid violence in any shape or form.'

'How does anyone avoid violence?' Orion wanted to know more. 'And what are you going to say?'

'I shall refuse to have anything to do with combat.'

'What, everything?'

'Yes. Absolutely. Even if I were to fail the medical.'

'And might you?'

'Well, I'm short-sighted and asthmatic, so they wouldn't enlist me anyway.'

'But why not use that as the reason?' he asked. Here was someone whose determination was stronger than his own, and it made him feel ill-equipped.

'No, I want them to have to accept my objection to killing people. I want them to hear what my conscience

59

says.'

'Well, they're more likely to listen to you than to me.' He blew out a puff of breath. 'I can't claim God is on my side though.' Feeling resigned he put his hands in his pockets.

'No more shall I. Good luck to you anyway. We'll all end up in gaol, I reckon.'

The air thickened. Men stood and moved into the next room as names were called. 'Mr Walter Cook!' 'Mr Thomas Lomax!' 'Mr Arthur Stockton!' The chap who looked like Leo responded and when he came back through the hallway he shook his head at Orion and, coming up to him, slipped a note into his pocket before disappearing out into the street. The note bore the single word *Arthur*.

And eventually his name was called. They mispronounced his first name, putting the stress on the second syllable and not the first. Inside the court room his heart was thundering in his ears, his skin tingling. He felt ridiculous with shiny sweat on his face. All the windows were high on the walls and light slanted into the room. Everything was made of wood: panelling on the walls, the seats, and the partitions between. It soaked up the sound of words into its polished grain and made every sound muffled – wooden. The fixed lines between the panels made it look as if all outcomes had been decided in advance.

When the mayor, who was sitting in front of the Union Jack, stated his name (pronounced wrongly again) Orion's remaining courage drained away. The mayor introduced the other members of the panel: two councillors on either side of him, and an officer in uniform who sat a little apart. He felt as if he had stepped onto a stage where a play was being performed but he didn't know his words or even what part he was to play.

Orion tried out his prepared piece. He had to read it out from the scrap of paper he'd written it on because his heart was pressing itself into the back of his throat. He hoped his voice would drown out the sound of it beating. When he first spoke there was a squeak and he wondered where it was coming from until he realised it was from his own throat. He tried swallowing it but it was like grit sticking in his larynx. Get a grip, he said to himself.

'That's not impressive,' said the mayor. 'You'll have to repeat if you want us to hear you.'

Was he referring to the argument or the delivery? Orion read aloud from his notes once more. He raised his voice a little but only a jot. When finished he lowered the sheet of paper and chewed his lower lip. The mayor leaned over the desk, his moustache looking tired, but his eyes were disconcerting, focussing on Orion's forehead as though trying to pierce his mind, 'You say you have a conscience which will not allow you to bear arms against your fellow men. You seem very sure about this.'

'Yes, sir, I made a vow when I was young. And you see, sir, my mother... when my brother...'

'Ah, your mother, and how will she feel if her son is deemed a coward? She won't bring herself to speak to you. And what if you carry this crazy idea through? How much worse will she feel if you were shot for cowardice, instead of on the battlefield?'

'Shot? But if I'm shot, sir, I won't be able to know.' The idea was new – he'd read that the Military Service Act recognised conscientious objection. A wave of panic flew through him. Oh, but perhaps it was just a bluff. Nobody was ever shot for this. Surely not?

'How can anyone distinguish between conscience and cowardice?'

'I know it to be my conscience, sir. It is close to my heart.'

'I see! I was not aware that the conscience was an

organ of the body. Whereabouts exactly do you say it is, anatomically speaking?'

'I didn't mean it was part of my body. It's like the soul, something indefinable.'

'You talk of the soul and yet I didn't hear you claim to have any religious scruples,' the officer spoke for the first time.

'No, sir, it's my personal belief in the value of all human life. I cannot take the life of another being.'

'But the Bible orders killing in a righteous cause, *Whoso sheddeth man's blood by man shall his blood be killed*,' interjected one of the councillors.

'I haven't studied the Bible. But I do believe war to be little short of murder.'

'War is not murder.'

'It may not be generally thought of as murder, but my conscience tells me it is.'

The mayor clamped his hands on the edge of table. 'Look, you're much too young to know anything about conscience. I will not be read a sermon by an overgrown schoolboy. Never heard such tripe. We dismiss your claim. Next case!'

Orion could not raise himself from the chair. Was that really all? Now what?

The mayor was speaking once more. 'I must say I'm reluctant to let you loose on the streets talking such barbarous nonsense. I warn you that if you carry on like this you will soon be behind bars. Out with you, please.' The mayor waved his hand at him, as if shooing away an importunate dog, and called to the usher, 'Next case!'

11

A few days later, Orion met the Ashamstead policeman cycling along the lane to the Pepperton driveway. The elderly constable placed him under arrest, asking him if he was ready to come then and there or if he needed a couple of days to get his affairs sorted. It was agreed he would report to the police station in Exeter in two days' time.

When the time came, he couldn't find his father to say good-bye to him and guessed he'd made himself scarce. Mother cornered him in the boot room and asked him to please re-consider for his father's sake, but when he said that he couldn't, she behaved as if nothing had happened. It was a relief to him. Perhaps she was assuming he'd be back when he realised the error he was making. Best to let her think what she liked.

He had resolved to walk to the railway station in Ashamstead until Cass offered to take him in the dog cart. As the cart jolted down the stony track into the valley, he said, 'I'm glad we're alone. I've been wanting to mention something… before they lock me up… that I hope you aren't too set on Frank.'

'What's it got to do with you?'

'Because… because… I think Frank Lethbridge may not be quite the man you think.' He didn't know how to put this into words. Suppose she was really in love with him?

'Crikey, Orion, you sound like a grandparent talking. Gone all snobbish all of a sudden?' The cart rounded a corner and up ahead they saw their father standing as though he was waiting for them. Cass drew up beside him and he climbed on to the seat without speaking.

They continued on their way in silence, the only sounds being the wheels and the pony's hooves padding along the dirt road, the gusty wind rattling the gorse, until they reached the outskirts of the little town.

At the station Cass hopped down to hug her brother goodbye. Tears were in her eyes. She said, 'I'm afraid of what's going to happen.'

Orion hugged her and said, 'Listen, Cass, you can get help if it's needed: make use of the Women's Land Army if the War Office starts piling on the pressure. The war can't go on much longer and I'll be back just as soon as I can. Look after this for me, will you?' He put Leo's pencil in her pocket. His father did not move from the cart and Orion leaned across and gave him a soft punch. 'Don't get the pip with me, Papa.'

At the police station he was taken to a cell in the basement where there was a bed of springs, a blanket and a slop-bucket. He tried to read the newspaper he'd brought with him until it was too dark to see and then he lay down but, partly from the cold and his own fears and the drunkards yelling incessantly down the passage, he slept very little. He was glad his cell door was locked. In the morning his eyes ached and he felt dishevelled and dirty. Or had the voices of the drunks been the sound of his own thoughts? In the cold light of day he couldn't be sure.

First thing, he was taken to the magistrates' court in handcuffs. He was locked in a room most of the day with a group of other objectors. They told him about the No Conscription Fellowship and said that there were thousands of other men who refused to fight in the wicked war, that the Fellowship would speak on their behalf, that they'd see it through together. He felt heartened. There were some other handcuffed prisoners in the room who taunted the conchies. One of them said he was 'a respectable criminal' because he was a burglar without a bleeding conscience.

In the court he was told to stand to attention as he had already joined the Army whether he liked it or not. The fine was £2. When he was instructed to report to the recruiting office they let him walk there on his own without a guard. Outside the office he joined a group of other men, some of whom he recognised from the magistrates' court. They stood side by side in a huddle, some wearing suits and hats, others in shirt-sleeves. To his relief Arthur was there, too, and he came across to shake hands just as a colour sergeant bawled at them to form a line to march to the barracks. 'Like this,' he yelled, strutting up and down in front of them, 'Left, Right.' They all stood where they were, looking at him blankly. 'I'm sorry,' said a tall man wearing a three-piece suit with a fob-watch, 'but I haven't joined the Army. And so I, for one, can't be ordered about. But I will come to the barracks if you ask me to.'

'Hear, hear,' mumbled the others and in a minute they formed a crocodile behind the red-faced sergeant. By the time they walked through the gates of the barracks they had all made friends. The fifteen men were locked into a room designed for ten, with a stench from urinals next door that seemed to have a leaking drain. There were three slop-buckets for the men to use. The bunks were also to be shared and where two men had room to lie down they were expected to fit three into the space, side by side. Each man was given a blanket.

Those who refused to wear uniform were forcibly dressed. When it was Orion's turn he helped by lifting his legs into the trousers and extending his arms. When they put a cap on his head he turned it round the wrong way.

He was told to muck out the horses but he said he couldn't do that if the horses were ridden by officers or soldiers. The sergeant said that those particular horses were used for bringing in supplies to the barracks. Orion thought perhaps that wasn't exactly aiding and abetting the war so agreed to do it.

As soon as he arrived in the stables he realised these were not draft animals. He sat on an upturned bucket for a long while though he felt sorry for the horses that needed cleaning out. When the sergeant came round to check how Orion was getting on and found he had done nothing at all he sent him to solitary confinement for three days on bread and water in the guard room. 'They shoot men in France for disobeying orders, yer know.'

Outside he could hear the sounds of soldiers drilling, their boots stamping the ground, the orders shouted as if at dogs. He felt fear creeping within him and it gave him an energy. He considered escape. But there was no hope of that, because he couldn't run home. There was only Cass's suggestion of living as a fugitive. Twice a day bread and water appeared at the hatch. To try and keep any body warmth he walked around the cell, which he calculated was about six feet by eight, and counted the number of stones in the walls but kept losing count. Eventually he also lost track of the hours. His chest ached for his mother and Cass and he wrote letters in his head to each of them, memorised what he would write on paper.

When he fell asleep Leo came into the cell. 'It's not your fault,' Orion said to him. 'I made you a promise. You never asked me, old chap, but I'll try and stick with it now, come what may. You'd be better at this than me. You won't leave me here by myself, will you? Please not.' When his weeping became audible the spy hole slid open and he heard whispers and laughter from outside the door. It takes only a short time to start thinking you're losing your mind.

A young lieutenant came through the door. One eye was sewn closed while the other glittered doubly bright in his white face. His lips were red beneath his moustache and his teeth flashed white.

'Why are you a conscientious objector? You are not claiming religious scruples.'

'No, it's not religion. But you don't have to be religious to believe that war is breaking the commandment, *Thou shalt not kill.*'

'Do you not think that applies to individuals, rather than to defence of the realm?'

'It applies to both the same.'

'I lost my eye defending the likes of you,' the soldier aimed between his eyes.

'You lost your eye trying to kill someone,' deflected Orion.

The lieutenant's face flamed, his sewn eye seemed to swell, his good eye flashed. Orion thought the man was about to knock him to the ground and he braced himself for the blow.

After a pause of several seconds the lieutenant said through his teeth, 'You belong to the Army now and you won't get away with this,' turning on his heel and slamming the door. He was ordered to suffer another three days of solitary confinement on bread and water for insubordination.

When he was released back to the communal cell, he was greeted by his comrades. Arthur said he looked starved as a lone wolf and handed him some bacon fat he'd managed to hide in a pocket. 'But don't bolt it. Eat it slowly,' he said.

He watched Orion eating and, when he was half way through, he prised it away from him, 'Finish that later. You don't want to make yourself sick.'

Later in the week they were ordered out on the parade ground. Nobody moved. Some new recruits entered, preparing by the look of it to give them a roughing up. The atmosphere zinged with tension until Orion's friend

Arthur cried, 'Look, we'll come quietly if you just give us a push.'

Outside, a corporal shouted at him, 'Private Forrester, you will carry a kit bag like this and hold your bayonet properly.'

'But I'm not a private. I'm a prisoner. I'm sorry… I won't do what you ask.'

'I don't ask anything. I'm giving youse an order, you insolent piece of shite.'

Buoyed up by what Arthur had said, Orion rejoined, 'I'm sorry but I don't take orders.'

'Stand to attention when I speak to youse.'

'I know I'm repeating myself – I'm sorry, but I won't do what you order.'

'Do as you're fucking well told or you'll be flattened out.'

'I don't consider myself in the Army. You can't order me about.'

'You are in the British Army whether you fucking like it or not. You can be court-martialled for disobeying an order given by a superior.'

'Then court-martial me.'

'My mother used to say don't-care was made-to-care and that's what's going to happen to you, you snivelling nancy boy.'

'If you think so.'

12

Upstairs in a drawer of her desk Cass had squirrelled some letters. She took them out and re-read them:

```
The War Office, Whitehall, London
Dec. 3rd 1914

Dear Miss Forrester,

Thank you for your letter of November 13th inst.
I regret to inform you that we are unable to
supply any information as to the whereabouts of
your horses. Please be reassured that they are
being well looked after and are making a great
contribution to the war effort on your family's
behalf.

Yours sincerely,

pp Major Sanders


The War Office, Whitehall, London
Jan. 8th 1915

Dear Miss Forrester,

Thank you for your letter of December 5th inst.
I regret to inform you that we are currently
unable to supply any information as to the
whereabouts of your horses. Please be reassured
that they are being well looked after and are
making a great contribution to the war effort
on your family's behalf.

Yours sincerely,
pp D. Callington-Jones
```

The War Office, Whitehall, London
Feb. 15th 1915

Dear Miss Forrester,

Thank you for your letter of January 10th inst. The only information I am at liberty to divulge is that horses from your area were all taken to one of the Remount Yards and were, after some weeks of quarantine and schooling, shipped to France. Your horses, being draught horses, will have various duties such as moving supplies and artillery. The British Army is highly skilled in horsemanship and has a fine reputation for care of equines. At present there is no requirement for civilian stable hands at the front as this work is undertaken by the Army Service Corps (ASC) and the Royal Veterinary Corps (RVC). In any case there is little likelihood of deploying females in this capacity. I cannot emphasise enough how very important horses are to the war effort. Their welfare is of paramount importance therefore.

If you are of the right age and experience, you might be considered for war work at one of the Remount Depots should the local policy change. I suggest you write directly to them and offer your services. Please find enclosed a list of such establishments.

Yours sincerely,

pp D. Callington-Jones

13

Cass had a question to ask her brother. So once he had been sent to a civil prison she announced her intention to go and see him as soon as the requisite visiting order arrived. She suggested Sarah accompany her, knowing it would be easier to speak freely with Orion without their father's presence.

But her mother did not want servants, not even Sarah, to see their family humiliation and said, 'Edward, you must go with Cass. Knowing her, she's quite capable of going on her own.'

As they left her mother said, 'And do your best to get the idiot boy to rethink this folly, will you? This can't go on, him being locked up with criminals.'

As their train pulled in at Exeter station another one stood hissing at the next platform. A row of men in ragged, blood-stained, mud-caked uniforms began to stumble out of the carriages. Their eyes were bandaged, heads lowered as if in shame, or as if listening. Standing in line with their hands on the shoulders of the man ahead they shuffled forwards, placing one foot in front of the other slowly, methodically. They seemed unable to walk without testing out the ground ahead with their feet. A sighted soldier in smart uniform walked at their pace in front of them and another one walked beside the last in line, a hand resting on his shoulder: two nurses also accompanied them, moving up and down the line, talking to each of the blinded men.

People in the station fell hushed, watching the cortege leave the station and file out into the main street. Someone raised a cheer and suddenly everyone broke into hurrahs. One of the men waved his hand, thumb up.

Others lifted their heads, looking around at the sounds. Two young women ran to the soldiers and excitedly pressed cigarettes into their hands. The woman standing next to Cass finished her cheering and shook her head, 'Poor lads. Heroes every one.'

'But what on earth's the matter with them?' asked Cass.

'Gas, that's what it is. They've been in a gas attack. Haven't you heard what it does?'

'I read about it in the paper. Where are they being taken?'

'To hospital. Specialist eye infirmary. They'll get proper treatment.'

'Will they be all right or have they permanently lost their sight?'

'Who knows, love, who knows? But there'll be more arriving tomorrow, and the next.'

Half an hour later, an elderly porter opened their carriage door and they stepped into a compartment with two other people. The train lurched, steam engulfed the view from the window. Her father shook out his newspaper and disappeared behind it. The sound of a whistle was like a cry that followed the train, as if its progress through the countryside brought distress.

Cass opened Orion's book of John Clare poems that she'd taken from his shelf, guessing he'd like to have it with him. She noticed they were now passing a flat plain between hills where a military encampment had churned up pasture into bare earth. The road leading to it scarred the meadows and a cavalcade of motor cars sent up a cloud of dust. She saw a large group of men on horses riding out from the camp across the farm land. That's where Orion should be, she thought. She turned back to watch the cavalcade until the train turned a corner and she could no longer see them. She wished she could see what lay ahead, rather than be a passenger about to enter a tunnel without knowing it.

Why had Orion brought this upon himself? Upon them all? She trusted him, more than anyone else. She knew he had made a decision he would not easily unmake. She saw now it wasn't something she should question. And yet…

'Tickets, please,' said the inspector standing in the doorway. Her father woke with a snort.

Neither of them could bring themselves to ask a passerby the way to the gaol so they wandered around the city streets for a while. Then, as they rounded a corner there it loomed: the gaol that was incarcerating her brother. The sight of the high stone walls, black with damp, made her flinch. But curiosity impelled her to step through the small wooden door in the main gate just as her father seemed to falter. In the gloomy light his face had grown ashen. He said nothing but drew her arm through his and clutched her hand as they proceeded down the passageway. Her fingers curled tightly inside her palms.

Inside, the place smelled of damp clothes, a mixture of old sweat and filth. The stink permeated the corridors, made her throat feel squeezed. She coughed. And the guards seemed to like jangling their keys, as they made a great show of swinging open the iron gates and then banging them behind. Voices echoed, rolling round and round the spaces as if there were no way out until the words lost impetus and faded away. She would give it to him straight – tell him that he must be mad to put up with this, allowing himself to be humiliated when other men left their homes as heroes. Ashamed of her own brother having to be held in this place, refusing to fight for his country, dishonouring his family among the neighbours.

The visitors were herded into a room with long tables and everyone sat there for a while until there was the sound of more jangling keys, a door opened and a man shouted 'Twenty minutes from now! Off you go.'

A vagabond with a shaved head and thin face approached the table. He was dressed in an ill-fitting uniform covered in arrows. He leaned across the table as if to say something and when she bridled he slumped in the chair. He opened his mouth and shut it. He bared his teeth in a crooked smile and at once she knew it was her brother. Nothing else about him was recognisable. Just that half-smile and his teeth. When he said her name she knew the timbre of his voice. But why so reluctant to speak? Wasn't he glad to see them? Grateful that they had travelled all that way? Her astonishment stopped everything she wanted to say for a moment. Was this really her brother? This filthy, bedraggled man in baggy, rough fustian was really Orion? He'd become one of those spectres she'd seen begging on the streets: crippled, deranged, sleeping huddled in rags and newspapers. A stranger from another world.

Her eyes blurred. She couldn't have explained what was the matter and was aware she was wasting the little time they had together, ruining the visit. She wanted to hug him but couldn't reach across the table because a warder was walking up and down behind the prisoners. Her tears embarrassed her. Her father was making no effort – and this embarrassed her.

When she blinked away the blurriness she noticed a strength in her brother. His face looked completely assured even as it looked so defenceless. She glanced round at their father who was sitting with his hands clasped and she thought he might explode. Orion leaned across the table, his grubby hand creeping towards her.

'What's happened to your tongue?' she asked in a wavering voice, through a runny nose. 'Has the cat got it?'

He snorted. Ice broken. She wiped her nose and

handed him the hanky.

'Mama sent you a cake. Will they let you have it?'

'No, they won't let me have anything.'

'You'd better eat it now then.' She pushed it toward him and he broke a piece off and ate it. He seemed to have some trouble chewing and swallowing. He rolled his eyes at her in enjoyment.

His mouth full, he said, 'Oh, it's so good to see you. Talk to me. You can't know how much this means to me. Talk, just talk.' His words sounded as though they were the first sputters of water that had been syphoned through a tube.

She passed the John Clare poems towards him and he opened it, turning the pages slowly and then shook his head and pushed the book back. She gabbled on to him about their new dog, about some girls from the Women's Land Army who had come to the farm, about Swan going lame after a nail penetrated deep into her sole and how difficult that had made things, about the lack of news from Fernley because all he ever sent were the regulation postcards. Orion nodded, eating as she spoke.

Her intention had been to say nothing controversial despite her mother's injunction. She knew now that whatever the consequences to herself or the family she would try to respect Orion's decision. But Father was saying nothing at all, keeping quiet while she spoke. She blurted, 'Is this worth it, Orion?' as if having to voice her father's thoughts.

'What? Prison?'

'Yes. What would happen if you changed your mind?' she said.

'Not on the cards. Whatever they do to me just makes me more determined.'

'You know, you never explained exactly why. We need to know. '

'Are people giving you a hard time because of me?

They have no right to do that. No right at all. I'm sorry, Father, but you mustn't let them bully you because of me.' His voice was so quiet it entered her as if he were whispering directly into her ear.

'You have never fully explained yourself,' Father said. He uncrossed his legs as if he were about to stand up. 'Giving us so much grief, humiliating us. We have to suffer because of this, I'll have you know.'

'Please don't waste our minutes trying to persuade me out of this. I needed to know how you are, how Mama is, and Swan.' He paused, as if talking was difficult and used up all his breath. 'It's so good to see you. I'm sorry I can't talk much about myself. There isn't much to tell you. I am as you find me.' He was leaning forward on the table between them, looking from one to the other. He looked down at his hands that had become fists, 'We have to keep silent… words aren't easy to say. So please, you talk to me.'

'We are owed an explanation,' barked Father. 'It's impossible for us when we don't understand. What the deuce is it all for?' Cass was relieved he had spoken at last but wished he didn't speak so harshly. He hadn't said anything warm or friendly. His own son!

'I took an oath.'

'An oath? What do you mean? What sort of an oath? When?'

Orion seemed to fall into a trance. He said nothing. The whites of his eyes glittered in their sockets. It was only a moment.

'… a long time ago.'

'When, Orion, when?' Cass shouted out. 'What was it about?' She couldn't help herself.

'Time's nearly up, five more minutes.' The hubbub rose, a baby keened.

Father continued, 'But you could take on other jobs in the Army. Ambulances, messengers, transport – things like that.'

'No, I can't support the war in any shape or form. I won't become part of the Killing Machine: I'm an absolutist now, Father.'

'Balderdash! An absolutist? What the dickens do you mean?'

'Yes, I can't just go picking out the bits that seem convenient. It would be against everything he stood for.' He looked round at the warder and hunched in his chair. He slid the handkerchief up his sleeve. He added, 'Look, I'll be released soon… but I won't make things worse by coming home. What happens is you get one hundred and twelve days for disobeying an order so that'll be over soon until…'

'That's it,' shouted the warder.

'But where will you go?' cried Cass.

'I've made some friends in here. I'll stay with them.' He was shouting over the din of rising voices and scraping of chairs.

'What? Confounded criminals?'

'No, Father. Conchies, like me.' She hadn't realised there was a network of them. 'They've made me a reservist and so what the Army does is issue orders again – which I won't obey. So they'll have to arrest me again. And so it goes on – cat and mouse. Until the war's over, most likely.' He stood up and looked across at the warder, swinging his keys.

'You mean they'll imprison you again? Your mother and sister have more of this to come?'

'Until the war is over, I suppose so, yes. Unless they change government policy.'

'Do you not realise Cass might have become engaged? That his parents now refuse to have anything to do with us because of you?'

'Who? Frank Lethbridge?'

'A thing like this can ruin a girl, ruin her prospects.'

'Well, no need to go that far, Father. It's not going to happen now. Forget about it.' As she spoke she realised she didn't feel as angry or disappointed about Frank as she ought to be. Not deep down. Was it a case of good riddance? He hadn't embraced her properly, not once.

The guard tapped him on the shoulder. 'C'mon. Time's up.'

'Oh, bother the time… look, write to us at least, when you're out, won't you?' Cass leaned forward to be closer to him. 'Mama would love to see you. Come home if you can.'

'No,' he said in an undertone to her, 'Father wouldn't have me.' A stricken look ran across his face, 'You can see what he's like with me. He'll never understand. She won't either.'

Cass stretched across the corner of the table to him. 'I do see a bit better now. It's all right, Orion my darling. It's all right.'

Grabbing his shoulders, she passed her hands around his neck and kissed his cheek. 'If only you could've talked about it…'

'And when they put me back inside again don't either of you come back. It's too horrible. Write to me. Just write. Write to me with Leo's pencil I gave you to look after.' The warder was holding his arm, jangling his keys on the chain. 'There's something else… don't think about Lethbridge… it's much better this way… I couldn't have borne… not him of all people!'

She couldn't hear what he said any longer, hauled away by the guard into the crowd of men. He moved into the line of other prisoners and she gasped out through her tears, 'You're talking in riddles.'

The prisoners shambled out of the door at the far end. As Orion turned the corner he looked back quickly and as the barred iron gate slammed behind him Cass waved. He wouldn't be home for Christmas as she had hoped.

Her father came up behind her and drew her arm in his again. They walked, without speaking, back down the dark corridor and out through the entrance into the daylight, stepping from one world into another. She heard sparrows cheeping and swifts screaming overhead. Beyond the gate a motor car rattled past.

Afterwards, his alien reek lingered in her hair and seemed to stain her skin even inside her gloves. She washed her hands twice in the cloakroom at the station but when she lifted her hand to her nose she could still smell it. Without soap and a scrubbing brush it would cling to her pores.

She put her father by the train window. He seemed helpless. She bought him a newspaper but he didn't unfold it. She left it on his lap and leaned her head against his shoulder. She slipped her hand inside his. It twitched incessantly. Against her fingers she felt the grain of his skin, the whorls of his finger tips fitted against her own. The palms were rough from working the land and yet handled horses with tenderness. He would not complain to her. Fathers do not complain.

She was glad he left her to her thoughts. She knew now there would been no point in arguing with Orion. He had his own agenda and was struggling to create peace on earth. That was the real point of his refusal and who could argue with him? Gas attacks, horrible wounds, dismemberment, death. What was it all about? Perhaps it would be better to let the Germans have the whole country if that's what they wanted. She could see that Orion wasn't going to budge from his position and that he didn't care what other people thought of him. That was his own particular battle. He was committing a heroic gesture, not a crime. She rather envied him his resolve, his conviction.

You have to feel out the choices you make. As a

woman she had fewer choices open to her. Orion had decided this course was the right path to take and he would not turn back, whatever the consequences. One thing would lead to another, to be sure. But she admired his determination: it set him apart as if he shone with an inner light.

She had to acknowledge she had been shocked by his emaciation. I expected him to look bad but not this bad, she thought. Maybe they ought to make enquiries. But of whom? I'll not be saying anything to Mother about how he looks.

For Orion might not come out of this alive. Or, at the least, not in good health. The authorities didn't care if he lived or died. His death would be just another one to add to the endless beastly lists.

As for herself, she was thinking as the train trundled beside the meanders of the river before arriving at Exeter, she would damn well go to the Front if only they'd let her. She could drive ambulances or look after the horses – maybe by now she would have found Silver or Punch or The Plough. She'd have gone through anything to find them and try to keep them out of harm's way. But women couldn't get to the Front unless they were nursing staff, and that wouldn't necessarily bring her close to the horses or to tomfool Frank. Her thoughts raced about.

She had to see Frank in person somehow. When might his next leave be? But she might not be able to see him. His parents wouldn't have it. If he had known about their likely reaction it really was too bad of him to have raised her family's expectations. And actually, when she thought of how he hadn't kissed her, his last letter wasn't at all surprising.

Sometimes it's the smallest things that seem to count the most.

14

As Orion is never going to lift so much as a finger to contribute to the war effort, it's down to me. He is pursuing his own notion of honour and I won't argue about it with him. Mother is going to object, of course. She will want me to stay here and knit socks, help about the place. But I have to do what I can with my own particular strength and skills, not just sit around at home being a lady. It's time for me to stop holding back and doing what is expected.

So what exactly, she wondered as she tried to get to sleep, was this knot in her stomach? If she tried to analyse it she couldn't work out what it was made of or where it had come from. It sat like a hard lump in her innards and always said *No*. It was only a tangle of difficulties, she decided, that needed picking apart bit by little bit.

Thinking about it logically, she knew Father could get other help for the farm: there are lots of women in the Women's Land Army now who can do what needs doing. My work lies with horses, not here where there are none left. Take one step at a time, see where it leads to... She pored over the map, tracing out a course across country not known to her, beyond the villages and lanes she knew, through places she had never heard of before, incomprehensible symbols. You just sat on the train until it got where you wanted. Not much to it really. She'd take a few clothes from her brother's drawer and Leo's mechanical pencil that Orion had popped in her pocket at the station. It might bring her courage, mightn't it? Or was it unlucky?

She got out of bed as the wind began rattling the

panes and rain beat against the glass. Her breath came in little puffs. Her hands were pink with cold as she turned up the light to re-read one of Frank's letters.

July 12th, 1916

My dearest,

I look forward to seeing your face in real life again and treasure the photo you sent me. I imagine you whenever I wake. Not that I can sleep much at night what with duties and one thing and another so I try and catch a little shut-eye during the day when the necessary trench repairs have been determined. We make such a racket with our cannon you have to be well-nigh dead with exhaustion to do more than doze.

You asked what it is like here and I can tell you the fighting has been terrific. Now, at every step we walk through the wreckage of war – mangles, pots and pans, old furniture, farm implements – worse still, discarded uniforms, tattered leather, wagons, shell cases – all flung apart. And of course, now and then a few bodies of those who have not made it to the dressing station to be bandaged back together once more.

We keep up a storm of shells. The horses are constantly overworked in order to maintain supplies to the guns and to the gunners. This means the ground is pocked and blasted and there is not one patch of earth that has not got a shell hole filled with water and rotting rubbish.

One day, when I am home, we will talk of books we have read and ride out to hounds once more and all these gruesome pictures will be things of the past. You can write sonnets and read them to me.

But now I must stop, dear girl. Hoping you are quite in the pink.

My fond love to you,
Frank

She flicked through to the last one she'd received a month ago. It was less crinkled than the others and was still in its envelope as if it had only just been opened.

Dec 16th, 1916

My dear Cass, for dear you will ever be,

I can barely bring myself to write the following for it is with more than some regret that I have to inform you my parents have instructed me to call off announcing our engagement. This is not what I would wish for myself as I am sure you must be aware by now and I trust it may only be a postponement.

Perhaps the Hun will soon be overcome, and I would then be able to persuade them out of their intransigence. Or your brother may yet change his mind and the obstacle my parents perceive will be removed.

I have one last favour to ask of you and that is that you give me permission to keep your photograph for a while longer to remind me of the young lady I once hoped would be my wife. It is too difficult for me to send it back quite yet and, in any case, I am hopeful that circumstances may soon change and that everything can be back to how we planned. But if this seems like a frightful cheek please write to me and I will send it back by return.

I am rather too upset to write any more at the moment. Please do not take this as any reflection on your sweet self.

My fond regards,
Frank

After the initial shock she felt annoyed with him for being so… so very obedient. Was his father his Commanding Officer? He couldn't really have loved her and he had never kissed her to make her feel breathless and tingling in the way she imagined Love would transport her. The whole affair had started as an accident with the teapot lid falling off at the cricket tea. Nothing romantic. And what about the photo? It felt like an intrusion that he should keep it but she could not bring herself to write and ask him for it back. She guessed she wouldn't ever be able to marry him – not after this exposure of bad feeling between the two families. After their objections to him marrying the sister of a conchie she herself would never be able to face his parents again. Even if they were to change their minds. But the photo didn't matter after all, she thought. He could be allowed to live in hope.

The thing that bothered her was what he said about horses being overworked. What she didn't know about horses wasn't worth knowing. Look at the countryside around them drained of its horses. Even the milkman and the baker delivered by motor these days. How many horses did they have over there? Who understood horses better?

At breakfast the next morning she said, 'I've been thinking, Mama.'

'Have you now, dear?'

'Yes.'

'You know what Thought did, don't you, dear?'

'You have told me.' Her mother glanced at her.

'I have decided… I'm going to take up an offer of work at a Remount Depot where the horses get taken before being sent to the Front. I might be useful there, exercising and training the horses. What would you and Papa think, if I did? You'd manage here without me, wouldn't you?' She hurried on, 'It is something I could be good at. Do my bit, you know, as you said…'

'I don't expect they'll take young ladies on.'

'Of course they will. They must.'

Every morning she watched out for the postman and

when he approached the house she managed to be around to intercept him. When an envelope with her name and address type-written arrived she guessed what it was and took it out to the stables to read.

Dear Miss Forrester,

Thank you for your letter of the 15th inst. If you have experience with horses I am prepared to give you a trial. Please report to my office for an interview at Pluckley next Wednesday afternoon when I will decide how long the probation period should be.

Yours sincerely,
Captain M.C King (RVC)

She rushed indoors calling, 'Look Mama, look. I really am going to go and work with the horses.' She decided she wouldn't tell her parents anything about wearing breeches and boots like a man, riding astride, mucking out. Not even if she was asked.

She asked them not to wave her off on the train. She had never been away from home before for more than a night or two on her own, and she did not want to disgrace herself by crying. She kissed her mother goodbye in the garden before climbing into the dog cart next to her father. 'I'll write and let you know how things are, Mama,' she said to her. 'Don't worry about me. I'll be fine with the horses, you know I will.'

'Have you got everything?' asked her father as she climbed in to the dog cart. He handed her two five-pound notes and said he'd send some more the following week when he had her address. 'Oh, riches! Thank you. But they'll be paying me, Father. Don't worry.'

She looked back at the farmhouse. Her mother had already gone indoors. The windows seemed to be watching her over the garden wall. When they reached the valley – the nexus of all their comings and goings – she said, 'Do you remember the old stories of this place? How Leo thought they were real?'

When he said nothing she looked at him and saw his eyes looked shiny. She grasped his hand and he pulled her to him and squeezed her. 'I never thought it would be you going like this.'

'Well, Father, this is the least I can do. Make use of all the knowledge and experience you've given me.' She was thinking: my bones are shaped to bend round a horse, my skin is accustomed to the feel of a horse's pelt. I can tell one horse from another from the sound of its hoof beats.

He pulled the pony up at the entrance to the station and made as if to get down, tying the reins up to the seat. 'No, Papa. We've had our tearful good-bye. You go on home now, look after Mama.' A number of young men and their families were milling about. She stretched back up to her father and kissed him goodbye, turning to wave again from the step. She watched him till he and the trap disappeared round the bend and knew that she was watching her past life part company from her.

When the train arrived, she found a seat in a compartment with some young men. She squeezed herself between them – Plymouth men, perhaps, leaving home after furlough, their eyes watchful, uncertain, hard like grit. One of them half smiled at her and offered her a cigarette. She shook her head. The train jerked out of the station.

She worked her way down the rattling corridor to the toilet. In her hold-all she had some of Orion's clothes: collarless shirt, breeches, jacket. In Cass went and out he came, hair shoved under the flat cap. She had to find out if he could carry it off. Would anyone believe in him?

With her clothes changed, she didn't feel any different

inside. Did a man feel any different? Try it out. Her stomach churned. No one was waiting outside the toilet and she slunk back in to look at her reflection in the small grubby mirror above the basin. She saw a very young chap looking back at her with serious eyes and slightly frizzy hair peeping out from under the cap. She pulled her hair tighter and thrust her hair clips in harder against her head to tame her wayward hair. She mustn't smile too much, if at all, because she thought it made her eyes look slightly girly.

She couldn't just go back to the same compartment, she'd have to find a new one. She unlocked the door and turned in the other direction into another carriage, where she spotted an empty seat. When she asked if the seat was taken no one more than glanced up. So she looked at her boots and out of the window, avoided catching anyone's eye, afraid she might blush, afraid she might see disbelief or, worse, puzzlement or laughter. She realised she had only a girl's history, and asked herself if that would be adequate. Was it really that much different? One step at a time…

Looking out of the window she noticed in the far distance a strange outline on a hillside. As the train drew nearer she saw that a gleaming white horse was inscribed in the grass. She gasped. Were her eyes deceiving her? The horse's head was low and it had a green eye and pricked ears, its tail carriage high. The man sitting opposite said, 'That's the White Horse. Been there since prehistoric times… a symbol of old England. If the blasted Huns invade they'll destroy it.'

'It's not a farm horse, is it? More of a riding horse.'

'You've not seen it before, I take it? You going far?'

'I'm going to work with the ASC on remounts. I'm on my way to Kent.'

'Jolly good luck to you, young man.'

15

She was the only person to alight from the train at Pluckley. She emerged from the station, with its busy sidings and goods yard, into a flat landscape: the sky above the trees seemed huge, with distant clouds in shades of white and grey like puffs of steam. Situated some way from the red-brick village with its neat railway cottages and gardens, the Remount Depot ended up being a longer walk than she'd imagined. The track ran through the woods and was marked and scored by the comings and goings of horses' hooves, with divots where they had sunk in the mud, stones struck white where iron shoes had clipped them. Walking along the pocked track was hard going.

Soon she could hear the horses. The sound of their neighing, one to another, grew into a bedlam with every step she took towards them, the whiff of horse dung and urine becoming a stench.

At the gateway, the place seemed empty – crowded with horses but devoid of people. Lines of horses were tethered in rows under long wooden shelters. Ropes rattled in their stays as some of them turned to look at her, and a bay pony standing in the stall nearest to her whinnied, its pink nostrils flaring. Other horses followed in chorus.

A sentry in a greatcoat emerged from somewhere and walked across. When he inquired of her business he called her 'Sonny'. She explained she would like to speak with the officer in charge about a job, and showed him her letter. The soldier looked at it and gestured to some shabby offices to the right of the entrance, a tin-hutment. Some older single-storey buildings stretched beyond. This must once have been a works of some kind, she guessed.

When she walked up to the door and knocked, a voice fired 'Enter'. The handle was wobbly and she twisted it one way and then the other. The door whipped open. Her finger was caught by the cracked door knob and the pain stung. She grabbed the finger in her other hand. At the open doorway, an officer stood over her as if he were on the point of leaving while she was standing in his way. Underneath the peak of his cap a shadow fell over his eyes, his nose thin as a blade, the skin of his cheeks oddly pale.

'What is it?' He studied her. 'Can I help you?'

'Captain King? I hope you can. You asked me to come for a trial,' she said, pulling the cap off her head. 'You said to report to you today.'

She handed him the letter he had sent.

'So, you came.' He glanced up at her. 'Right, Miss Forrester. You have experience with horses, do you?'

She explained how she'd been breaking and schooling horses since she was young. 'But can you muck out a stable and groom a horse? That kind of thing – the basics?'

'Yes, I've always had to take care of my own horse. I wasn't allowed a groom. I can do whatever is required,' she answered, looking past his shoulder at a cabinet full of hunting whips and spurs.

'And you have led horses before, I take it?'

Cass nodded.

'Is that a Yes?'

'Er, yes… sir.'

'I don't mean one at a time though. I mean three or four.'

Cass suppressed a half-smile and replied, 'I'm sure I could do that. It doesn't put me off.'

He sniffed and walked back across the room to open a cupboard from which he snatched a piece of paper.

There were piles of forms neatly arrayed in rows on the shelves. His hand shook slightly and seemed to hover in the air for a second before descending on one. On his cuffs were two rows of gold braid. From the centre of the desk he took a pen and dabbed it in an inkwell. 'Read this and sign at the bottom, if you would,' he jabbed with his finger where she should sign.

'This letter says you claim that you can ride competently and that you're experienced with all types of horses. We'll give you a week's trial. If you pass, you get paid ten shillings a week.'

He stood, and looked down at her. She realised that the interview was over, that he was dismissing her, so she was flummoxed when he extended his arm and shook her hand, holding her fingers tightly.

'Well done, Miss Forrester, you've arrived at the right moment if you really can do what you say you can.'

He put the form she'd signed in a drawer which was full of unfiled pieces of paper. 'Now you'll need to find Corporal Fox and ask him what needs doing. He'll be busy in the stables right now. You can put on a saddle and bridle, can you?'

'Yes, sir.' She didn't take offence. There were lots of women from families like her own who had grooms to prepare the horses for riding, so it was quite possible that others wouldn't know how to tack up a horse even though they rode to hounds every week.

'Well, that's more than some people can do,' he said more warmly as he walked back to his cupboard. He thrust a booklet in her hand. 'Here's a manual for you, costs 2d. It'll come off your first pay if you stay. Tells you what you need to know: times of day, what to do when, that kind of thing. Someone that-away will come over to show you the ropes,' and he pointed up an avenue of stables as he opened the door. 'You'll soon get the hang of things.'

She walked in the direction Captain King had indicated. Round the corner at the top was a group of soldiers of her father's age. They all stopped talking and looked round at her approach. 'What you doing here, son?' one of them said as he strutted towards her. His face shone as if he were hot – which he might have been, being so tubby. There were two stripes on his arm. She explained that she had come to work.

'Oh, my giddy aunt! I was told to expect a lady somewhen. Come along with me, Miss. I'll show you what's what. Thousands wouldn't bother round here but I will. Sergeant Maddox will be here any minute and you'd better look sharp, I tell you that for nowt.' He turned round and winked at the other men. 'Don' s'pose Captain King mentioned him, did he? Nor where nothing is, for that matter.'

'No, he didn't. Thanks, that would be awfully kind of you.' She fell in beside him.

'There's three horses in need of a thorough grooming, hooves picking out. Can you manage that?' She nodded. 'Right, and as you finish each one they are to be tacked up, ready for exercise.

'Get going on those ones yonder. Lightweight hunters, for the cavalry. You'll manage them. Not the big boys. Get the kit from the saddler's store over there.'

He was striding ahead of her, talking over his shoulder. He continued, 'Between you and me – not quite all there, our Captain ain't.' His voice dropped. 'Bit of a dreamer. Irish. Not quite up to the job… shell-shock case – lost some of his mind so back here for a bit of R and R. But we don't talk about it.'

'Shell-shock? What's that?'

'Can't stand the sound of shelling any more. Here we are.' They arrived at a grey door that led into an old warehouse. Inside were rows of saddles and bridles with numbers on tallies, bags of grooming kit dangling below.

'Excuse my asking, but you know how to saddle and bridle a horse? Other ladies who've been here couldn't really tell which end to put the nosebag on, they couldn't.'

'Really? So what were they here for?'

'Oh, they said they knew horses, but obviously they didn't know the rudiments.'

He reached up and took down a bag containing brushes and a cloth. 'Tell you this for nowt – what the Sarge likes is coats shining and tails combed through. We've got new young cavalry officers this afternoon, coming in to choose their mounts. They need to be looking smart. A quick, hard grooming, sleeves rolled up. I'll show you which ones. And I'll come back and give you a hand soon as I finish.'

'Thank you,' she said. 'That would be terrific.'

'Stables is till 3.30 in the afternoon. So best get cracking. Sarge allus gives new recruits too much to do. Means they allus fail. He'll be round any minute. Oh, and use the curry comb on the coats.'

'Thanks for the advice.'

'And what do we call you, Miss?'

'I'm Miss Forrester. And what should I call you, sir?' She knew what two stripes meant.

'My name's Corp'ral Fox but you can call me Foxy, dearie,' he said with a wink. His eyes were bulgy and the winking lid didn't seem to quite close. It felt as if she were under surveillance even when someone was apparently trying to be friendly.

Alone with the horses, she felt more at home. The first one was a chestnut mare, edgy, nervous – the touch of the brush seemed to irritate her and she sidled away. The steel curry comb wasn't going to be tolerated. Her eyes rolled and she flung up her head when Cass's hand came near. Cass lowered her hand and stood in the stall, talking quietly to the nervous mare, not looking her in the eyes, waiting for her to show curiosity. The mare's head dropped and she stood licking her lips for a while. The horse next door put his head over the rail and nipped the mare on her neck. She flung her head up, jerked back by the halter rope. Jumping sideways she almost stamped on Cass's foot. The stall was too cramped, so Cass led the horse outside and tied her up to a rail. Her mane was long and her tail stringy. No one had combed them out for some time. She wondered if what the corporal had said was correct. She'd noticed the other man wink at her. What had that been about? Was he trying to make things difficult? Or was it just blokes being blokes? Being friendly? You could never tell what men were thinking, especially when they got together. They never meant what they said. Everything was always a joke, she thought, banter or innuendo, especially the ugly ones.

Outside in the open air the mare was more compliant but was easily tickled and her skin flinched whenever the brush ran over a new area. Her head kept turning and she continuously stamped one or other of her hind feet. It was easy to see why her tail hadn't been properly combed out. Cass was aware that a horse feels through its fur, every hair on this one expressing its discomfort.

She saw a number scrawled in chalk on the stall and went back to the saddler's store to find the tack. The mare didn't like the feel of the cold leather on her back either. She put her ears back and hunched herself up. Cass managed to do up the girth and eased the bit into her mouth and then put her back in the stall to await collection. She wasn't sure how much time she was supposed to spend on each horse. What did the Manual say? Looking it up she saw it was an hour. But he'd given her three horses to do and there was only an hour and half to do it all in. And she hadn't yet had a bite to eat.

Footsteps approached. The mare's ears twizzled round. 'Afternoon, Corporal said you'd arrived.' A feminine-sounding voice spoke. A huge figure blocked out the light in the stall. Against the light, she just made out his shaven face. Funny how large men have such high voices sometimes, Cass thought. She felt like a child being admonished.

'I don't know about ladies. I really don't. Just because you go huntin' an' that and can stay in the saddle doesn't mean you know about Army remounts, with a war on, Miss… er…'

'Forrester. No, I don't suppose it does, Sergeant.'

'You have a lot to learn. A lot. You report to me, Miss Forrester, and you ask me whatever you need to know.'

'I will, sir. Thank you, sir.' She didn't know what needed to be known.

'Well, let's see. You've not done too bad a job. But look – these legs aren't what I'd call clean. The tail's all rat's tails and the mane must be trained to fall on the offside. Put your will and weight into it. And look here, tap the fuckin' curry comb out on the ground behind the stall as you go through the coat so I can see how much dust and scurf you've pulled out.'

'Right-oh!'

He continued, 'Use the curry comb as if you fuckin' mean it, see. Over in France, there's a lice problem so they must be groomed hard to make sure there's no sign of that when they leave here. Remounts go downhill rapidly with lice. Have you seen lice? Or mange?'

'No, sir, I haven't.'

'Well, you'll fuckin' know 'em when you do.'

'I'll keep an eye out.'

'You must actively look for 'em. Report any to me. Sergeant Maddox is my name. Got that?' He started walking away. 'And watch out for that next one. It's got fuckin' teeth. I'm doin' my rounds during Stables and I'll be back in a jiffy to see how you're gettin' along. Oh, and beg pardon for my French but you'll just have to get used to it.'

She wondered what he meant by this as she hadn't heard any French, or, at least, not recognised it as such, though his sing-song accent wasn't the easiest to understand. He wasn't from Devon, that was for sure.

The next horse in the row turned its head and bared its teeth when she approached, lashing out a corkscrew kick that nearly landed on her belly. She jumped sideways to avoid the hoof. After that, the horse settled down as if it had made its point and only turned round to threaten her now and then.

The third horse was clenching the wooden partition with its teeth and sucking air into its lungs. Its eyes rolled around in its head. Its fur was dry and scurfy and it would be impossible to produce a polish on the staring coat. None of it was easy. No cavalry officer would choose this one. Her father wouldn't keep one like this, however handsome it looked, as its curious wind-sucking habit would be transmitted to other horses in the yard. She'd have to report it to Sergeant Maddox. A pity, because it had good conformation, which meant it could perform well in the field. What would be its fate, she wondered?

'I came to tell you, Miss, it's teatime and you're to come and have a brew with us. You must be needing a break by now,' said a voice.

'Oh, thanks. Yes, I could do with one.'

'Me too,' the soldier said. He came into the stall and edged towards her with a pronounced limp. He wore spectacles and his eyebrows and moustache were faded like ash. She felt uneasy. He slapped the horse's rump so it startled aside, leaving nothing between him and her. 'So, what's a pretty young lady like yourself doing in a place like this?' He looked down at her, grinned. The gaps between his teeth looked orange and his breath smelt of mice.

'I like horses,' she said, cleaning off the brush she had

just been using. 'I've grown up on horseback. Thought I could be useful here.'

'Did you now?'

She picked up the grooming bag and ducked under the rail to slip out of the next stall and into the daylight. 'I need that tea,' she said and walked quickly away down the row of horses. 'Where is it?'

In the canteen a large group of men sat smoking. At the counter a man in a grubby overall was pouring tea from a large metal teapot into chipped blue cups. 'Hello, Miss,' he said. 'You'll be the new girl. We'll make sure you're all right. Biscuits and sarnies on the table.'

A woman in a print house-coat was selling cigarettes. 'You'll be staying at my house down the road,' she said cheerily.

'Oh, thank you. I didn't know about that.'

'Sergeant Maddox fixed up the room for you. Didn't think you'd want to sleep with the men in the bunk house. Cost you two and six a week in advance, please, ducks. Barf night on Wensdy and you gets your meals up here.'

'Right-oh,' answered Cass, wondering what the room would be like.

Foxy jumped up and offered her his chair, but she shook her head and put her cup on the table while she fetched a chair from the back of the room and sat down on that. He introduced her to the other men, who nodded at her and carried on talking in an animated chorus of different accents punctuated now and then by guffaws and snorts of comprehension. Foxy winked at her again. The man with the limp appeared in the doorway, picked up a teacup and sat next to her. 'Where you from, dearie?'

'From Devon. And what about you?'

'Oh, the Army is my home. Haven't known much else. I been wounded so many times – last one was in South

Africa – but I won't take my ticket. I've alwiz been a soldier. I volunteered for this partic'lar job because the doctors wouldn't let me go to the Front. Too wheezy, they said, too rickety on my pins. But I'm not too long in the tooth, not yet.' He nudged her and snorted with laughter.

He looked round the group and seemed pleased with himself. 'She done a good job on they horses, Sarge. Knows what she's doing, this 'un.'

'My name's Miss Forrester,' she said. 'I hope we work together,' she said.

'Right then,' said Sergeant Maddox, stubbing out his cigarette as he stood up, 'better get the show back on the road. We've some fuckin' horses to get moving. You keep this little lady with you, Mrs K. I'm sure she's tired of cleaning up after mucky nags. I expect you'd like a hand in the kitchen. Roll-call at 5.50 sharp. You can't be a second late.' And he vanished out of the door.

Mrs K pointed up the stairs to Cass's room. When Cass opened the door she thought she might have mistaken what was meant, as it seemed to be a walk-in cupboard with nothing but a bed in it. The window was blacked out. The planks creaked beneath her feet, and from the room below she could hear men's voices. Later their cigarette smoke seeped up between the gaps in the floorboards. 'Is this where adventures end up?' she thought to herself. The bedding felt slightly damp and when she lay down the sheets smelled of coal smoke: they must have been dried beside the steam trains.

All night the railway line outside the house was busy with trains on their way to and from the docks. At the back of the terrace lay the goods yard, where the sound of chains clanking and the screeching of wheels against rails woke her up constantly. Torch lights and raised voices punctuated the night. An acrid smell of damp coal permeated the room. One way and another she had little sleep, and when the alarm went off in the dark she managed to get back to the depot only just in time. A bird or two began to chirrup as light broke on the horizon.

First job was to water the horses in batches at the trough. It was very orderly and under command. Not before the words 'Dress up' could any horse get to the water, however thirsty. Every group of horses was given six minutes at the trough – they had to start getting used to conditions at the Front, Sergeant Maddox said. Then each horse got a nose-bag. Rations were strictly measured. In case Cass should get it wrong, they put her on the machine which cut the chaff that bulked up the oats in the nose-bags. At first she thought that this was an easy option; that she was letting the men down, not pulling her weight, but soon her arms ached. She felt crestfallen to hear how much work had been going on during the evening after she'd been sent to her billet.

After a week of broken sleep she approached the table at breakfast and found herself saying, 'Before there's any misunderstandings amongst you, I'd like you all to know I'm here to do the same job as you men. I don't want any special favours. I just want to be treated like one of you and do the same work. I don't need to be given easier options. I will dress like a man and can manage horses as well as anyone.'

In the sunshine the smoke in the room had turned blue. Apart from her immediate neighbour, faces across the room looked like pale medallions. 'Let's hope you manage this lot, too, dearie,' said the man with a limp, unaccountably called Quagmire.

Cass frowned at the plates on the table. 'I'm spoken for already, anyway.' No harm in a little lie. She had been, once upon a time.

'And another thing – very kind though it is of you,

Mrs Knowles, to put me up in your house, I think I'd better sleep where everybody else sleeps. I need to be here to make an early start and not finish before everyone else does.'

'Try telling that to Mad Dog.'

'Who?'

'Mad Dog Maddox. He'll have a thing or two to say.'

'He won't have it. He'll go mad dog over that.'

'Anyway, well done, Miss. We'll remember what you said,' a big-bellied man laughed, raised his tea cup as if cheering her.

'And don't any of you dare read anything into that.'

'And what might that be?'

'Just forget that I'm female, all of you, please. No door holding, no standing on ceremony of any kind. Nothing. I'm not a lady.'

'Well, you prove it by coming to the pub tonight with us and see if you can down a beer or two. We'll stand it you. Then we might believe you.'

16

Maurice King felt he was a marked man: a horse had saved his life. But he was a damned vet, for God's sake. He should not have been skulking on the wrong side of a patient. It was pathetic. When the horse fell he had crouched low beside the deep belly, its back and hind quarters sheltering him from the force of the fire. Tucked in there, he'd been shielded from blasts of shrapnel and the raking machine-gun bullets.

It had happened while one of the teams was feeding shells to a battery on the Somme. Horses with their heavily laden wagons often had to stand around in exposed positions, while the *toffee-apples* and the shrapnel cases were unloaded into shell-pits near the heavy field guns. It wasn't enough for the pestilential Boche to destroy munitions; they had to harry the innocent horses, destroying the means by which the guns were reloaded, making it clear how perilous it was to keep supplies flowing to the Front. Cannon fodder, the lot of them.

A message was phoned through to his Veterinary Unit, stationed at Mamcourt, that one of the supply horses hauling a general service wagon had been pulled up when hit during cross-fire. It would be impossible to unhitch the horse and wait for a replacement without leaving the rest of the team exposed. In the fire zone a horse couldn't be changed over for a fresh one, even if there were one close enough to use. And at a slow walk behind this wagon the rest of the transport convoy would be exposed and might result in the rest of them being blown to bits or cause team mates to slip into the mud. On top of that, a working draught horse was too valuable for the Army to lose. It was worth at least £40, while a man cost a shilling to replace.

On this occasion Maurice, being the veterinary officer on the roster for that night, was called out to give a shot of painkiller so the animal could finish its job in the traces. He jumped in the mobile horse ambulance with his usual driver, Jed, a young recruit from Co. Donegal. Jed knew horses inside out because his family, like many others in the area, bred a few ponies. Both Maurice and Jed were used to approaching the firing line with its continuous thud and roar of guns, the explosions of mountains of mud and tree limbs. They came in and out of the line at all times of day and night. Slung over Maurice's shoulder was his leather satchel containing chloroform, scissors, scalpel, needle and silk to perform small operations, mostly inadequate to deal with the wounds he encountered.

Once it had been a grey mare unable to move but looking uninjured. When he walked round the back he lifted her tail and found her anus was completely excised, as if by a surgeon's knife. How this could have happened leaving the rest of her unscathed, particularly the tail, was a brief cause for wonder. He and Jed concluded she'd been hit by a piece of shell as she'd lifted her tail to defecate. Standing there looking inquisitive she seemed unharmed but they both knew she was beyond the help of either chloroform or the new cure-all, BIPP paste. He used the cattle killer on her. Before Maurice flicked the lever, he said to her, 'It's the best thing for you now.'

When he was a lad, some IRA men had shot the family dog. His father had carried the black and white spaniel home in his arms and laid him down in the stable, asking young Maurice to fetch his gun. His father had stroked the dog's head, murmuring 'It's the best thing for you now' before pulling the trigger.

Bullets sometimes flew through the horses' bodies, the point of entrance looking as if it had been drilled by

101

an auger, the point of exit exploded. Depending on the velocity of the bullet the bone might be shattered, or it could get lodged inside. One such horse had a bullet wound on the side of its neck, in the very same spot where he would inject against the disease of glanders which could splutter its way through the horse lines, causing umpteen deaths from septicaemia. The bullet had entered just there and passed through to the other side of the neck as far as the skin and then became deflected over the shoulder and along the thorax, leaving its course clearly marked like the weal produced by the lash of a whip. Palpating with his bare hand, the Captain traced along each of the ribs: between the fourteenth and fifteenth he could feel the bullet rolling about subcutaneously. He removed it quite easily with the scalpel from his satchel and after he'd applied the miraculous BIPP paste, the horse continued its job as if nothing had happened.

On this particular night, while he was examining his new patient at the battery, the German gunners sent up flares and the brief stalk of silvery light revealed the motionless group of horses and wagons behind the British lines approaching the gun emplacement. Something whistled downward through the night sky onto the position and erupted just beyond them. He and Jed and the Transport men were instantly engulfed in a whirlwind fury of shells. The air burst into screams, hisses and bangs. The earth around them seemed to be blowing skywards. The exploding shells gave off successive pulses of hot gas.

He, Maurice King, survived because he took shelter behind the bulk of one of the heavy horses. Its body was riddled with bullets, slicing through the air to burrow and batter into the flesh, blood spurting like a syphon, a hind leg half torn away.

He floundered back into consciousness – firstly to a

stomach-turning stink: iodine, alcohol, blood, vomit. His stretcher was lying on soft earth, or something mushy. A candle flame was flickering. Was he imagining this? Or was there something wrong with his sight? Every few seconds the walls shook as a shell struck somewhere not far away. Sometimes a rain of small stones fell on the roof above, and the occasional thud as someone's helmet hit the low ceiling, startling him each time.

An orderly said, 'You was lucky, sir.' Apparently the stretcher bearers had found him lying in a deep pool of blood. They had hauled him out thinking he had bled to death, but when they found a pulse they brought him back here to the medics at the dressing station. A nurse brought a tray with some tea: there must have been something in it because he fell asleep again.

When he woke once more he found himself in clean sheets and apparently floating. He had a thirst like a layer of gritty beach-sand in his throat. But where was Jed? He was only a young man, hardly more than a lad really, and had never before been anywhere away from his own townland, let alone Ireland. His family were Republicans and the news of the Easter Rising had shaken him up, but he'd said he was only in France for the sake of the horses and he was sticking to his post. With his horse-kind eyes, he was as dependable as his name suggested, like good wheaten bread. He would wipe away tears whenever they had to destroy a horse, too badly wounded or too sick to recover, or when it had slipped off the roadway and couldn't be hauled back. He wouldn't be consoled by Maurice's mantra, 'It's the best thing for you now'.

Maurice lifted his head to see if Jed was nearby, and called his name. But he had no breath for more than a croak. No sign of him. Only other poor blighters jammed together like sardines in beds. When Maurice had last seen Jed, he was holding the reins of the courageous ambulance horses. Perhaps he'd got back somehow.

Overhanging trees were slowly passing the windows and he heard a steady buzz of engine, not vibrating, not close but ceaseless and irritating. A VAD nurse came by and saw his eyes had opened. He tried to sit up and ask her about Jed, but she went away to fetch him a glass of water. When he pulled his head up from the pillow to drink she said they were travelling on a hospital barge, being towed down the River Somme to the port. He would live. Might not return, though. And what about Jed? She hadn't heard about anyone called Jed but she would check. What was his number?

The man in the next bunk often sang. Even in the dead of night he sang. Always the sound of heavy footsteps going back and forth. Maurice asked all the footsteps about Jed. But nobody answered. Only the sound of singing. He called out to a nurse as she passed because he couldn't sleep with the dreadful tuneless moaning and she explained that no.48 had had both legs amputated and he wasn't able to sleep either. 'Pity you people can't do the best thing for him,' he said. In the morning a long line of eyes staring at the ceiling, the pillows grey and spotted.

He survived the Channel crossing: this hospital ship wasn't torpedoed. He then spent some time in hospital near Guildford. The War Office must have got him muddled with someone else because they sent a letter home stating that he was *Missing*. Then they'd written to tell them where he was. Confound it. He quickly wrote another note to say that he wasn't missing so far as he knew. He supposed some part of himself had indeed gone missing: he couldn't understand why sometimes he started crying or why his limbs trembled at inconvenient moments. It was humiliating. He'd have to keep it quiet.

His parents didn't need to have assumed he was dead. It was easy to get separated out there. The letter they'd received made it clear: 'The term *Missing* does not necessarily mean that the soldier is killed or wounded. He may be an unwounded prisoner or temporarily separated from his regiment. Any further information received will be at once sent on to you.'

Later, even when his physical wounds had healed, they refused to send him back to his post. They must have noticed his infernal effeminate habits. He'd get the quivers from time to time, couldn't easily hold a match to light a cigarette. The MO gave him a fortnight's leave but he wouldn't show himself at home in this state. Anyway, even his home was no escape: his father wrote to him about the sightings of U-boats surfacing off the coast, about a ship torpedoed off Rathlin Island, about the corpses of the crew that were occasionally thrown up on the beaches and needed to be buried.

To recuperate from his shakiness he went to stay in a cottage in Wales. He started writing a long letter to Jed's parents and found it hard to drop it in the postbox, thinking of the family reading his words. How could he adequately explain what had happened? It was all a question of trust. He and Jed had come to rely on one another, but the damned War meant he had failed him when the chips were down. He hoped to clear his head by walking, to keep his thoughts at a foot's length, as it were. The paths across the Brecons were, he thought, lines of human freedom, made by footsteps that had carried the weight of another person's history.

17

Steam lay among the trees as if trapped by the branches. Small puffs began to drift upwards into the dusk. The red ball of sun was shining behind a cloud and the evening sky was turning orange. In this flat countryside you could see for miles. There was a distant booming sound. Foxy sat on his drowsy horse smoking a cigarette.

'Hear that? Not very far away, is it?'

'The Front, that's what that is,' replied Driscoll, who was on foot. He never mounted a horse if he could help it. Before the outbreak of war he had been in charge of the horses at a fire station. It had been his job to keep them up to the mark for the emergency bell. With this experience he had done a stint at the Front and had been wounded when artillery fire reached the horse lines, almost destroying a battalion's supply chain.

'Must be beating the hell out of each other for us to be hearing that here.'

'A right menagerie, blackbirds, turtle doves… oh, that one there must be Big Daddy.'

'Do you s'pose it'll ever end?' asked Quagmire. His cigarette was glowing in the almost-dark. Above their heads, stars were beginning to show in the gaps between clouds. The horses were becoming restless, rattling the bits between their teeth.

'The only way to end it is to win it,' said Foxy, swinging his horse round to keep its quarters away from the others.

Cass, who had been looking up the long straight railway line in expectation, turned her eyes towards Dover and half expected to see flashes of light in the sky.

'What's it like?'

'What?'

'Being bombarded.'

'Like hell on earth. Puts the wind up yer, it does. You long for a nice wound just big enough to get you sent to hospital, or even home. While you're waiting yer hands shake and shake but when yer out there on an attack all you can do is listen. You hear the shells and the gunfire with every fibre of your being, right through your bones.'

'An' you haven't a bloody clue what's going on. It's allus the likes of us what gets killed.'

'Captain King seems a bit shaky,' Cass prompted.

'But he in't a proper soldier. Not his true vocation, like. He's just joined up to do his bit for king an' country even though he's a Paddy.'

'What do you mean... not a proper soldier?' she asked.

'You don't become a soldier just because you put the uniform on, Miss. The Officer Training Manual won't help much, if you're proper windy,' said Holmes, who was one of the Boer War veterans.

'He may be a 1914 man, I grant you, but he's not what a soldier calls a soldier. Not a real officer, dusn't know anything about musketry, dus he? '

'If this war was being fought by reg'lars it would be over by now.'

'But there aren't enough left,' said Holmes.

'Exactly, it's being going on too long. All the officers are dead or wounded out.'

'Do you mean, it isn't winnable?'

'That's not for the likes of me to speculate upon,' said Foxy. 'It's not like any other war I was in before, sticking men in trenches, bogging 'em down, making 'em wait for shells to blow 'em up. Fritz is too far away to reach. What's needed is some good, honest open war... bayonets, man to man killing each other. Killing should be more personal... much more satisfying to kill someone at close quarters, innit? These new-fangled Lewis guns just blast the enemy lines at 500 rounds a minute so it's pot luck who gets killed or even if they hit anything at all. And half the time these days, you sits in a rat-infested trench waiting for Fritz to lob over a grenade or for a sniper to catch youse out.' A boom like approaching thunder interrupted him, 'Fuck me, that were a big 'un... they gunners must be having a field day.'

'So,' said Cass, half thinking aloud, 'if Captain King isn't a soldier, what is he? And how come he's a captain?'

'Good God, Miss. Questions, questions. Most gents aren't anything in partikler, are they? A toff's a toff. But Captain King is a vet'narian. Knows a thing or two about horses, but nothing about waging war.'

'Oh, and what's more, he's from Ireland. Plucky, I grant thee, but gormless.'

'He were giving succour to a wounded horse hauling ammunition to the guns. Front-liners they are. Got caught in a bombardment himself, right out in the open,' said Holmes.

'Got to hand it to him. Perilous work.'

'While he's convalescing, he volunteered to run this depot, only temp'ry like, I'd say. Swinging the lead for a bit.'

'They says he used to play the violin. Concerts, Mozart, that sort of thing. Hearing's almost gone so he mightn't play no more. Gets the shakes he does sometimes, has to hide away in th' office.'

'Oh, I've heard music being played on a gramophone late at night sometimes.'

'Not my idea of a good time, but it do take all sorts, don' it?' Holmes's voice broke into song:

Any old iron? Any old iron?
Any, any, any old iron?
You look neat. Talk about a treat!
You look so dapper from your napper to your feet.

'These nags ought to be tucked up in bed,' Quagmire said.

'Yes, how much longer we going to have to wait? When do we give up?'

'We stay all night if needs must,' Foxy barked. After a few seconds, he said, 'Getting parky now though, I grant you. I don't half fancy a pint. Or three.'

Trains carrying horse freight travelled slowly and were subject to hold-ups making arrival times unpredictable. This particular consignment was due to coincide with feed and watering time at the depot, and only four staff had been spared by Sergeant Maddox. 'Bring them in nice and easy at a walk and the kraal gates will be ready and open,' he instructed them.

A whistle seemed to call up the moon as it appeared through a gap between clouds, which smouldered round the edges like a bullet hole. From way back along the line, the train's lamps shone on the rails as it approached the station. As it shuddered to a stop, pandemonium broke out and spread through one after another of the wagons. The noise was a contagion. One horse had kicked out the boards and by the platform light they could see its hind legs flailing, blood pouring.

The wagons were opened and one by one the horses were unloaded and turned loose in the paddock. Rolling their eyes, they wrenched themselves away from their handlers. Some of them huddled in a corner while others kicked up their heels. Some bent their heads to drink thirstily from the muddy puddles.

'Instead of leading 'em, we'll drive 'em orderly fashion down the road. When they gets a whiff o' the stables they'll work out where to go.'

'Right then!' Driscoll undid the gate and swung it wide open. Cass mounted her horse and stationed herself to make sure the horses turned in the right direction away from the village. With the gate now open the horses didn't make a move at first, as if afraid. Corporal Fox rode round the back of the paddock and yelled at them.

Cass's stomach lurched as she realised how many of them were heading towards her. A riderless cavalry charge. To try and turn them she waved her arms and kicked her mount forward. But they streamed past her, their eyes shining with terror, their iron shoes sparking on the stones. Her legs became pinioned between her own mount and the mass of moving animals. It occurred to her that she could be seriously injured.

'Stupid cunt,' shouted Corporal Fox as Cass turned her horse to give chase. Just as the front of the stampede reached a bridge over the railway line, another train whistled and steam engulfed the bridge. At this, the flight of horses halted, the ones at the back careering into the rumps of the ones in front. Cass seized the chance to edge past them and get herself on the far side. She would have preferred someone else with her to help prevent the horses running past her again, but by then the whole panicky herd was swivelling round and round to escape. Snorting and blowing hard, some were snatching at green twigs in the hedge banks.

When the locomotive whistled as it reached the station, the stream of horses surged back down the way they had come, fanning out in all directions in their urgency to get away from the monster train – over garden gates, crashing through fences and palisades, galloping across lawns, leaving behind a swathe of devastation among the cottages beside the railway station.

Holmes and Driscoll waved their arms to rush them past the goods yard and down the track through the woods to the depot. They followed, whooping them on until the whole lot charged through the gates, milling around among the horses tethered near the entrance, who were straining at their ropes, lashing out with their hooves. One of the kraal gates lay open and men came running to herd the hurly-rush of horses through it.

'They'll find the water trough and after they've cooled down by morning we can feed 'em,' breathed Foxy, lighting up a cigarette and drawing the smoke into his lungs. He passed the packet round the others.

'A tub o' shite you've made of that,' Sergeant Mad Dog came up, yelling. 'How many horses are goin' to be injured and how many others do you think you lost?' His voice fell, ringing like a hammer beating out an iron shoe, 'I've a good mind to dock your pay for each and every damaged and missin' horse as well as for the damage to property. We'll see tomorrow when all the complaints come in a ruddy deluge.'

Holmes said, 'Look, Sarge, it weren't our fault. They took fright, but it were Miss Forrester who got herself in the right spot and turned them. If it hadn't been for her, they could have galloped into the town, doing God-knows how much damage. We might have lost the lot.'

Before day broke, Cass roused herself and as the dawn lit up the herd of horses – of all types, light hunters, heavy draughts, small pack ponies – she started trying to count them.

She had nearly finished when Taffy, the elderly draught-horse master, spoke behind her, 'How many do you make it, Miss?'

'It's difficult because they keep moving about.'

'I make it forty-three. But it can't be – I thought it was a consignment of forty?'

'Well, I make it forty-four. Let's try again.'

After a minute, Cass said, 'Forty-three, you're right.'

'Well, I'll be jiggered. You haven't lost any. You've gained some. Half the countryside roundabout will be here claiming the best horses are theirs unless we get this sorted out.'

'But at least none were lost,' laughed Cass.

18

Cass knocked on Captain King's door. 'En-ter,' snapped his voice. She rattled the wobbly handle until the door was snatched open and pressing his hands against the doorframe he seemed to be caught by surprise.

'Yes?' he asked.

'You sent for me, sir?'

'Did I? Oh, yes, come on in. You've been on leave. Glad you didn't give up. Take a pew.' He offered her a packing case to sit on. 'Cigarette?' he said, a silver case open in his palm. She saw it contained a row of coloured Turkish cigarettes. 'Thanks, but I don't.'

'Do you mind if I do?' She shook her head. His hand jiggled as he tried to light the tip of his cigarette. His face contorted a moment. 'What I wanted to know, if you don't mind my asking, Miss Forrester, is this – what do your people think of you being here, working with the men?'

'I don't rightly know, sir. I do my best not to ask.'

'You don't think they object…?'

'I'm here, now, sir. I won't be leaving whatever they say. Why do you want to know?'

'It's just rather unusual for a young lady like yourself…' He seemed reticent.

'They don't know I'm dressed like this. They don't know I'm the only woman here. There were two women working on our farm during the summer.'

'Wouldn't they rather you were just at home?'

'Maybe, sir. But I'd rather be here, doing what I'm good at.'

'I wondered what brought you here. That's all.'

He was being quite persistent, she thought. What

could she say? She couldn't bring herself to explain about Orion. He might well never speak to her again. Best not to tell that bit of the truth. But there was something about this tall, lanky man who smoked black and gold cigarettes and whose eyes slipped away from looking at her whenever hers met his that made it difficult for her not to spill the beans. She sighed and said, 'My brother, sir, my brother is… he let the family down. My father's furious with him. He's a conscientious objector. He's in prison. It was up to me, you see, sir, to do something… and I do know quite a bit about horses.'

'I am aware of your brother. Letters in and out of the base are censored, I'm afraid. A senior officer reads everything. Your brother… he has taken a very hard road.' His pause let her wonder what was coming next, 'I had to ask because I want to know what you think, Miss Forrester.'

So it was him checking the letters. Had she written anything that she wished she hadn't?

Her heart seemed to be pounding in her throat. 'What I think?… er, I hope that isn't a problem.' She was both surprised and relieved to know that he knew, but dreaded hearing what she supposed would now be her marching orders.

'Look, I'm putting in a recommendation that more ladies be sent to work here at the depot. Your being here has made me realise that there are so many like yourself who are experienced around horses it would be a waste not to utilise them… provided their families are agreeable and don't make things difficult. The women can look after the horses and exercise them, releasing soldiers to go to the Front or to work in supply.' Trying to slip his cigarette case into an inside pocket, he didn't seem able to get it back in. His teeth seemed to grind as he spoke. Eventually his fumbling fingers dropped the case in the slot.

'That's a very good idea, sir.' She wanted to smile at her own relief, at his awkwardness, which made him look as if he didn't fit inside his own skin.

'It's all so temporary round here. There's around a hundred personnel on this depot and I never know, from one day to the next, which men are staying and which are being transferred across the Channel, apart from the few elderly or wounded. A few females would give the place stability.'

'But not be considered fit for active service.'

'At least that way they won't be snapped up by the Remount Bases in France.' He rose and started walking about the room. She noticed that his eyes were brown like a labrador's.

'When do you expect them?'

He steadfastly didn't look at her. 'Oh, I've got to wait for a reply from those damned men in suits at the War Office. They haven't a clue in the corridors of power how to run a war properly.'

'Not if they keep sitting at their desks. I can imagine they wouldn't.'

'All they want are reports – reports about movements, reports about figures, reports about forage, reports about fatigues, reports about losses and breakages. I spend my day recording things and filling out forms. If I don't I'll be hauled over the coals.'

He seemed to be about to lose his temper but thought better of it and opened a drawer, stood up to rummage through it and flung it shut again.

'Oh, one more thing, there's… ah… to be separate sleeping accommodation, so a new bunk-house is to be made out of one of the stores.'

'How many girls were you thinking of?'

'About five or six, I think, to begin with. To give the idea a trial run. And I'll be wanting you to see to them and train them up, Miss Forrester. I shall rely on you to tell me or Sergeant Maddox if anyone is unsuitable after, say, a month's probationary period. Earlier, if necessary. Is that all right with you?'

'It feels like an order.'

'Well, I thought it more civil to ask first.' He stood up and under his peaked cap she saw his eyes were fastened on her. The telephone started ringing but he refrained from answering it.

'Thank you, sir.' She smiled to hide what she was thinking – I'm getting used to taking orders by now. It was on the tip of her tongue to ask if he was yet used to giving them.

'Oh, and you can stop calling me "sir". You're not under my command,' he muttered as he picked up the phone. 'Pluckley Remount, King speaking…'

She would have answered, I don't think that would be a good idea, sir, even if I'm not considered eligible to have a CO. But she saw the frown on his face as his hand covered the mouthpiece and he said to her, 'Thank you. That will be all for now.'

A fortnight later, four new female recruits arrived on the afternoon train from London. Cass waited on the platform for them to arrive. She noticed a flapper stepping from the carriage in a fancy blue suit, hemmed at the ankle, sporting neat lace-up boots with pointed toes. Cass decided she couldn't be one of them. Two other girls stood on the platform together in crocheted rose-bud caps. Only one of the four arrived in sensible breeches and boots. She shook Cass's hand vigorously and introduced herself as Florence. She was a large girl and looked as if she could handle the chargers and the heavier draught horses. Cass warmed to her at once. She was less certain of the other girls, saying, 'I hope you've brought some work clothes with you. To be honest, I don't quite know when you'll be needing those again.

We'll have to find somewhere or other to stow them.' They would have to pick their way in those shoes through the mud to the bunk-house where she left them to choose their own bunks. There were no cupboards: they'd be living out of their suitcases.

Later in the canteen when they were all dressed in breeches and work clothes, their hair tied back in gypsy scarfs, she explained their duties.

At the end Florence asked, 'How are the men going to take to us doing some of their work? The land girls haven't had an easy time of it.'

'Yes, good question. You'll notice how the men take a bit of time to relate to us women. At first they like to think we're here for only one thing and that they'd like some slap and tickle. Don't worry about it. Treat them like naughty boys and just concentrate on doing your jobs.'

'God, we'd have to be desperate.'

'We just have to prove that we're capable of doing anything they can do and maybe even better. And oh, if they ask you to go to the pub make sure you drink beer and knock it back.'

'Beer?' said Amy of the blue suit. 'Yuk.'

'That won't be hard,' said Florence.

'Have you heard of Flora Sandes?' asked Amy. 'She's an Englishwoman who joined the Serbian army. There was an article about her in the paper. She's a soldier, a sergeant even. She's allowed to fight alongside the men'.

'Oh, really? But she must be one in a million.'

'Yes. One in several million actually, said Cass. 'The point is that she does what the men do and they believe in her because of that.'

19

The rule was to keep silent – some of the 'respectable' prisoners had done so for months, others for years. After a while, the enforced silence seemed to be slicing away at his memories as if with a bacon cutter. His arbitrary thoughts took on a life of their own. Continually dwelling on all that he had lost, and ruminating on the horror he saw in the heart of the world, gave him a strange measure of comfort because he no longer felt so isolated from the national despair.

On Sunday afternoons a bell sounded for a half hour of talking practice. Sometimes, after all that waiting, it was impossible to think of anything to say. And who would want to hear a list of grievances, especially when they also wanted to talk? Although he was looking forward to it, counting down the minutes, his mind fell shut like a lid when that bell rang. The connection between lips and brain was shattered. He was aware that the minutes were ebbing away, that he was not communicating.

During the week he began to practise speaking alone in his cell, and found it came burbling out in little spurts – bits of words, syllables all jumbled up at first as if his mind were unravelling. With his back to the spy-hole in the door, so that the warder would not see his lips moving, he mouthed nursery rhymes, snatches of poems he could remember from their governess, Miss Sowden, the part he'd once played in *A Christmas Carol* at Colonel Westwood's house. His mind seemed to have forgotten the mechanics of articulation but words flowed out from some store of memory in his body and the lines

Little trotty wagtail he went in the rain,

And tittering, tottering sideways he neer got straight again
came back to him. His father had given him a book of
poems by John Clare. Those poems had inspired a new
game between the brothers: he and Leo began to
transcribe bird song into words or sounds, using a human
alphabet just as the poet had 'translated' the nightingale's
song into *Chew chew chew chew chew... up cheer up cheer
up... wew wew wew... tee rew tee rew tee rew... gur-chew rit
chew rit-chur-chur chur... tweeet em jug jug jug jug*. So
Orion had attempted to notate the blackbird's song: *whee,
whee, gudge, gudge, du dee, du dee, weeee, weee, chweep, chweep, chu-
weep, chu-weep, churr, churr, chaw chip-chip, chaw chip-chip*. Leo
guessed it easily because he, of course, listened to it too:
he had also tried to put it into words himself but had lost
himself in the bird's flutings and trills. Like Clare, Leo's
poetry was in the fields but, unlike Clare, he could not
write it down. Later, the two boys tried to imitate the
nightjar's churring, but neither could begin to find a way
to notate that. They simply made droning noises until
their throats were sore. Trying to replicate bird song in a
human way made Orion – even when only young and
unable to express the thought – aware how language,
with its limited alphabet, fell short of expressing one's
innermost thoughts. Those old poems came back to him
now:

The badger grunting on his woodland track
With shaggy hide and sharp nose scrowed with black...

By the autumn of 1917, after reports of brutality reached
a head, the Home Office offered the thousands of
conscientious objectors the chance to transfer to
dedicated detention centres and undertake *work of national
importance* not connected with the war. Orion signed up to
be transferred to the Dartmoor Work Camp, not very far
from his home. It was located in the old Napoleonic
prisoner-of-war gaol at Princetown. From the outside the

118

prison looked like a Satanic mill, a factory, a warehouse. Inside, the walls ran with damp and the corridors smelled of sour clothes. The rules were more relaxed; the cells were not locked; you could leave your cage and go and speak to someone. Still, the landings were almost mute, as if the privilege might be rescinded if exercised too much. The cell itself wasn't any better – a plank bed, a blanket.

On the first evening after his arrival, he poked his head round the door and took some steps down the landing, to try and find out where others who had arrived on the same train as himself were to be working the next day. He had liked the look of some of the fellows in his train compartment and they had agreed to try and wangle working together. One of these chaps raised his fist as if he were a Communist. He didn't seem to know the others and introduced himself – 'Known to one and all as Len. Good to meet you' – and he solemnly shook hands with everyone in the compartment, offering cigarettes.

The freedom to make any choices at all made Orion feel that blood could reach the ends of his chilled limbs. He dawdled past the unlocked doors to see what his new neighbours were doing, introducing himself to see who might be friendly. His immediate neighbour was engrossed in making a model out of matchsticks and didn't seem to want to talk. Orion noticed heavy cobwebs dangling from the ceiling like drapes and withdrew. He caught the sound of a song coming from the end of the landing. A man leaned by the open window, singing quietly to himself, his voice a little cracked:

Some of these days, you're gonna miss me honey
Some of these days, you're gonna feel so lonely
You'll miss my huggin', you'll miss my kissin'
You'll miss me honey, when you go away.

He turned round at the end of his song and grinned at Orion, shooting his hand out towards him. Perry was a stocky man with a long face and a short, quick smile. He wasn't one of the latest arrivals and had acquired himself a larger cell at the far end of the landing. He said, 'Good morning to you. I saw you beating a retreat... your neighbour, Stan, is a cautious man: he won't talk to you till he knows you better. He loves spiders more than people.'

'Yes, the webs were a shock. Bit like Miss Havisham's in there. Doesn't he want to clean them out? Makes it seem rather sinister.'

'No, Stan is an arachnophile... won't harm a spider nor their webs. Ask him about spider webs one day when you have plenty of time to spare! The Cobweb Chamber, that's what we call it. Hey, tell you what – I was going to come and tell you new lads that on Sunday we go to church in the town – if you happen to want to come with us.' Orion shook his head, but Perry continued, 'Singing is good for you. Helps free up your voice. Only a short walk from the prison gates. Several of us go each week.' Orion must have still looked doubtful because Perry persisted, 'Look, we need people to go... unless you're a Quaker or a Methodist or an atheist? What happens is, you see, the vicar chooses the most martial hymns and psalms to try and provoke us. We have to keep going and stand firm.'

'He doesn't want conchies going?'

'No, that's it. But we have a right to worship and so we must exercise it, whatever he throws at us. We have our own battles to fight but without fisticuffs.'

Orion said he'd think about it.

Going beyond the gates without being escorted by guards or being hauled off immediately to a military training camp would be a gift from heaven. Was everyday life really going on somewhere beyond these imposing dark walls? It would be strange to rub shoulders with ordinary people once again and do ordinary things. Still, venturing into town needed some nerve – the space of it, the smell of car exhaust, horse dung, the sky so huge. He'd experienced it on the march from the station. Perhaps he'd rather not go.

In the end, the temptation to walk out of the prison gates like a free man to somewhere – anywhere, even just the church – was too strong to resist: the leaves on the trees, sounds of bird song, clouds in the sky. Once they were outside, the few people he saw passing back and forth made him flinch at first – their own conspicuous garb, ill-fitting and worn thin, must look ridiculous.

Through the fog the moors were invisible. A light drizzle fell on his face. He flung back his head as he walked and opened his mouth to taste the freedom of rain. Cold fingers of wind prickled through the gaps in the weave of the fustian uniform. He liked the feel of it against his skin. A flock of jackdaws and rooks spiralled in the gusts overhead, rising and falling.

The birds landed in the tops of the bare trees in the churchyard, cawing. Chack, Leo's pet jackdaw, which he had hand-reared from a chick, pecked into his mind. Unlike other boys of their age, Orion and Leo never stole eggs from nests. They hunted for them and climbed the trees to look inside but it was enough to find the different kinds of nests – the feather- and wool-lined nests of the sparrows; the perfect mud bowls made by the swallows in the barns; the collection of sticks that herons make their nests from, leaving holes at the bottom for the chicks' long legs to dangle from as they grow. They thought it a fine thing to climb a tree to see the eggs lying inside the nest, to admire their beautiful colours – the blackbirds' greenish eggs with brown speckles; the house martins' white eggs shaded with reddish freckles.

Without even speaking about it they left the eggs alone to hatch and grow into the birds they loved to watch. Tiny eggs that looked so delicate but contained within them wings, beak and feet that would, when fully grown in only a few weeks, enable the bird to fly and to migrate across the sea, they did not know where – but surmised it was to some sunlit other-place.

They never found the nest of the yellowhammer though they saw them on the heath and heard them singing in the cornfields. John Clare had called them *writing larks* because their ash coloured eggs, covered in black squiggles, looked as if written all over with a fine-nibbed pen. After Orion had read Clare's description this had been the nest he most craved to add to his list, as if he imagined he might find in the squiggly writing a new language for him and Leo.

He was glad to be in the middle of the group as they chatted together about food, football, their occupations. Perry had been a tailor, and clean-shaven Stanley, the spider expert, was a carpenter. There was an Irishman who said he was born a Catholic and lived in London, and another man who wrote poetry. Len, who had been put in a cell opposite his on the landing, joined the group. He said he was going to be an accountant.

Their conversation made Orion's head spin. What was to be done about Ireland? Would the aims of the Easter Uprising succeed in the end, despite the brutal executions of their leaders? Didn't he know that Eamon de Valera, no less, had just left Dartmoor prison and had been re-elected?

He became aware that only a few of the men he'd seen on his landing had come with them: the Quakers were going to their Meeting which took place within the walls, while the Plymouth Brethren and Jehovah's Witnesses kept to themselves. The Anarchists and Communists apparently refused religion... so why, he wondered, was Len one of the group?

As they neared the church a group of teenage boys

moved out from a clump of trees and came towards them to pass close by. Their hands were deep in their pockets and they spat on the ground as they passed the men. A few steps further on, one of the lads yelled, 'Hey, conchies, gutless cowards!'

'Don't take any notice, walk on,' warned Perry. But Orion was already turning round into a volley of grit. He felt the particles land on his cap, and one stung his cheek and another caught his lip, drawing blood. 'Whatever you do, don't react,' murmured Perry, dragging him by the forearm.

Surrounded by its own high perimeter wall, the church's dark, jagged-edged granite stones resembled the prison walls. The huge tower rose up high to stare out across the moors. He didn't want to attend the service any longer, but wasn't confident that returning by himself would be possible. He'd have to stay, see it through. He needn't come ever again.

The inside of the church was like a huge empty ship. Footsteps echoed. Voices were indistinct. They took a pew at the back. He went through the motions: stand up, sit down, kneel. But as soon as it came to the singing, his own voice rising out of his throat, *Fight the good fight with all thy might…* brought back some strength.

He didn't know the next hymn. The organ played some unrecognisable tune and he opened his mouth: *Rise at the cry of battle…* the words made him fidget. *Fiery and fierce the conflict…* He stopped singing and read through the rest of the hymn:

After the well-fought battle
Join in the victor's song…

He wasn't going to join in with that tosh, so he shut his hymn book and looked around. A stained glass window depicting St Michael fighting a dragon, a crucifix at the altar with the usual handsome figure of Jesus being crucified. The symbols of his own religion felt inimical to him.

He rose to his feet, sat down when required, felt alienated from his friends, looked forward to being out in the open air again. When he noticed Psalm 144 on the board he flicked through the book to find it.   At the words *Blessed be the Lord my strength: who teacheth my hands to war, and my fingers to fight* he would not open his mouth. Why had he let himself be persuaded to come? He glanced sideways at Perry and the others, who sang on. *War*, he knew, was being used as a metaphor but not many would get that and so it wouldn't count as a metaphor, would it? When is a metaphor not a metaphor? When everyone takes it literally. He sat down, folded his arms.

He was interested to hear the sermon. The vicar started with a quote from the Bible:

And take the helmet of salvation, and the sword of the Spirit, which is the word of God. Praying always with all prayer and supplication in the Spirit, and watching thereunto with all perseverance and petition for all saints…

Orion felt relief that he'd decided he wasn't coming again. The whole service had been designed to cause discomfort to the conchies and to show Christian support for the war. He couldn't listen to any more of it. In his bones he had never been one of the faithful, had never felt the power of belief. He had an overwhelming urge to be with his brother, who, in that moment, seemed to squeeze in beside him in the pew. Orion shuffled slightly to one side to make a little space for him. He felt the warmth of his brother's leg, heard his intake of breath. Orion thought of Leo's funeral when he had vowed never to pick up a gun against anyone.

He remembered how on shooting days he and Leo

would get irritable and scratchy with one another, picking a fight. On one occasion, when Leo copied what he himself had mocked, 'Cracking shots, young fellow,' he had thumped him in the ribs. Leo managed to spring away from the second blow. 'Who is going to eat so many dead birds? Well, I've asked you before, stupid,' Leo said. 'Many times, in fact. Why do the birds get shot? It's always just bang, bang, you're dead. Good for cracking-shot me.'

Leo had pretended to be sick, making realistic retching noises in his throat. They'd been good at that. Orion didn't remember how it happened exactly but soon they were rolling on the ground punching the hell out of each other, struggling against the other's weight and heat. They ended up sore and badly bruised and crying hot, stinging tears. Both were angry about the slaughter of so many birds, but Orion wasn't going to admit it. Instead, he wanted to feel how much it hurt. Somehow it helped – to feel this physical pain – which took his mind off the torment caused by the futility of minding.

But he had started the fight and now he couldn't recall why. Leo hadn't fought him at all until he'd had to defend himself. He'd never hurt his younger brother in his life. Orion was so embarrassed he hadn't been able to explain himself at the time. They didn't speak much all day after that. Had Leo been avoiding him? Had he gone with the village boys on the beat to get away from his own brother? Orion wondered, If I hadn't picked that ridiculous fight perhaps I might have stayed vigilant, kept Leo out of harm's way.

Remembering this made his head throb, the space beneath his rib cage ached. He found himself rising to his feet and pushing past the other fellows towards the end of the pew. In his arrowed fustian he knew he was drawing attention to himself but he couldn't easily shuffle past them. One man clutched his elbow and shook his head at him. Perry, sitting at the end of the pew, stretched across and yanked him down. The commotion made people twist round in their seats. Angry faces were turned towards him.

'You'll get us all into trouble. Sit down, will you,' hissed Perry. 'Forget it for now.'

He had to sit down again, feeling a fool. The pews creaked as everyone settled back into position. From the lectern, the vicar's eyes remained on them, firing his sermon in their direction, but Orion no longer heard the shots. By then, the sensation of Leo's presence had gone. At the end of the service, Perry muttered, 'C'mon, let's get going.'

'I did try to warn you, old chap.' Perry tugged Orion's sleeve. 'You won't take it amiss? But your creating a scene is just what they want us to do. Everything we do gets noted. We must remain peaceful, whatever they do to provoke a reaction out of us.'

They were approaching the door. Orion could see the sky outside, and heard the sound of voices as they shook hands with the vicar. As the conchies came through the door, the vicar turned on his heel and moved ahead of them. A group of people was waiting for them to come out into the daylight. A man with a long moustache and a black hat shouted, 'Get the 'ell out of 'ere, bloody shirkers.'

'Yes, you in the Cosy Club, you ought to be ashamed of yourselves, miserable cowards, how dare you show your faces in the house of God?' ranted a woman, in a grey felt hat and a Sunday suit. 'Look what our boys are going through,' she opened a newspaper and shook it at them as if they might catch sight of what it said. 'You're not welcome here. Not welcome, don't you understand?'

Meanwhile the vicar stood on a gravestone behind this group, as if taking sides, the wind catching his cassock, blowing his vestments while he gesticulated with his arms. Orion wanted to stop and talk. He started, 'If you'd let us explain…', but the woman in the felt hat advanced towards him, the point of her umbrella thrust forward. 'They should have shot you all, you are worthless… worthless, do you hear me?' Her eyes looked as if they might burst.

At the gate, the stone-throwing lads were waiting again. Len clenched his fist and said, 'Let's give 'em a taste of their own med'cine.' Perry took hold of Len's upper arm and hauled him away along the roadside. 'The better part of valour in this case, old chap, is discretion,' he said. Orion turned to look round and saw the vicar still standing on his perch, looking like some demented demagogue. As they ran up the hill towards the safety of the prison gateway Orion put his arms over his head to protect himself from the missiles.

When he was back in his cell, Stan knocked on the door and, stepping in, silently proffered a paper bag. Inside were assorted fruit gums. Orion took a red one from the top and Stan nodded and left. The sweetness on his tongue brought tears to his eyes.

So much for a taste of ordinary life, thought Orion. But life inside the walls was a community of its own, the prisoners organising committees for everything: hygiene, laundry, a court to mediate disputes, and access to health care – one prisoner was a doctor, and it was common to consult him before submitting yourself to the prison doctor who had a reputation for being brusque and unconcerned. To get off work you needed a sick note, and he rarely gave those out.

Two prisoners, who had been grocers, ran the prison shop, donning warehouse coats to look the part: on display they had Pheasant margarine, chewing gum, Lyons' cocoa, and loose hazelnuts and cashews – all carefully laid out like a child's toy shop. You could buy by the ounce – Rowntree's fruit gums in black, maroon, green, yellow. The shopkeepers seemed to squirrel other things away behind lids, stored them under the counter.

When his old pal Arthur turned up on the same wing some weeks later, Orion told him that he should watch out for the professional spies, sent in by the Home Office. They wore the same clothes, ate the same food, but they never stayed long. They might even act as *agents provocateurs*. With the doors unlocked, they could search through your things when you were out on a working party, looking for evidence that you were a traitor or were plotting sedition. All new arrivals were looked on with suspicion by the other inmates until they had passed through some kind of initiation rite. Arthur said he would be left alone, as he was a Friend. He was working on getting himself released early.

20

'Cass, don't look now, but who is that fellow with the Captain?' asked Florence. They were in the store room, some weeks after the arrival of the new girls. 'Now, he looks fairly presentable, top-notch, in fact.'

'He's just come across from France. Looking for the pick of the nags for one of they bigwigs,' said Foxy who was always listening.

'It's getting a bit thin on the ground to find much by way of good horse flesh. S'all gone across by my reckoning,' a cigarette was stuck between Taffy's lips as he filled up hay nets for the evening feed.

Florence said, 'I don't know about that...'

''Spect he'll go for one of the new batch o' Irish youngsters. That's what I'd choose,' said Foxy.

'He'd prefer something less green for a brass hat.'

'But we can give them some training. When does he want it by?' asked Cass, who was turning the handle of the chaff cutter.

'He wants two, I've heard said.'

'And he wants them before the Big Push they keeps talking about.'

'They're much too inexperienced at the moment, but they'll come on quite quickly,' said Cass. She went outside when she had finished the chaff cutting and walked over to a line of horses, recently crossed over from Dublin, and whose coats were still plastered in mud. They were used to running loose in all weathers, but now they were tethered to a picket rope slung between poles while two of the girls were standing in a cloud of dust trying to brush them down. Cass walked up and down the line looking at their conformation, and mentally chose three or four.

'Would you work on these ones?' she asked Amy and Sylvia. And she grabbed a curry comb herself and began dragging it through the stiff coat of one of the horses she liked the look of. Minutes later, Captain King appeared with the adjutant. 'Ah, just the person to speak to,' said the Captain, beckoning Cass.

She trotted up the horses she'd chosen to parade. 'They're not remotely battle-ready, Sir, but they have the right temperament, I'd say,' said Captain King. 'They were broken in where they were bred in County Waterford, and schooled on in the depot at Dublin. But we can put some condition on them and get them near as dammit.'

The adjutant, with waxed moustaches, immaculate boots and colourful ribbon, selected two of the horses and sauntered off. Such men did not converse with Other Ranks, or with civilians unless from the War Office, let alone with ladies to whom he had not been formally introduced.

'I'm putting you, Miss Forrester, in personal charge of these,' said Captain King as he summoned her into his office later. 'I want them schooled up and exercised across country every day. They must meet with every kind of hazard we can throw at them. We've got eight weeks. Corporal Fox is going to accompany them to Base Remount in Abbeville and then he stays on with them to make sure they get safely to their Brigadier, and aren't snaffled by some other CO who happens to take a fancy to them. You've made a start on the mud. Right. First job: farrier. I want him to attend to them every week. They won't have had any work done on their feet as yet. Second: hard rations, hard exercise. And I want the sergeant in Saddlery to measure up for brand new saddles and bridles and they must be broken in and oiled so there's no stiffness, no squeak. I'll advise Sergeant Maddox what your duties are. We can't give new horses battle inoculation as we haven't the wherewithal here, but we can test their mettle. Corporal Fox can make sure they get more of what they need when they are stationed at Base Remount.'

So black his coat, he seemed to glow blue. M1980 branded on his wither. She called him Magician, after the horse that helped the princess save her father's kingdom in the fairy story she used to love, 'The Girl who Pretended to be a Boy'. He had one white sock on a hind leg and a small star between his eyes, which were grained like wood. His forelock was thick and heavy and his mane would not be persuaded to lie on one side. He always sidled away from being saddled and then stamped a hind foot, his tail lashing like oaths.

No.M2016 became Sunlight, after the second horse in the same story. He was also black but had brown hairs in his mane and tail, which gleamed in the sun. He had a white flash down his nose and two white socks. He was calmer and more affectionate. He liked to have his face rubbed and he leaned his head against her shoulder. She'd circle his ears in her hand and pull them gently. His mane fell neatly on one side, and stayed like that after she had shortened it.

To ride, both of them were like silk. She schooled each one in a manège, going through dressage routines to make them supple and obedient to leg and voice. She erected obstacles out of fence posts because Foxy said the officers wanted horses they could enter in the show jumping competitions that were put on behind the lines. She rode bareback, knelt on their rumps and slid off their backsides to dismount. In the afternoons she rode one and led the other across country, jumping every obstacle in sight and at speed. She would gallop through a gate on which she had placed a handkerchief, and lean from the saddle to pick it up as they passed. At weekends, if it wasn't too icy, Mad Dog Maddox set up a game of polo in a field, saying the horses needed to get used to the hurly-burly of the game, as the battalions played against each other behind the lines.

They had to become accustomed to heavy motor traffic and other hazards, so back at the depot the men would shake tarpaulins at them and drive artillery horses hitched to gun carriages past them at a gallop. They beat an old drum to simulate gunfire and they let off balloons to sound like shells.

When staffing allowed, Cass took Florence with her so that both horses could be ridden in the snowy fields. Florence was well accustomed to riding astride and was a fearless, agile rider. Sunlight never wavered even if he had to slide down into a ditch and jump a fence on the other side. But Magician sometimes stopped to look about him, to size up obstacles he'd never encountered before, and then he would jump them, sometimes from a standstill: you needed to be agile to stay in the saddle. It was a joy to both girls as they watched his courage grow with experience. Cass knew full well it wasn't a good idea to get fond of either of them: they wouldn't be staying.

'Do you know something… I don't think I could ever love a man as I love these horses,' she said to Florence.

'I know what you mean.'

A tractor was pulling a trailer full of manure towards them. Cass wondered how Magician would react. The driver slowed to a halt and waited for the riders to pass. The engine backfired as it started again and Magician charged forwards, ears flattened. Cass crooned to them in the horse words Fernley had used.

'What do you think you might do after the war?' asked Florence, as they rode back in the dimpsey towards the depot. The snow light was turning everything blue. More flakes were beginning to fall.

'I think that girls are supposed to find nice husbands

and live happily ever after, aren't they?' laughed Cass, bending down to check Magician's snow-filled hooves. They periodically filled with compressed snow and a large clod would loosen and be flung sideways. But sometimes the clod stayed in the hoof, making the horse walk tall as if on stilettos.

'That's what I used to hope for until I joined the Suffragettes. Wedding dresses, bridesmaids, babies, all that. My mother wanted me to do the season in London. But I kept refusing.'

A flock of crows flew overhead, their wing-beats whamming like gas igniting.

'You're a real Suffragette? How exciting.'

'I've been on lots of marches. It's always terrific, the atmosphere. And I went on the Women's Pilgrimage on a horse. I rode all the way to London from where we live in Oxfordshire. And I was there at the Derby when Emily Davison threw herself under the horse.'

Snow slid from a branch and landed with a flump up ahead.

'I read about that. It was incredibly brave.'

'It was really terrible actually.'

'But to believe in something that much… You wouldn't go nearly that far yourself, would you?'

'Women must get the vote. I say, shall we trot on?'

'Yes, we'd better get back.' The horses stepped out eagerly. 'But what are you going to do after the war is over, Florence?'

Starlings exclaimed from the tops of bare trees as if the snow spoke.

'I'm going to study for a degree in Archaeology. Then I want to excavate ancient remains and find out how people used to live.'

'Do you think they'll let you?'

'Who's going to stop me?'

They were approaching the buildings of the depot,

the long roofs covered in snow; it was falling more thickly now as if the daylight was crumbling and might never come again. Flakes were settling on the horses' manes.

'You haven't said what you want...?'

'You've made me think, Florence. I'd never thought of going to university but I think I'd really like to try. I'd never thought that far ahead. Not until now.'

'The world is your oyster, Cass. Just go ahead and do what you most want. The chances are that there aren't going to be enough men left to marry all of us anyway. So that will no longer be the only option.'

'Never get married, though?' She was about to ask Florence what she thought about Frank not kissing her when he had suggested getting engaged. She was on the brink of telling her how his parents called off the engagement before it became known. But she held back, not wanting Florence to find out about her brother being a conchie. She might disapprove and stop being a friend.

'After this, can you see yourself being a fairy-tale woman living happily ever after?' asked Florence. 'Perhaps we should all just have love affairs!'

Mad Dog met them at the gate. 'Where the blazes you been? I was beginning to think you were lost, I was. And no, I wasn't going to send out a search party in this. Not for you, anyway.'

'You might be needin' this one day.' It was Mad Dog speaking, holding out a package loosely wrapped in brown paper. She had just arrived back from early morning exercise and was walking the steaming horse round and round on a loose rein in the manège to cool it down.

'Whatever is it?' Cass asked.

'You take a look-see.'

She pulled open a corner of the brown paper to reveal

the contents. 'Khaki? Oh my heavens, you're giving me this? What for?'

'Aye, Miss. If you don't mind my sayin', with all this work you're doin' you look like a lad anyway in your fuckin' breeches and boots, ridin' astride and all that.'

'I expect I do.'

'You can do the work of any man. But you're not one of the lads so I've brought you this. I thought it'd keep you safe one day. You might be needin' it. There's too many louts comin' and goin' and one of them might misunderstand.'

'You think I might be needing it? How come?'

'Lads get transferred to other depots at the drop of a hat. New blokes transferrin' through might not treat you right. If things ever got rougher, or you have to move yourself, you'd be better off wearin' this. Uniform makes you look like one of us… at least from the outside.'

'I suppose it does. As if I've enlisted. That's very kind of you. I'm most obliged. I don't know what to say…'

'Not enlisted, Miss, if you don't mind my sayin' – no, not fuckin' enlisted – but it makes it look as if you have, to those that don't know. It doesn't have insignia or anything like that so you won't be had up for wearin' it. I tell you there's a bloke at one of the base remount depots who never enlisted and he's in khaki.'

'You've thought of everything, Sarge, thanks. Save the wear and tear on my own clothes too. I don't get paid enough to keep buying new togs to work in.'

'Wear it for the time bein' but also keep it between ourselves where you got it, if you don't mind.'

'I'll not mention it, don't worry.'

'Best to look the part. And I know how dedicated you are to your equines. You would do fuckin' anything for any of them, you would.'

21

Wind rocked the landings, roared as though towering waves were breaking against the walls. No one knew if the roof would hold, and the floors seemed to heave like a deck. Only one man, a fisherman named Bob, enjoyed these storms and he stood with his arms crossed by the window on the top landing, as if keeping watch for the first sight of land.

Until lights out, Orion read whatever he could get his hands on – the Bible, Darwin's *The Origin of Species*, Shakespeare's collected plays, *Sir Gawain and the Green Knight*. Cribbage tournaments reverberated up and down the halls, adding words to their speech, salting their days with the invention of strategies. And on the Continent men were waiting in dugouts and trenches playing the same game of chance and skill by the light of a stubby candle, using the same rules with the same repeated calculations passing their lips.

Twice a week the Education Committee arranged lectures on different subjects drawn from the pool of knowledge among the conchies. One such speaker was a Socialist named Ted Flanagan who started by quoting from *Henry V*, his address to the soldiers:

Every subject body is the King's
but every subject's soul his own.

Ted switched tack then to Darwin's concept of the biology of conscience, and said that one day when they located the moral centre in the brain they would conclude that it was made of animal tissue and was part of the body, not evidence of the soul. There was noisy argument that night and some of those fired up by their religion said the Socialist speaker was damned to hell for voicing such opinions. 'What about the morality of the Good Book?' someone asked. Flanagan shook his head and said that all religion is based on imagination and that morality is a simple human attribute, like a heart or a part of the brain.

Other speakers gave lectures on the history of pacifism, the history of the Dartmoor Depot during the Napoleonic Wars, the causes of war, fairy tales and their origins, Georgian poetry, Naturism, Methodism, Buddhism, Tolstoyism. The Tolstoyan had grown a long beard like a Russian priest, resembling a little the great writer himself. Orion was excited by the ideas of pacifism and community but wasn't certain he wanted to be celibate or even vegetarian, or even grow a long beard. Would he have to go that far to be called a Tolstoyan?

The quiet voice of the Tolstoy apprentice wasn't easy to hear because someone was always coughing or blowing their nose, but one phrase caught his attention: *A man may cease to do what he regards as wrong, but he cannot cease to consider wrong what is wrong.* The bearded man was reading quotations by Tolstoy, his head bowed over a tatty little cloth book.

Orion envied the man his strong belief system. He had only this quiet voice but everyone was listening. Orion thought he would rather leave behind the Orion he had been and become a different one. He might have to give up on some of his hopes: riding to hounds in the fields back home with his sister, eating roast beef, drinking whisky, not being celibate. *Universal service is the extreme limit of violence necessary for the support of the whole state organisation...* Orion thought he could go along with this anarchism. The argument took him a good step further in his thinking, and gave his own reasoning a decided ring to it. He could hear himself quoting these phrases. Could he make the necessary changes? He doubted it somehow but it would be the right thing to have a go. Later that week, he found a copy of *Anna Karenina* in the small library: the words *Rummaging in our souls, we often dig up something that ought to have lain there unnoticed* stuck in his mind. He was rummaging in his own soul and unearthed the feeling that he wasn't at all certain the Orion he knew himself to be would fit this new person he couldn't yet imagine. He would finish the book and see if the urge lasted as long as it took to read. He began to feel the necessity of growing a beard.

Later that winter, Stan fell ill. He vomited whenever he ate or drank anything and he hadn't the strength to go to his job on the farm. He looked almost cadaverous and his friend Ted Flanagan brought a cup of fresh milk straight from the cow every day to the Cobweb Chamber, hiding it in a pocket and walking very stiffly so as not to let it spill. Because the milk was deemed to be prison property, Flanagan was technically guilty of theft, and so when a guard discovered the cup in his pocket the offence was reported to the governor and an adjudication was held.

During morning assembly in the central yard the governor announced that Flanagan's punishment was to be transferred back to prison for stealing milk to give to a felon. 'Let this be an example…' he said, but could not finish, for a low murmur grew loud and soon swelled into a roar of disapproval from the prisoners. The guards stepped forward, pulling their truncheons out from their belts. A voice yelled, 'Let's stone them'. The hubbub fell silent. Everyone waited, the moment drawing out while no one moved or spoke. Len grinned and folded his arms as those beside him turned to look at him. The exhortation had been a shibboleth, creating an ever-widening ripple that opened out across the crowd of men. Sometime during that evening he was seen entering the governor's office, and he never appeared again.

From sunup to sundown, jackdaws and rooks circled

the roofs, paced up and down the gutters. Unafraid, the blue-eyed daws strutted along the sills and peered in at the windows. The varied tones of their voices sounded as though they were exchanging views.

After the incident in the church, Orion had determined never to waste words. Maybe now that I'm freer than I was, he thought, words should cost me less. But I can't spend them. There are plenty of men who are not free to speak. He could not forget those who had complied and were now dead. He had held out for freedom of speech and been silenced, but had lived. Plenty of others were now silenced by death, not by choosing a crime. He would spend the rest of his life making up for this. But how? He'd look out for some opportunity.

In the new work camps writing was allowed. When he had some spare money from his daily 2d, he saved up to acquire pen and paper from the prison shop... thinking wistfully of Leo's mechanical pencil which he had given to Cass. Between his thumb and forefinger it was a joy to hold a pen and scratch words along the lines. Because the ink was not good quality the pen needed dipping frequently and the shop's loose sheets of paper were not exactly Basildon Bond.

Now he could write as many letters as he could afford to buy stamps for. To ensure that the press and the public knew the conchies were being suitably punished, the post was often curtailed. So as not to give the censor an excuse to hold it back, he was warned to be mindful about what he wrote – he would never know which letters got through and which did not, as they weren't handed back. There was some debate about what happened to the stamps and who might steam them off the envelopes. He wrote hopefully.

Hall 9/4/1189
The Settlement
Princetown
South Devon

Dearest Mama,

Thank you for your letters. Please keep writing to me as I love to hear from you. Every letter helps to keep my spirits up. It upsets me greatly to hear that people should be so offensive to you on my account. I can't understand why neighbours and acquaintances would take it out on you. I really do feel for you.

As you can see, I have moved. This is an old prison but is now re-christened a Work Camp. I was brought here after I agreed to do Work of National Importance. There are only us conscientious objectors here. We work for more than 9 hours a day, whatever the weather – biting winds, lashings of rain and the clothes we are issued do not keep out the cold even when we manage to stay dry. Some days the views are grand – blue peaks in the distance as if I can see all the way to home. But most days the fog rolls in and suffocates us or the wind blows rain or snow that gets indoors, through the cracks between walls and windows or doors! Sometimes the rain runs in rivulets down the corridors and into the halls where we sleep. Home Office rations keep us from starvation. After work we stay in the halls, where we play cards with each other or sometimes have little concerts or lectures on all kinds of interesting subjects. I am getting educated.

I will send you a picture postcard of the town as soon as I can get one for you.

I miss you very much as well.

Orion

140

Hall. 9/4/189
The Settlement
Princetown
South Devon

Dearest Sister,

Thank you always for your missives. I do not know what I would do without them. But Leo's pencil tells me more about you, you know, than you might think. I am glad you are using his pencil as it makes me feel he is keeping us together somehow.

I imagine that letters will be nice to receive where you are now so I keep writing even when I have little new to report. My chief news is that I have grown a beard! Its colour is admired though some have been observed to laugh. It is a ginger brown of the most approved tint, and makes me look like a version of the great Russian writer Tolstoy or, equally distinguished, a French decadent poet. Can you imagine that?

There was a tremendous thunderstorm here the other night and the lightning was right above the prison walls with thunder sounding like cannons blasting off. I thought of what you said about hearing the battery across the water from where you are and it made me realise it must be like that for you a lot of the time.

I hope this finds you in good health. I had a letter from Mother, who said she was mortified to be handed a white feather on my behalf. The flappers are handing out white feathers to conchies' families as well now. I hope it doesn't get any worse for you but there must be things they are not telling me. Are they telling you perhaps?

Your devoted but difficult brother,
Orion

22

It was late March and the Irish horses were scheduled to be entrained for Dover the following afternoon. Everything had been rehearsed several times, including walking them along a gangway so that they would not baulk at being boarded onto the ship when their time came. The ferry was scheduled to leave port as soon as it was loaded some time after 10pm, but the animals had to be inspected by a Veterinary Corps inspector on arrival at the dock before being led into the ship's hold. So the timings were critical. Foxy was going to escort the horses to the dock and see them safely delivered. Cass was to entrain Sunlight and Magician and then ride Foxy's mount back to the depot.

She knew that her horses, as she had come to think of them, were looking their best – coats shining, eyes bright and curious. Inquisitive and fit, but not hot and pumped up. She wouldn't know who would be riding them, or whether he would be confident handling them and kind to them at the same time. So she was nervous for them, hoped they would be brave and not too spooked by what lay ahead of them. They were trusting animals, and if they liked their handler they would try to please. But if he were to be rough or feel anxious when handling them she knew they would play up. A brigadier would stable his horses and have experienced ASC grooms. Sunlight and Magician were going to be parade horses, and not deployed to charge into the line of fire. They would make a fine spectacle on regimental inspections, would lift the hearts of any Irish Guards or cavalry troops.

Still, her own heart weighed as heavy as an anvil at

having to part with them. She hoped she wouldn't weep when they left. She tried to be calm for their sakes, knowing how they could pick up on how she felt. But all the horses were in a state of alarm and maybe she was catching it from them.

Cass led Sunlight and Magician down to the holding pen in the goods yard. About thirty other horses were travelling with them. Cass and Florence and two soldiers were at the ready, together with Foxy. But it was long past the appointed hour. There were no puffs of steam across the still expanse of countryside, no phone ringing in the station master's office. The confused trail of voices around them grew quieter. Dusk was gathering and lights came on, a phosphorescent yellow of acetylene. Cass wanted to soothe the horses onto the train herself, to see them safely depart and so stop worrying about them. It was the final service she could perform for them.

They were restless in the paddock, at risk of being kicked by others. She wanted to take them out and walk them up and down quietly, let them graze on the few blades of spring grass on the road verge. She admitted to herself she had become too fond of them – her father wouldn't approve. She could hear what he'd say. And she'd even made the cardinal mistake of giving them sentimental names.

As the train finally pulled into the siding in the goods yard the steam whooshed and the nearest horses shied away violently. As if they were one creature they all barged sideways, a tremor running from one to another like ripples merging. 'Whoa, whoa,' crooned Foxy.

Foxy's mount was tossing its head and was uncharacteristically trumpeting through its nose. The other two mounted horses drew themselves taller and taller, infected by the atmosphere. Foxy wanted to wait till calm had been restored but the driver, who had come across to see the horses being loaded, pulled out his fob watch and pointed at the time. 'We must be on our way to the docks,' he called, 'we're running late. The ship won't wait – it only sails under cover of dark.'

Cass and the men managed the trembling horses out of the compound and up to the train to load them one by one, tethering six inside each wagon. Difficult to avoid getting feet trodden on, toes broken. Cass led Sunlight and then Magician herself so that they were safely boarded together, nose bags attached to their headstalls along with the instructions about their destination. Inside the wagons the other horses crashed about.

Those in the compound grew fewer but their strength seemed to grow as they objected to being loaded into the mouths of dark, uninviting wagons. Some jerked their heads against their ropes, squealing, eyes rolling. The ones inside the train were neighing. Two lead ropes were whipped through Florence's hands and the runaways charged off in the direction they had come from. The gate swung wide and the remaining horses bolted. 'Fucking idiots,' shouted Foxy as his nervous horse bucked violently, catapulting him like a sack over its head, dumping him on the stony ground.

Cass, who had just tied up a horse, rushed out of the wagon, saw what had happened and ran over to him where he lay crooked, at a strange angle, motionless, a wound opening in his head. 'Foxy', she said to him, touching his hand. 'Are you all right?' She wished he would speak or open half an eye. 'We'll get you some help soon,' she added, wondering how.

The fireman hurried over – not a man, but a woman – 'What the bleeding heck…?' she began, but didn't continue when she saw the corporal's body. Cass sent her off to the station office to ring through to the hospital for an ambulance, and told her to ask the station master to get the Captain to come at once. She couldn't abandon Foxy in this mess, bent and bleeding, War Office timetables or not.

After some minutes, with the entrained horses lurching in the wagons and the others vanished into the night, both of the crew returned and stood lugubriously smoking in the dim lights. 'Poor bugger, what a way to go,' said the driver. 'Looks like one for the rest camp. Not much we can do. Fucking shambles 'ere tonight. See if we can pick up time somewhere on the line once we're under way. Can't leave without a signature though. I'd best turn up the draught a little,' said the driver as he turned on his heel towards the footplate. Just then, to Cass's relief, headlights raced through the darkness from the direction of the depot.

'Captain King's on the way,' she said to Foxy. 'Soon there'll be an ambulance to take you to hospital.' She was murmuring whatever small comfort came into her mind, bending over his chest to feel if he was breathing.

She shaded her eyes from the dazzle of the headlights as she gestured at the pale face of Captain King through his windscreen. 'We've called for an ambulance. He looks badly injured. Still breathing though.'

'Good. Well done.' He squatted down, put two fingers to Foxy's throat for the feel of a pulse. 'Corporal Fox, we'll have you more comfortable soon.'

Captain King stood up, hands on hips, and looked at the train. 'Look, I'd best sign off the t-train load and send it with what they've got so far. And someone must t-travel with the horses to keep a check. Who is left here?' In the light from the car she noticed a trickle of sweat running down from his head. He seemed to be trembling, his hands thrust deep in the pockets of his greatcoat.

'Only myself, sir, I think, now. The others chased after the horses.'

'Right, y-you'll have to escort the, ah, horses and make sure they get to D-Dover all right. Report to Captain Woods, the veterinary inspector at the d-docks, and tell him what's happened and then hand them over. I'll wait here with Corporal Fox for the ambulance.'

'Me, sir?'

'Yes, you, Miss Forrester. You're not in m-mufti. You'll make it there and b-back. Make sure they understand what's happened and t-tell them the rest of the consignment is following as soon as we can find space on a train. Make sure the Irish b-blacks are b-boarded safely and get them a good b-billet as high up the ship as you can get them. It's worse down b-below.'

In the distance she could hear the ambulance bell. She supposed Foxy was indeed a goner. She hadn't seen much sign of life in him, his neck must be broken, his head badly injured.

The train drivers were getting up a head of steam so she grabbed Foxy's pack with his mess tin, cutlery and mug, his bivvy bag and other requisite paraphernalia and, as the train pulled away, she swung herself up through the doors where Sunlight and Magician were stowed. As the train got under way the horses fell quiet, concentrating on keeping their footing with the unfamiliar shaking and jolting motion. It was more than she'd ever hoped for to be able see them onto the ship.

When they arrived at the docks she could hear a hubbub of neighing as rising panic once more spread from wagon to wagon. As soon as the train had shuddered to a stop the doors were pulled open and a couple of ASC men jumped aboard. They promptly started untethering the horses and leading them off the wagon.

'These two here are a special consignment for

Brigade HQ', she said. 'I'll bring them out myself. You deal with the others.' Neither of the men so much as looked at her. An idea opened up before her. Report to Captain Woods and see what happens. Take one step at a time. Say nothing unless challenged.

23

To carry out the Work of National Importance, Orion and his fellow prisoners were escorted by two guards, mounted on Dartmoor ponies, along a track that led across the moors. Their task was to lay a firm path through the bog, and for this they needed to build foundations. Their designated way passed through an ancient burial ground of cists and cairns, whose stones they had to plunder in order to line the bed of the track. The route was to end up at a crossroads where the tinners once turned west to the mine at Whiteworks or went straight ahead to Swincombe. To reach Huccaby, travellers also came this way to ford the river at Swincombe. Both Whiteworks and Swincombe were no longer inhabited, so the track was leading nowhere – even as they began to build it.

In one of the lectures an historian had explained that Bronze Age people had farmed this land when the climate allowed, creating their own paths across the moor, burying their dead in stone-lined chambers in the bog. The prisoners worked daily in this ancient landscape where stones lay pocketed in the earth, labouring at their own crossroads, measuring time by the number of stones they could heave out. The guards left them to it, returning to count their charges once or twice and to fetch them back at the end of the day, knowing that any absconders wouldn't get very far across open moorland in their uniforms.

Perhaps, thought Orion, the powers that be were hoping that a Herculean task would force them to change their minds – or that the assassin wind would drive them into being assassins.

Down in a dip, one of the moor's orifices opened like a sump, the barely-moving water as black as tar, stinking of sour old age and rotting vegetation. The men groped through this to find a firm surface to lay down stones. Their arms and hands were oiled with mud, shining with sliding ooze, their boots weighted with it. They caked themselves with wet bog-earth to keep out the wind – they blackened their faces, their names being already blackened enough. No one could tell one from another. Yells of laughter. Mud slinging wasn't in it. They couldn't have sunk any lower.

Someone was having a coughing fit – Harry lay on the tussocks, craning his head, pulling, scrabbling. 'There's something down here,' he called. 'Help me. Get him. Pull him out.' All the dead on the moor have long vanished, thought Orion. Not a bone to be found. The peat consumes them.

A leathery form shrouded by mud was hauled from the suction and lay shape-shifting on the quivering ground. 'It looks like my grand-dad's old mac, when he came in from a storm one night on the farm.' A crowd gathered round the crumple. Someone slapped away the clots of sodden earth revealing a hand. A collapsed face emerged. A head with a slit, not healed. 'That's justice for you,' he said. Everyone gathered round and watched the creature emerge from its coating of mud.

'I think we should bury him properly,' Henry, a Methodist preacher, called out above the wind. 'He was buried and now we've exhumed him. He must be re-interred.'

'He wasn't necessarily a Christian,' said a voice.

'He wasn't buried with any ceremony, was he?' said someone else.

'We can't know what he did to merit this. Might not be anything. Might have been an accident, mightn't it?'

'But surely it's a matter for the police? Looks to me

149

like a crime was committed.'

'His clothes have almost rotted away. Maybe he was wrapped in a sack. Who knows when this might have happened. It'd be a hopeless investigation.'

'They'll find a way to blame us, mark my words.'

'Shouldn't we just bung him back where he was? Perhaps he's a curse.'

'Or perhaps he was like us and spoke his mind once too often. Perhaps he was a victim.'

'Not for any of us to mete out justice. Let's bury him the way we think it should be done. It might free his soul. He's been alone so long – let him have the company of footsteps over his grave, the few who might walk by here in the future.'

So they dug a deeper hole in the shape of a crouch and lined it with stone. They lowered the remains into the hole. Henry paused for a moment and a psalm came to his mind:

Many times they have persecuted me from my youth up... Nor do those who pass by say, "The blessing of the Lord be upon you; We bless you in the name of the Lord."

Bob, whose hair stuck up on end and whose face now looked yet more hirsute with drying mud, said, 'We saved a soul today. We looked death in the face. I feel honoured. We don't often get the opportunity out here, shut away so no one will hear us.'

'I like the idea that a man from a bog will bring luck to those that pass even though they don't know it. I've never associated luck with God before now,' said Harry.

24

She felt draggled with sea-sickness. The sides of the ship trembled and seemed to draw closer, move further apart. She sat on the tilting floor with her head in her knees for what seemed like hours. The horses stood with their heads bowed, ears back, their sweat-darkened skins quivering. When she managed to stagger over to feel them her hands became sticky. They took no notice, intent on keeping their feet.

The ship's engines laboured as they rose and plunged through the heavy sea. A horse in the next stall to Sunlight threw up its head and wrenched at the rope, pulling and pulling. It slithered on to its haunches and sank to the floor, its hooves scrabbling in panic at the partition. A Veterinary Corps sergeant took one look and brought out a cattle killer with a long tube. Its thud coincided with the ship landing in a trough. The horse's body shuddered to stillness.

In the distance a line of light was opening as they drew into the harbour. After a time, the bows bumped up against the quay. The horses lifted their heads and whinnied, their calls running up and down the length of the hold. Cass felt relieved that at least her charges were on the top deck and would not have to wait as long as those stowed down below.

But it took an inexplicably long time for the gangways to be hauled into position. Plenty of time for Cass to start worrying about what was going to happen to her when they found she didn't have the right papers. She knew security was tight. The Red Caps had a fearsome reputation. Now she had arrived she wasn't feeling at all sure what to do. Wouldn't the light of day be certain to expose her? What might happen then?

When the order to disembark came, she led Magician down the gangway. A private led Sunlight and she took hold of him again on the quay. Her legs felt like jelly, her brain seemed to swirl. She spoke quietly to them so that no one else would hear. She would just follow the man in front, do what he did: it was easy enough. The morning light looked grainy.

The long cavalcade of horses moved away from the harbour and through the cobbled streets to a huge old warehouse, where a group of men in trench coats and peaked caps stood at a holding bay lit by kerosene lamps in the half light. Each horse was brought forward for inspection by the veterinary officers: teeth, eyes, legs, skin. A corporal checked the numbers inscribed on their withers and ticked each horse off as sound. He called 'Lead away'. No one had asked her for her rank or number, demanded to see papers. The ASC chaps knew where to go and had already gone on ahead of her. Her heart was pounding in her ears, but she knew no one else could hear it above the clatter of hooves. Magician's eyes were bulging.

Somehow the horses seemed to know where to go – it must have been the smell of the others – and they almost dragged her down a narrow alleyway, which led to a cavernous warehouse. Rows and rows of empty stalls, filled with hay and straw, stood waiting. A sergeant came up and grabbed their head stalls. He reached round to take out the notes in the bag dangling from their necks. 'Special consignment,' she said.

'Walk them up and down till they've cooled off, will you? They've got overheated: we don't want them coming down with respiratory problems. When they've dried off, fill up their nosebags and give them a feed. They need watering: I expect they're dehydrated. Rough crossing, I gather. The ones down below will have suffered more.'

She was kept busy all day, settling in all the new arrivals, filling haynets, taking horses to water, mucking out. Knowing the normal daily routine of a remount depot helped her not draw any attention to herself. She had no time to think about how she would explain her presence but, as the day passed by, she found herself hoping that she wasn't going to be discovered after all. Even now, nobody had questioned her. The horses themselves were her passport.

After Evening Stables she made her way along with the ASC men to the Mess. Many of their voices were Irish. She forced herself into looking confident even as she mumbled her thanks to the ladies who doled out a ration of ham and eggs into Foxy's mess tin as she shuffled past in the queue. At the table, the men she sat with nodded at her, introduced themselves and she tried to remember their names: Dan with a curly moustache, Jack O'Keefe with broken front teeth, Rorky with a rash on one side of his face. She shook hands with Rorky and told him her name was Forrester.

'We'll be out to the boozer, Forrester, soon as yi loike. If it's beer yer after, the Frog stoff here is loike piss but gets yi canned. Gotta moind the Red Caps though. The place is fairly crawlin' with the boogers.'

Cass declined. Said she was teetotal. After that Rorky and the others proceeded to ignore her and their conversation weighed up which boozer they would make a start in – where the prices were lowest, where you might find a willing Frog bitch or two. These boys were rowdier than the men back at Pluckley. They were on edge, nervous, charged, as though the proximity of the war made them wild. The lads bolted their tea in order to go out and spend their pay, getting themselves sozzled on beer or cheap French wine or brandy. As wave after wave of men coming off duty entered and left, she finally got herself lost in the general drift for the doorway. It wasn't so hard being invisible in a large crowd and there were men coming and going on various duties all the time.

Afterwards she found she could sit in the canteen down the street, where you could buy mugs of tea or coffee, both tasting exactly the same, served up by one of the exhausted but jolly Cockney women in the WAACs. In the steamy atmosphere she huddled in a corner, keeping her face hidden in the newspaper, like a horse enjoying a nose bag.

She dragged herself off to a bunkhouse and slept in her uniform, having managed to use the latrine while the others were out. They didn't arrive back till much later, disorderly and drunk. At Reveille they roused themselves like zombies. No one noticed that Forrester didn't take the time to shave. A lot of them seemed to stay hung-over through the day as well. They were used to strangers among them, didn't bother with a boy who wouldn't compete against them in the drinking stakes. She had no need of friends. She spoke very little, kept herself to herself, pointed her nose at a book and made herself out to be an unsociable and silent type. She took a widdle in the stable occasionally. She often had to hang on for long periods hoping she wasn't going to wet herself. She had the stinking holes of latrines to herself only when the blokes had gone to the *estaminets*. Lucky, she thought, my Auntie Flo's visits are light, not like those of Florence, who called it the curse and bled like a stuck pig, suffering from terrible tummy cramps.

Every morning, she exercised both horses in the manège, and every afternoon she took them out in the streets to familiarise them with heavy traffic, gun carriages with caissons rattling along behind, heavily laden service wagons, motor cars, trucks – all the noise and bustle of life behind the lines. She didn't know how long this would go on for.

Nearly three weeks after she had arrived, the Major in charge of the yard approached her. She thought, My God, it's all up now. I've been rumbled. She saluted. He said, 'These horses you brought over – I've been watching them. You've done a good job. They've got plenty of bloom without too much oomph and I think it's time they moved on, now.' She had noticed his calmness around horses. He had a bit of a reputation as a nightly reveller who enjoyed a bon time as much as any of the blokes, she'd heard tell. His tipple was said to be champagne. He never lost his temper and he had the respect of every man at the depot. Both horses and men seemed to eat from his hand and he ran the place like clockwork. They called him an honorary horse. He had been in the Hussars at the start of the war. The story went that he had found himself on a course parallel to that of a troop of German cavalry whose stallions started whinnying at his mare. He had made the mare lie down in a trench, putting his hand down her throat so she couldn't respond until the coast was clear.

He said she was to prepare numbers M1980 and M2016 to be entrained the next day to the rail head at Arras and from there she was to ride them to their destination at the brigade HQ. 'We'll supply you with a map and a *sauf-conduit*. Go to the orderly room just before 6 o'clock.' He started walking away, 'You'll get to see how the other half lives, anyway,' and he laughed. A lance-corporal was busy writing down the horses' numbers and he stuffed a form in each of their headstalls. Even he didn't think to ask her rank or number.

At the station there was a mêlée of horses and mules bound for Transport duties at supply depots, and artillery horses were going out to front line battalions. The spring offensive was beginning. She noticed the three acquaintances from her first night having trouble with a line of mules. The animals were meant to be loaded on to the train via a gangplank, but every time one stopped they all did. 'Lead a pony in front of them and then they'll follow,' she called to them as she passed. 'A grey one, if possible. They like grey best. Dunno why.' Rorky straightened up and raised his hand.

Each horse was led up the brow by one man. The momentum was kept up so that potential shirkers were not given the chance to hesitate, refuse, or back up, and the whole consignment of horses was entrained in short order. During the journey the train shuddered to a halt every so often. Each time, the horses started neighing as if they were sending messages to one another. Horses that had stood drowsily began to fidget, teeth gnawing the ropes. One set up a rhythmic kicking on the steel-reinforced partition. Others grew restive and yanked on their ropes, the whites of their eyes rolling.

At the rail head, once they had all been unloaded down the brows, everything became more chaotic. Soldiers and supplies were moving in every direction. It was hard to keep track of companions. Keeping an eye on the man in front of her, Cass checked the harness, tightened the girth on Magician and readied herself and the two horses for the ride ahead.

25

Cass rode Magician and led Sunlight in the line with the transport and artillery horses as it moved out of the town, along cobbled streets with tram rails worn so smooth it was difficult for the horses to keep a footing. The buildings in the town might once have looked quite splendid, but the stonework was blackened, the windows grimy. The dingy streets were now filled with horse droppings from the comings and goings of war traffic. The muddy country lanes were less slippery – not that there was any let-up in battle preparations there.

She almost laughed aloud at the sight of London buses and removal lorries; a delivery truck marked *Waring and Gillow Removals* overtook them. A stream of casualties, sometimes sitting in the buses or in horse-drawn wagons and sometimes walking along, flowed back towards the rail head.

German prisoners, some limping, some bandaged, were being herded slowly away from the Front by men on horseback. The prisoners looked exhausted, the whites of their eyes shining in their grimy faces. This is The War, you idiot, she said to herself. What on earth were you expecting?

At first, the countryside looked normal enough: trees, villages, people working in the fields. Wood pigeons clattered out of trees as they passed, sounding like rounds of sniper fire. In the distance she sometimes spotted a hare across the grass. But as they drew further away from the town the landscape slowly began to empty of civilians. Nobody was working in the fields or gardens. As if a malignant tornado had passed by, houses were abandoned – here, a wall blown out; there, a roof missing. At first the woods looked dilapidated, then trees were blown to shreds, fallen together like heaps of bones. Fields which should have had crops in them were quagmires full of craters. Church towers looked like broken teeth. The grumble of shelling in the distance became a slow crescendo of thunder.

Rain drizzled and accelerated into a downpour, then relaxed back to a mizzle, but never stopped. It must have been raining for days as the road surface seemed alive with liquid mud; maybe it was a trick of the light, but it was difficult to tell what was road and what was field. Puddles reflected what light there was in the sky. The yellow stems of willow trees shone bright with wetness.

They came to a village which was surrounded by tents and makeshift huts laid out in a fan pattern: a rest area for soldiers in reserve. Further on, she passed a burial ground where soldiers were digging graves, and bodies were laid out in row after row. The horses snorted, and shook their heads at the cloying smell, turning their heads as if about to go back.

A stray shell landed some way off with a crump; earth and debris flew into the air making both horses back away, and she had a deal of trouble controlling the two of them. It was a relief that the artillery horses in front remained calm: they had been out here before, she could see that. But she hadn't reckoned on being so close to the action, and as the thudding of guns grew louder all the horses became jumpy and difficult to control. Even the battle-proof artillery horses danced about. Bangs and crashes shook the ground. And all those noises – whines and pops and shrieks. Nothing could have familiarised her two charges with these. Indeed, nothing could have prepared her. It was like approaching a vision of Dante's hell that she'd seen in pictures in the schoolroom. He must have been in a place like this.

From the top of a ridge she could see the plain laid out below them. All around were battlefields, a blasted landscape pitted and mined, its trees broken and burnt, villages in ruins. The furthest horizon looked as though it were still ablaze: a frightful tumult as if the sky were exploding and the ground were being pulverised.

When night came they found a billet in an encampment, where they were fed and given somewhere to sleep. No one thought of taking their clothes off. Spending a penny – or something more – was another matter. Sentries stood at the gate so she couldn't leave the camp for fear of drawing attention to herself. But within the perimeter fence and near their tent was a small copse, and after everyone had turned in she managed to relieve herself, bursting as she was by then.

The next morning, the transport horses peeled off in one direction and a sergeant-major directed her to take the other fork in the road. She had the map and the military pass and the copy of a *sauf-conduit* from the mayor in her pocket in case she were challenged by military police. She found herself alone in the middle of a war. Had she lost her mind? She had only herself to blame: no one had sent her here.

Around her lay the remains of people's homes – abandoned piles of rubble. An old woman, dressed in a man's coat with a sack over her head like a hood, was standing outside one such ruin. She seemed to be guarding the patch of grass where her three cows were grazing. Cass stopped to speak to her, but the woman looked at her strangely for a second and then shouted that her cows needed the grass and that it was all that was left for her – and no, the horses couldn't walk across it or eat it. That little island of grass, thought

Cass, must be all that lay between survival and starvation, for her cows and for herself. 'I have no intention... ne vous inquiétez pas...' she repeated. At this, the old woman swore and broke off, a look of something like recognition in her eyes. That expression made Cass ride hurriedly on, fearing she might be discovered, telling herself it must have been a woman's intuition.

Soon after, she came to another encampment of huts and tents – another battalion's rest area. She showed her papers and the *sauf-conduit* to a sentry who stood on guard in the doorway of a ruin. He directed her to a chateau in a valley not more than a mile away – her final destination.

She rode into a courtyard of stables, a coach house at one end. She slipped off Sunlight, saluted the sergeant and handed him the horses' paperwork. He directed her to a line of stalls where some horses were tethered. She pulled off their saddles and a young lad took them from her without saying anything. She felt responsibility for the horses slipping from her hands. Seeing them soon afterwards pulling hay out of the rack, she reflected that she probably wouldn't see them ever again. The place seemed safe, and the ASC grooms here must know their job. They were working for a brigadier, after all.

The sergeant returned with a clipboard and filled out a form. 'Take that back to Major Porteous.' He directed her to the local ASC mess so she could get something to eat before finding her way back to base. There was even a washroom in the old servants' quarters. She washed the mud and dirt from her skin and hair in cold water. She felt relieved but exhausted, drained by the journey. She was wondering how on earth she would get back on her own through what she had just experienced. The job is done, she thought, as she fell asleep fully clothed on a spare bunk. Tomorrow would bring the problem of finding a way back to Pluckley; but fed and washed for now, she would sleep perhaps for a little time.

Almost immediately, someone yanked her awake. A voice said, 'The brig wants you. Pronto.' Was something wrong? Did he not like the look of his new mounts? She ran to the yard and found the horses already saddled up. 'Take them to the manège and put them through their paces.' The brigadier was standing there, together with the adjutant who had come to Pluckley and chosen the horses. She hoped he wouldn't recognise her, but then he had never taken any notice of her. Other ranks were beneath the notice of senior officers.

The guns had fallen silent and the horses were thoroughly exercised and behaved well. In the little manège she jumped them over some stick jumps with her arms folded, and she vaulted on and off on both sides while the horses stood still. The brigadier slapped Sunlight's neck and walked round Magician, who was tired by then, standing with one hind hoof tilted. He didn't say anything at first, but she could tell he was pleased with them. He lit a cigar and looked at her, said he wished he rode as quietly. Then he got on and rode them about himself. He wafted the lit cigar in one hand the whole time so he had only the other hand on the rein, but she saw how both horses attended to him.

Afterwards, when she had put the horses back in the stables, she was sent to his office. The adjutant was there again and his presence made her nervous, but she must have saluted competently enough, for the brigadier, who didn't seem to mind she wasn't even a NCO, shook her hand and thanked her. He reeked of whisky, his eyes shone. As if to no one in particular he drawled, 'A commander must be mounted on a good horse. If on foot he will be lost in the crowd: if he goes in a Rolls he passes so quickly no one knows he is

161

there...' Flicking open his cigar case, he waved it towards the adjutant and then at herself before selecting a cigar. He continued, 'These horses that Major Winstanley selected and which you have brought across at his instigation are good enough to be seen leading a charge from the front... now, when the time comes, I shall be decently mounted.

'You have dispatched your duty in delivering me two of the finest to be seen in the final battle to come.' He walked over to the window and spoke as if delivering an utterance to his own reflection. 'I am ready to make history on either one of these two magnificent steeds.'

His words made her heart quail. Have I gone through all this, she thought, for these two animals to be brutally shot down? All for the sake of a suicidal brigadier's self-glorification?

She just managed to control her face and leave the room without being rumbled. Outside the room a corporal told her she was to bed down at the chateau before being given a lift on a motorcycle back to the rail head the next morning.

One more night near her horses. One final night...

26

Before turning in, a lance-corporal with a ginger moustache said to her, 'Don't take no notice of the noises out there, kid. Fritz won't bash up an HQ.'

'Oh? Why ever not?'

'Gentlemen's agreement. They don't attack each other's.'

'That's very polite.'

'It'll be over soon. Stick it out.'

But the bumping of shells accelerated. Glancing round, she drew some comfort from the troopers who were continuing to chat and smoke as if nothing unusual were happening. Exhausted, she felt herself sucked into a blank sleep, but woke frequently because of the racket of shelling and machine-gun fire through the night. The floorboards sometimes shook. It might not have been directed at the chateau, but even so she didn't sleep much because she couldn't convince herself that it wasn't.

Early the next morning there was a terrific blast as though a thunderclap had burst directly above them. But long-drawn-out and far more powerful. Then a series of sharp whistling sounds. More explosions overhead sounded like iron doors being slammed, and a hail of metal and fire rained down in the yard outside the window. Plaster was falling from the ceiling onto Cass's bunk. There was a commotion all around her as men hurried to get their kit together. Someone yelled, 'Bloody Huns misfiring.' Her thoughts flew to Sunlight and Magician. The corridor was full of noise and bustle: men in great-coats carrying bayonets, and with huge kit bags dangling from one shoulder, made it hard for her to nip through.

Out in the stables she found the horses in a sweat and trembling. When a whizz-bang zipped overhead and exploded on the far side of the courtyard she knew they weren't safe shut in the stables, and having shoved bridles on them both and thrown a saddle on Sunlight, she undid their head stalls and led them towards the door. Magician ripped the reins out of her hand and yanked himself away, galloping out of the yard. She could barely hang on to Sunlight. Gripping his reins she vaulted into the saddle. She couldn't hold him back after that and let him have his head. Just as his hooves clattered over the cobbles a shell screeched for a second and, after a pause, the walls of the stables burst apart. Splintered wood and metal flew into the air.

She clung to the horse for her life. In the mottled early light she tried to keep an eye on the ground just ahead to anticipate where he might slip or stumble. All she could do was stay on board and trust that his instinct for self-preservation would keep them away from obvious danger.

When he finally slowed, she had no idea where they might be. She'd managed to stick on, but all hope of finding Magician ever again was draining from her. Had he been hit by a shell, fallen in the mud? It was her stupid fault, letting him go like that; but if she hadn't undone the rope he would have been felled in the stall. Oh, good luck, good luck, my friend.

She steered Sunlight down a lane that seemed to take them away from the immediate horrors of the Front. For a while she and the horse wandered past some fields that were still green – wood anemones, germander speedwell, wild mint, a twinkling of goldfinches overhead. But on the other side of the road the ground was littered with dumped packing cases and wrecked equipment, and had been sliced into deep ruts by armoured vehicles and artillery – a frieze left behind by the war as it had passed by, to which it might yet return.

She slid out of the saddle and let Sunlight graze the roadside grass. She had nothing else to give him. She chewed some grass herself and sucked the moisture from the sappy stems. From somewhere, she wasn't sure if it was up ahead or across the fields, came a rumble of voices. The horse's ears pricked and he stopped chewing. Barely audible at first, like some animal grunting, and then the undercurrent of boots striking the stones of the road. Who was approaching?

Some dishevelled Tommies came round the corner. Now you're for it, she thought. It made her heart beat to see human beings again, and she was relieved they weren't Germans. Closer up, she could see their uniforms were torn: one had blood seeping through a filthy bandage and their tin hats sat askew. They seemed exhausted and disoriented as well and, on seeing the horse, must have assumed she was an officer, because they lined up and prepared to stand to attention until they realised there were no badges on her uniform.

'You're not the only one who's lost, mate', one said when she asked them if they knew where they were. 'We're just following on behind. Our battalion, or what's left of it, is up ahead, somewhere in this gawdforsaken 'ole.' One of them offered her half a cigarette and she smoked it gratefully while they shuffled off and the horse continued to tear at the grass and munch it, the bit clinking in its mouth.

Only a short distance further on, the land on both sides lay ripped to shreds. Tangled piles of barbed wire squeaked in the wind. The flash of shells in the distance turned the skyline yellow. The smoky daylight blurred Cass's vision and the meanings of words in her mind seemed blasted and torn.   She wandered on past abandoned ruined farmsteads, past deep shell holes full of black and stinking water, through a landscape that would have seemed inert but for the fluting of a single thrush from the top branch of a blasted tree.

She chose a ruin with half a roof to spend the night. It had some mouldering straw she could lie on. Cigarette butts and an empty sweet tin told her that soldiers had sheltered here. Cass's stomach was growling. As darkness fell, it started to rain and Sunlight lay down on the soggy straw. Cass, who had been shivering against the damp wall, crawled over to him and laid herself gingerly against the warmth of his belly. He sniffed at her hair as if it might be edible and then his head fell back. She drifted off to the sounds of his hunger, his heart beating, his digestive tract grumbling.

She was shocked awake by the horse rising to his feet. She cried out. Someone was coughing. Something was scrabbling about on the other side of the dilapidated building.

'Who's that?' she gasped.

'Only me.'

'You gave us quite a turn.'

'Sorry about that. I need to kip. It's raining out there.'

'It's raining in here.' She scrambled away from sitting between the horse's feet.

'Yeah, well… how many are there of you?'

'Me and a horse.'

'A horse? My God, I thought there was a squad in here.'

'No. Look, you'd better come over this side. The roof has holes but there is some cover over us. What's your name?'

'Name? er… Jim.' A minute later there was a pinprick glow of a cigarette close to Sunlight and she heard the small putt of his lips. 'Ta,' he said. 'Sorry, but this is my very last fag. You can have a puff if you want.'

'No, you finish it yourself. I don't suppose you've got anything to eat, have you?'

'If only I did. But who are you? What's your name?'

'Forrester, Orion Forrester.'

The orange glow brightened and dimmed. Within seconds Jim started snoring, while Cass was kept awake till dawn: there was a catch in his every breath and something about him made her wary, fearful that he could steal the horse from her if she was not on her guard. It occurred to her to creep away in the dead of night, but without the light of a moon she knew this would be too dangerous. In the half light the Tommy roused himself. He stood at the crumbled doorway and said, 'If they get hold of you and ask you anything, best if you don't mention meeting me.'

'Why? What do you mean, Jim?' She noticed now that he wasn't lugging a kit bag on his shoulder. That was odd, because it wasn't permitted to go without. He must have lost it somehow.

'They'll be after me. They're going to shoot me if they catch me.'

'Isn't that the idea?'

'No,' he shrugged, 'you haven't twigged, have you? The Red Caps...' and he vanished into the grey light.

After he had left, Cass mounted Sunlight and continued down the road. The barn must have been full of lice, because her skin itched incessantly. She wondered about the stranger. Seemed a bit desperate. And was he really called Jim?

About an hour later, a sentry stepped out from a stone building, its roof intact. As she approached he called out, 'Halt!' She pulled out her creased papers and told him the horse had bolted with her and now she had lost her way. The sentry pointed the way back to the chateau and they saw a pall of smoke hanging over the hills in that direction. He shook his head and said that

Fritz was showing those poor geezers a lot of hate this morning and that it'd be better to delay arriving until later. 'I'd lie low for a while if I were you, laddie.' And he scribbled on a form he then handed to her. 'Go an' find yourself a place to sleep an' get yourself a tot of rum. Over there,' and he pointed out the way to an encampment. 'They'll make room for youse.'

By midday she found herself in another valley, full of tents in rows. Mules were tethered in long lines. Men with packs on their backs were on parade in the drizzle, stamping their feet while turning and turning about. A few others were washing and shaving in front of the tent flaps. She did fancy the idea of a sleep in a tent because her head was so heavy with tiredness, but she couldn't leave Sunlight without finding him a nosebag and some hay. For that he'd have to wait till the others were fed and watered: his own nosebag had been left behind at the chateau and she'd have to sort something out for him. Afterwards, she joined a queue at the Salvation Army canteen for a cup of coffee and some bread and dripping. The food tasted good but landed in her stomach like lead, exhausting her as if digesting it took up all her energies.

She unrolled her wet puttees and, despite the dampness of her kit, she fell into a deep sleep. She woke with a start. The tent roof billowed and thwacked, making her feel giddy for some moments. She clutched the bedroll and peered round the space. Stale cigarette smoke, coughing, voices not far away. Someone guffawing close by made her shut her eyes, pretending to be asleep still.

Had Reveille sounded? Two men at the back of the queue for a wash grinned at her as she ducked out through the tent flap. One said, 'Stick to it, kid.' He shook her hand and the other, patting her on the shoulder, said, 'Good luck, chum.' Most of the others barely glanced at the stranger in their presence, busily talking amongst themselves: maybe not unusual for soldiers to become separated from their detachments, or even to be a sole survivor.

She made her way towards the mule lines, anxious to check that Sunlight was where she had left him. A smell of breakfast was emanating from a tent and she ducked inside to find herself among a crowd of soldiers eating ravenously. At the end of the trestles there was a spare place so she found some boiled bacon and a hunk of bread. The man next to her shifted a little on the bench and grinned at her, 'What's eating ya, buddy? Looks like you've got the heebie-jeebies. So where are you from?' His manner made her almost tell him the truth.

'The ASC. Delivering horses,' she said, trying to speak as little as possible. 'And you?'

'Me? With the Canadian Corps. Yup. Been with 'em somewheres around four months now and still live an' kickin'. Good luck, fella.' He stood up to leave.

At first she felt she couldn't eat a thing, but she was aware that she didn't know where the next meal was coming from and that she must fill her belly while she could. 'Lonely, your job, I should think,' said her neighbour, who lapsed into silence, shovelling his ration into his mouth.

As she ate, she overheard snatches of conversation down the table:

'Blown to bits, he wor...'

'Shrapnel in his head...'

'Mopping up operation...'

'Only a kid an' all...'

'Four fuckin' weeks without a bath...'

'Nothing left of him, only a hand...'

Their conversation seemed full of shrapnel. So as not to fall inadvertently into the muddy depths of the military's systems she needed to plan her next move. But what to do now that she was here? Give herself up? Turn Sunlight in? Would that be best for him? A supply depot was probably not the best place. But if not here, where? She wasn't going to take him back to the brigadier after what he'd said. When the stables had been shelled they would have assumed the horses had scarpered, so that was covered.

The men continued talking around her. One was reading from a newsletter called *The B E F Times*. 'It says 'ere the Great Army Peace Movement is going to have an anti-war demonstration at Passchendaele. Look. We're all going to lose our jobs soon.'

The man sitting next to him replied, 'Don't worry... it says the president is D. Haig and the speakers are R. Tillery and T. Atkins.'

When she'd finished eating she went outside again to find Sunlight. He whinnied as she drew close to him and she went back to fetch his saddle and bridle. He had at least been fed, as he had an empty nosebag attached to his head stall. But he couldn't have had much rest because the mules were so noisy and the line to which he was tethered was swaying. Had he been watered yet? She didn't know whom to ask. His legs were slathered in cloying mud. When she felt his ears they were cold. His coat was wet.

After showing her papers to the Transport Officer she saddled Sunlight and then led him away from the misery of the supply lines. She wanted to find some clean water. A puddle on the road would be better than the filth she assumed the mules were having to make do with. The stink the mules left in made her determined he wasn't going to end up in the hands of the army. The men looking after the animals were not knowledgeable enough and no one was cleaning up after them. The lines needed to be moved to higher, drier ground: they'd be contracting mud fever, and disease could spread through here like wildfire.

Her plan was to get Sunlight away to a place of safety. Her grandparents had owned a house in a village somewhere near Albert and she knew the place from the summer holidays they'd spent there, so she thought she would see if she could find it. Perhaps she could hide herself away there until the war was over. This shambles can't go on for much longer, she thought. What she had seen and heard in so short a time made her feel quite sick at heart.

The countryside that she remembered from summer holidays was devastated. On the skyline she recalled seeing a windmill from her grandparents' house but there was no sign of anything now. She couldn't be sure she could find the way to the village: they were all children when they used to come. Now there was no one about but herself and the horse. She talked to him: 'There's an orchard at my grandparents' full of grass – you can live in the stable. Until this is over. We'll be safe there. Safe.' She thought she could pretend to be French. 'No one would guess and if anyone does they won't say anything. Need to get rid of this uniform soon as I can. There'll be clothes I can wear in Grandmaman's wardrobe. Only summer clothes of course. But not this uniform. And we must get rid of your Army-issue saddle.' Talking about it to Sunlight made it all seem possible, a gamble worth taking.

All around the maze of lanes, the fields and buildings were blown up, torched, desolate. At one place she thought she recognised the lie of the land from the view of hills in the distance. She spotted a pimple of a ruined church tower. A river lay between, and when she thought it might be shallow enough, on a long bend, she pushed Sunlight into the water. He stepped in willingly. She had taught him well. The water was deeper than she thought and he had to swim across the current. On the other side, he clambered out through a boggy pool between willows sprouting green shoots. She let him nibble them. She saw the ruins of the church further along the bank and headed for that.

When she came up to it, all the other buildings around it lay shattered, the rubble lying in piles. Corpses of horses still attached to their wagons lay in what must have been the square. Where houses had stood, she found burnt and broken bed frames, smashed pictures and furniture. An old stove still stood against the remaining wall of a kitchen. She dismounted and walked Sunlight across to where some grass was pushing up between the stones. When he'd had a bit of a nibble she rode aimlessly on again, following a track that seemed as though it might take her away from the sound of shelling.

She heard the snarl of a motor cycle some way behind her. After a while it came into view along the straight road. A British soldier anyway. Instead of overtaking, the motorcyclist held back, idling along beside her. Sunlight didn't like that and threw up his head, nearly pulling the reins from her hands. The soldier had a red band round his cap and she realised he was a military policeman. She'd heard enough to know she was about to be thrown on the mat. He drove on slowly, then looked round and stopped the motorcycle in front of the horse.

He pulled off his goggles and said, 'I'll take a look at your papers.'

She said nothing to him as she pulled her pass and the mayor's *sauf-conduit* out of her pocket. He studied them and then looked at her. The man's attention was almost a relief.

'What the fuck are you doing here?'

'I think I must be lost.'

'You think you're lost? We'll see about that,' he said.

27

The bed in the guard house was unmade and the sheets unwashed. There was a very smelly tin bucket in the corner of the room. Outside, she heard voices – clipped military ones, slurred drunken ones. Further away a man's voice was wailing, or singing. Through the night, outside her blacked-out window was the tramp of marching as troops moved from one position to another. She slept, but only fitfully.

Soon after daybreak, the guard opened the door and told her to follow him. He gave her tea, sweetened with too much sugar. Then a door was flung wide and a red-capped military policeman leaned into the room. 'Miss, you're to be questioned. Now.'

They entered a room with high windows. It had obviously been a school before the British Army had taken it over. He indicated that she should sit on an ammunition crate in front of a cluttered desk in the middle of the room. Across the desk a Welsh sergeant lilted, 'It has come to our attention that you are not who you say you are. You have been trying to impersonate a private in the British Expeditionary Force. You were also caught mounted on a horse belonging to His Majesty's Armed Forces without permission. What do you have to say?'

'I can explain…' she said. She could see his moustache twitching but couldn't see his face properly when he was leaning over what he was writing about her. He wrote quite slowly and in pencil. It occurred to her that he could erase it later.

'You will have to do a lot of explaining. Your papers are not in order. Impersonating a member of the armed forces carries serious punishment as does being in possession of a mount belonging to the King's Army. You cannot deny all this. The horse bears the Broad Arrow mark and its Remount number.' He looked across the table at her. His eyes met hers briefly.

She looked away. She was very tired and her mind didn't seem able to concoct a better story than the truth. Was that going to be good enough? She really was in boiling water. This man was never going to be convinced, whatever she said. His belt with the pistol in it glared at her. She felt a lump rise in her throat and her eyes start to go blurry. If she wiped them with her hand it would look as if she were going to cry and, if she looked up at him, he would see that she was. Let him think what he liked. Inside she was defiant, if also terrified.

'So, why don't we start at the beginning, shall we? When first apprehended you gave your name as Orion Forrester. What is your real name?'

She hadn't heard from Orion. Of course, she had received no letters while she had been in France because nobody knew where she was or, indeed, who she had become. She felt very alone. She could be lost in this world, disappearing under the mud without trace, a blip of liquid at her last exhalation. The last letter she had received from her brother was about his becoming a Socialist or something, and said he was thinking of going to some far-flung place with an unpronounceable name. He wasn't in France, so her using his name wouldn't get him into trouble.

Her mind could not find the beginning of a thread to pull out from the tangle of events and actions that she had lived through. It had all begun long ago with visiting Orion in prison that time, seeing the gassed soldiers being led from the train in Exeter, wondering how she herself could best make a difference. The Red

Cap wouldn't want to know about any of that, but this was how it had started.

She gave him her own name and he asked her if the uniform also belonged to her brother. How had she come by it? Where was her brother?

'Miss Forrester, explain your reasons for impersonating a member of the British Expeditionary Force.'

She was used to being with men in uniform, had learned their swear-words. She had slept beside the soldiers, had listened to their snores and sleep-worn mutterings, had rolled out of bed at Reveille. She had worked beside the ASC men, grown accustomed to smelling constantly of horse sweat and dung like the rest of them. She had remained with her charges as instructed, had hardly let them out of her sight, knew the sound of their breathing, their hoof-beats, their bit-champing. She had learned how to drill with the ASC men and had eaten alongside them. She'd travelled in convoy over the mudscapes of the Front to deliver her charges to the brigadier, who had personally thanked her, never guessing that the grubby jockey whose small hand he shook was a woman. She had stood in uniform without flinching very much while the shells screeched overhead and fell beyond the half-ruined chateau, and while the *ack-ack* of machine guns rattled from the trenches beyond.

So it had become easy to forget she was female and the rules didn't permit her to be here. How would the military policeman in front of her ever see things from her point of view? How could she communicate to him how she felt? Tight-lipped and short of time as he was.

She began to feel some concord with Orion. The war looked like a shambles. Men were being randomly marched from one place to another to stand in front of machine gun fire. A multitude of human beings lived as though buried up to their necks in a landscape criss-crossed by trenches. Everything in her mind had become muddled. She couldn't think why she had come here.

'It's the horses,' she muttered. After a pause, while the Red Cap kept his eyes pinned to the table with his pencil poised, she continued, 'I was delivering two remounts to the HQ of the Third Cavalry Brigade. I don't know where exactly. I followed the instructions given to me. Some chateau in the middle of nowhere. There was a bombardment, lots of shells, the building was damaged and I escaped on one of the horses we had brought. As it's a valuable animal I thought I'd ride it back to Abbeville and then you chaps found me while I was getting there.'

'The papers you have given me refer to your mission to the Third Cavalry Brigade at their HQ.'

'Yes, that's correct.'

'But you say you were returning the horses to Base Depot. Where is the authorisation?'

'The chateau was being shelled. I had to get the horses out of the danger zone. I couldn't wait for the form to be signed and sealed.'

'So, no document, no pass. Nothing.'

'No.'

'You expect me to believe this?' He looked up from the writing and she saw the glint of his eyes beneath the peak of his cap pulled down low over his brow. His chin was white and newly shaven and his lips were thin. He kept on licking them. His eyes were fixed for a moment on the wall behind her as if he was used to being patient in dealing with imbeciles. 'That's all, is it?'

'I had to get them out of the firing line. Valuable horses like that. Nobody asked them to volunteer.'

'So you're an animal lover?' he said with mock pity.

'And what if I am?' She swallowed back a nervous

giggle, the absurdity of the situation striking her. 'Is there something wrong with caring for horses? They never asked to get involved with this. *Schadenfreude* is a human emotion, it isn't experienced by animals.'

As if he had just realised something he fidgeted and sucked in his cheeks. 'So you speak German? Who are you really and why did you come here?' he pursued.

'I thought I could make a difference.'

'Did you? What did you have in mind? Sending signals to the enemy maybe? Collecting evidence of movements, ammunition dumps, supply lines?'

'No, that's ridiculous. I told you, I just wanted to get at least the one horse to safety.'

'What system had been agreed on?'

'System?' She shivered. There was a pause while she heard his pencil running across the paper as if it had a life of its own. 'Signalling?' Suddenly the questions seemed completely irrelevant. From the pit of her stomach rose the words, 'All this is such unnecessary waste, don't you think? It's carnage.'

'It's not my job to have opinions.'

'But how can anyone want this to continue?' She shifted her feet and gripped the edge of the table. 'Do you?'

'My job is to investigate you. Not me. You!'

She sighed resignedly, 'I'm not a spy, if that's what you're getting at.'

'Where you were found wasn't the Abbeville road.'

'Wasn't it? Well, I got lost. You people have taken all the signs down.'

'Who ordered you to return to Abbeville?'

'The brigadier, actually.'

'But not with the horse?'

'No, that was my idea.'

'So, to get this straight, you acted on your own initiative when you took the horse out of its stable?'

'Indeed, I did.' She could see exactly where this line of questioning was leading. 'But, hang on, I'm not a soldier. I don't have to take orders.'

'But you wear the King's uniform.'

'It keeps the rain off and gets me about.'

She watched his pencil move across the page, tried to read what he was writing upside down, but couldn't decipher any of the words. When he looked up at her again, the page looked like a mirror but not one she could see herself in. Even if he was writing what she said verbatim it would include the snap opinions he was clearly making about her. There was a pause. She sniffed, fidgeted her backside on the squeaky crate.

'You speak French, too, I understand?'

'Yes. My mother taught me.' She was thinking as fast as she could, 'But what do you mean by *too*?'

'You have French contacts?'

'My grandparents were French. They had a place near somewhere called Albert. I wanted to find their old house.'

'You know Albert then? What are your grandparents called?'

'I thought we were friends with France. Otherwise, why are we here?'

'That's a matter for the COs to decide. There are plenty of things the French would like to know that we don't want them to know. And you aren't supposed to be here.'

'I only spoke to some French people to ask the way or to find some food for myself or the horse.'

'What exactly did you convey about our sentry positions or troop movements to your French colleagues?'

'Nothing. This is a bit steep, you know.'

'I believe you were gathering military information.'

Nonplussed, she heard soldiers passing close by

outside, glanced at the window, saw figures through the lace curtain. Laughter spilled into the room and she wondered if it was about the girl prisoner. She desperately wanted to know what they'd done with Sunlight. And where was Magician now? Caught up in all this and alone?

Her inquisitor jumped up from his chair and banged on the window. 'Get away from here,' he shouted, pushing aside the curtain. The men outside seemed to melt away. 'What the blazes is going on?' he muttered to himself as he strode out of the door, slamming it behind him.

She heard the words, 'Slippery cunt, that one… French bitch. Speaks German, too.'

A sentry slipped in to the room, stood to attention inside the door. She heard the Red Cap's footsteps creaking away.

'Any chance of some more tea?' she asked the young man by the door. He looked startled at the sound of her voice.

'I'll ask in a few minutes, Miss,' he said confidentially.

'Aren't you allowed to talk to me?'

'Not allowed to communicate with prisoners.'

'I'm an official prisoner now, am I? I suppose I must be. It's all right, don't answer that.'

She went up to the window to see if she could peek through a gap in the curtain. The sentry came up behind her and pulled the curtains tightly shut. She sat down on the crate again. After a long silence, she heard footsteps approach and there was a knock on the door. 'Come in,' she called, nervously standing up. Two officers walked in, with an orderly carrying a tray of tea and toast. The sentry boy at the door drew himself up and saluted. 'We thought you'd need some fodder before they take you to HQ,' said one of the officers. 'That'll be all,' he nodded to the sentry. The young soldier saluted and marched

179

out of the room.

'My name's Hutton, Lieutenant Hutton. And this is Lieutenant Robinson.' They both shook her hand. 'How do you do,' she said, noticing how both men held her hand with no grip. She couldn't quite trust either of them.

The older-looking officer was thin as a thorn tree bent by the wind, his face creased with tiredness. What might happen at HQ, for heaven's sake? She didn't have the strength left to ask. Is that where the lightning would strike her?

'Jolly decent of you to think of bringing me some breakfast. I'm terribly hungry.'

'We wanted an excuse to come and meet you,' said Robinson with a grin. He took off his hat and his black hair looked wet and shone with some glutinous preparation. He propped himself on the edge of the table. 'I say, can't they get you a proper seat?' He dragged the chair the Red Cap had been sitting on and changed her crate for the chair. 'Do tuck in, please. Don't mind us.'

'You're quite the talk of the town,' giggled Hutton. He walked over to the window and squinted through the curtains. 'Everybody wants to meet the girl who's ridden here on a cavalry horse.'

'Jolly brave of you. What the deuce do your people think about you being out here?' asked Robinson.

'Oh, they don't know. Otherwise, they'd never have let me come, would they?' She was buttering the toast and spooning out marmalade from the pot. She crammed toast into her mouth and the crunching embarrassed her.

'Where are you from?' asked Hutton. The question had an edge to it. It wasn't just conversation. She guessed that they were here to form an opinion about her and that they'd be reporting to someone later.

Hutton took out his pocket watch to have a look at the time.

'From the middle of Dartmoor,' she said with her mouth rather full.

'Let the poor girl eat first,' said Robinson. 'Then we're to escort you to the General at HQ.'

'Why's that?' asked Cass. A sense of foreboding crept through her hair.

'It's a matter for top brass, now.'

'Before I go anywhere, could you possibly find out what's happened to my horse? I'm very attached to him and I want to know if he's all right. I'd be so grateful.'

'I'll make a phone call, it won't take a jiffy. But if I were you I'd try and remember, Miss Forrester, the horse is not yours. It'll be in limbo till its paperwork has been sorted, I should think.'

'Any chance I could see him?' she asked, feeling miserable.

'I'll see what I can find out. What's its Remount number?' She told him and Hutton left the room.

Being left alone with a man can't count as bad form if you yourself are dressed as a man, Cass was thinking as she drained her tea cup.

Robinson stood up and walked about, then plumped down on the crate and offered her a cigarette. She noticed his long fingers with their clean nails, and how his buttons sparkled, even the one on his revolver case. 'Thanks,' she said, taking one. She decided she needed something to calm her. He lit it for her and for a while they said nothing. Her first cigarette. She coughed on the smoke in her mouth. The first puff made her feel light-headed.

He confided, 'I really can't imagine how you got past the sentries.'

'I had my papers,' said Cass elatedly, 'told them I was delivering urgent messages.'

'Nobody stopped you then?'

'Nobody at all,' she smiled at him. 'Why should they?'

'I gather your pass is out of date.'

'Is it? Perhaps it's the French handwriting. It's not so easy to read and the papers had been in my pocket all the time and while I slept so they'd be creased.'

'Still, the system really isn't working very well,' mused Robinson. Fiddling with the buckle of his boots, he paused for a while. He continued, 'Being on horseback, I suppose, rather puts you above suspicion.'

'Look, I'm not a spy. How am I going to make you all believe me? It's the truth. I don't know anything anyway. Why are you people so fixed on the idea?'

'Well, the manual warns us about female spies.'

'What manual?'

Hutton reached into his side pockets and pulled out a well-thumbed booklet. 'The Officer's Manual. I'll find the bit I mean.' He thumbed through it. 'Look, here it is – in the notes on espionage it says: *Several women spies have been caught collecting information regarding names and numbers of regiments, numbers of officers etc.*'

'That looks pretty bad, then.'

'That's not the end of it either – underneath that it goes on: *Spies have been caught at rail heads observing entrainment and detrainment of troops.*'

'Oh, I see now how it might look,' she gasped, covering her face with her hands. The shock of it curdled in her stomach, making her feel suddenly faint. She gripped the table. 'But how can I prove to you that I've not been spying? I swear I haven't!'

'I think the spies are usually French women,' said Hutton, pulling hard on his cigarette.

'But I thought the French and British were allies.'

Robinson got up and walked to and fro. 'You'd think so to read the papers, wouldn't you? But reality is a bit different. We don't trust them and they don't trust us. In fact, they hate us. We never work together, and if we do we let each other down.'

Hutton rushed in again and said he'd phoned around and discovered the black horse had been taken to the stables until the brigadier demanded it back. It was probably enjoying a nosebag full of oats. He apologised, but orders from on high were that she wasn't permitted to leave the guard room. She opened her mouth to remonstrate but knew she was beaten. He gabbled on, 'Now, we must be getting you away from here. Pronto. Sorry, we can't offer you some decent clothes.'

Cass thought to herself that she felt quite decent enough, thank you, in Army uniform, though a clean set of undies would have been nice. A motor arrived at the door and all three of them climbed onto the back seat, Cass in the middle. She supposed sandwiching her in like this was a precaution against possible escape.

'I rather feel for you. But why did you do it, er, Miss Forrester?' asked Hutton as they jolted off down the potholed road.

'Feel for me?' Cass felt indignant. 'Why me? Don't you people see what I see? The horses, poor things, just got sent here to put up with all this… this horror. It's so unfair. Trees blown up, a nightmare landscape, war, war, war everywhere you look. I… I just wanted to save Sunlight,' she said. 'I didn't think it would cause so much difficulty. Magician was so frightened he took himself off somewhere. You needn't think about me.'

'Sunlight and Magician? Is that what you said?' Robinson was fishing through his pockets for his cigarette case and started laughing. 'Who gave them those names?'

'I did. Horses have names even in a war.'

'Miss Forrester, how come you got into France at all?'

She had forgotten it wasn't obvious – she was wearing khaki uniform but she hadn't deceived anyone. She hadn't realised that they couldn't know about her work at the Remount Depot at Pluckley. When they arrived at this HQ she guessed they'd be reporting to whoever was going to interrogate her next. So she told them how she had volunteered to work there and had eventually been given the responsibility of training up the two Waterford horses; how one thing led to another and she'd found herself at Abbeville, in charge of two of the Army's finest horses with a motley column of nags bound for a transport corps, and how she was then to ride to the regimental HQ of the cavalry regiment further on. She was careful to avoid saying anything about Sergeant Maddox's gift, said she'd simply bypassed everyone. She kept saying that her actions were motivated only by the horses' welfare.

'Do you know a chap called Frank Lethbridge, by any chance?' she asked. 'A lieutenant, I believe.' He might not want to marry her any more but he would surely vouch for her, in her hour of need.

'Second Lieutenant Lethbridge?' said Hutton.

'You know him, do you?' asked Robinson.

'Well, yes. We used to hunt together.'

'Oh, I saw on the list… Lethy's been reported missing, I'm afraid,' said Hutton. 'It doesn't mean he really is missing or even lost. It means they don't know his whereabouts at this point.'

After Cass and her two escorts were given tea and biscuits in a small study of the old farmhouse used as their HQ, she was escorted by a sergeant to a chintzy parlour where the general stood up to greet her. The sergeant stamped his feet a great deal in front of the desk and turned on his heels before marching out of the room. The general shook her hand and gestured to a Louis Quinze chair. He was a wizened elderly man with a short moustache that was grey in patches and yellowing. His jowl was droopy like an old spaniel's and his eyes, blinking and ringed, reminded her of a hen's: his whole face was like a reflection in the back of a dessertspoon. Gold braid was dripping off his shoulders and a clutch of red tabs was sprinkled on his tunic.

When he found out where she lived, he said he knew the county well and had once spent a week hunting on Colonel Westwood's horses. 'Are you aware that Yvo and Alexander have been out here?' He made it sound like a holiday.

'Have been?' Were they not still here? Might they be able to speak for her?

'I'm afraid to say Yvo was recently killed by mortar fire, and Alexander is apparently dangerously wounded and in the hospital at Rouen. So I gather from despatches.'

She cried out in horror. The war had reached as far as home – two men she'd known as children. They had all grown up together… maybe in somewhat different social circles, but on the periphery of each other's worlds. They hunted together, danced at hunt balls. She staunched her tears, wiping her eyes with her fingers. With poor Frank listed as missing as well, was everything she'd thought of as secure now in a state of total collapse?

'Young lady,' he said, 'now that I meet you, I cannot believe the cock and bull they tell me about you – that you are some sort of a spy. But those Red Caps are decent clever fellows and I have to take this seriously. You understand me, I hope.'

'Yes, of course,' replied Cass, looking across at him. She heard a clock chiming a tune in the corridor outside. Footsteps reverberated down the corridor.

'Can I offer you a little glass of something, Miss

Forrester? A whisky or a sherry, perhaps?'

He poured her a generous slug of sherry into a cut glass and took a great gulp from his own whisky tumbler.

The general said, 'Now, then, tell me, my dear, how it is you have made fools of us all?'

'I didn't intend to. I never had any plan, beyond trying to find my grandparents' place, on the road from Albert to Le Boscin.'

'Highly unlikely they'd have stayed there. No civilians anywhere near that town any more. It was behind the Boche lines until the British advanced. The Germans destroyed everything when they retreated. What was left of the town has been used for target practice for the last two years.'

'Oh.' She knew her grandparents lived further south and had not been to their country retreat since troops arrived in the area, but now her plan to get to the house and hide there, catching fish from the river and feeding the horse in the orchard, sounded so feeble she couldn't bring herself to explain. She would rather have shot Sunlight herself than let the Army take him from her. Maybe it would have been the best thing she could do for him. But could she have carried it out?

'The house was our holiday home. We used to stay there in the summer sometimes with our grandparents when we were young. It's how I learned French. I wanted to see how the place was. Thought I might stay for a while.'

'But you can't just wander about when a country is at war. It's madness. You've been in the firing zone.'

'I know! I didn't exactly plan that either.'

'How ever did you get here, a young lady like yourself?'

She gabbled quickly about how she had come to be in France. Finishing the story she said, 'Sir, I must speak in my defence. I had no wish to be a problem. I had once simply wanted to serve my country and be a soldier. I'm as strong as some men. I shoot and ride as well as anyone. I have been working on my family's farm, and I'm fit. It really isn't my fault that you won't allow women at the Front.

'But then when I got here and it all seemed so terrible... and then I thought... I was thinking... I thought something must be done to stop it.'

Leo would have worked out a way to stop war, if he were still alive, she thought. It sounds impossible but he might have done something. Look at the mess this countryside is in. He'd know what to do, if anyone did. The thought of him rose up in her mind: she missed him terribly, as if he had died only yesterday. She tried to cough. And she wanted to say that if women were allowed to run things, this war would have been over long ago, but the words would not come out. What was it all for?

'But why would anyone want to stop the war? Before we've won it? You aren't thinking logically, my dear.'

'But then what? What will you have won? A... a morass?'

'Miss Forrester,' he hesitated a moment, his face reddening, 'We're here to fight and win a war, not stop it prematurely. Not now we've started, and not now that we've got the Boche on the run. They will be brought to their knees before we're finished or they'll drive us back into the Atlantic. We are ordered to fight by the King, so we serve our country and fight to the end.'

'Is it because you've all got used to it? Are you going to lay waste the whole of France? It was once such a beautiful country. Flowers everywhere, trees and woods and now everything looks like... like hell and worse.'

'Commendable as your intentions may or may not be – we do not have ladies in the Army for the simple reason that the gentler sex is unable to bayonet a man. It takes considerable strength to insert a bayonet into flesh and even more, sometimes, to remove it. You have no idea.'

'Yes,' said Cass, feeling admonished. 'But if women were able to help by negotiating or making bridges we could put an end to all this strife.'

'It may even be construed in some circles that your motivation was to become a camp follower, heaven forfend. The British Army does not countenance such things. If you were a man we would be court-martialling you for this, but as it is we would rather you returned home. Go and knit socks for the men at the Front, or grow hay to feed the horses if you prefer.'

'What on earth are you suggesting, sir? I don't understand what you mean.'

'Go and get yourself married before this comes out, young lady. And riding astride is not good for ladies. It can damage... things, private things.' He rose to his feet and walked over to a sideboard. Her mind felt like that of a charger having to wade knee-deep through mud. Every step made things worse. She saw that the general's legs were thin as a spider's. He filled his glass from one of the decanters and picked up another and offered her more sherry but she shook her head. One sip had made her feel giddy. She looked out of the window at the trees blowing in the wind, at the cloud shadows passing over the mown lawn. She was aware of him taking a turn around the room. Footsteps came and went outside the door. He looked at himself in the mirror briefly.

Falling back into the comfort of his chair, he continued, 'If – and I emphasise the *if* at this stage – we were to permit you to go home, I must add that there would be a condition attached to this. You must on your honour swear never to say anything to anyone about all this. If it were to get out to the press or become common knowledge, the powers-that-be will come looking for you, and your name will be blackened. They will make sure no one believes a word you say. '

'I didn't ask to be protected. I can do as much for my country as any man.'

'Miss Forrester, enough – stop arguing. I strongly recommend that you take up any offer we make before we change our minds. For one thing, it would ruin your chances of a decent marriage if it became known you might be a free and easy type of woman. I'd get home to the farm, if I were you. When you have given back your uniform and changed into some civvies – a corporal has been sent out to find you some more suitable apparel – a sergeant at the guard house attached to my billet here will be instructed to conduct you straightaway to the station. I must add that nothing has been decided yet. But that is the best offer you may get.'

She already knew enough not to trust the top brass. It hadn't been at all difficult, getting into the Army. It was staying there that was the problem. They were the ones with red faces now. She'd got to and from the Front, past the sentries, without any papers.

She wasn't going to admit defeat. Not yet. She could do what any man could do so long as she didn't have to take her clothes off.

28

Maurice King's application to be transferred back to France finally went through, soon after the tragic death of Corporal Fox at the railway station. Better able to control his reactions and reflexes at long last, he felt it was time to be putting his knowledge and battlefield experience to good use and not be kept hanging about while others stood their ground in the firing line – did he not owe as much to young Jed? The Front was where he should be himself, and was the reason why he'd joined up in the first place.

The threat of his own death had haunted him when he first got out to France. But once he had become accustomed to staying in one piece even during a strafe he knew he had only himself to face – that dark inner space where he met his own personality as if it were someone he could see in the distance. Not someone who would hide behind a horse to save his own skin. Getting through each day had been a matter of finding small but slippery footholds along the track, albeit running in bloodied mud. He mustn't let his body's fears sabotage that inner core. He must get a grip on himself, be a man like the rest of them – or at least pretend to be.

The medical officer wouldn't let him go back to the Front. After his spell at Pluckley he had gone up from B2 (fit for garrison service at home) to B1 (fit for garrison service abroad) but the MO said he would never make A1 again. Just the noise of a car backfiring sent him looking for cover. Any strong smell he could not immediately identify made him flush with heat or become chilled. Voices and certain quick movements reminded him of the days back home when he had feared the IRA lads might be lying in wait outside their house.

From his new billet in the grounds of the horse hospital he could smell the sea, it was so close. It reminded him of his Antrim home perched on a hill near the coast with his dinghy drawn up on the dunes on the edge of Whitepark Bay, where eider ducks swam between the white limestone cliffs and the black basalt rocks. And the curragh in which he used to paddle out to see the seals wailing on the skerries, the cormorants perched high on Sheep Island. Often he used to ride his old bay mare along the beach at low tide, passing the cows munching seaweeds, lengths of it dangling from their mouths, the smell of their dung mixed in with the sea air. He could almost taste the salt on his lips.

But here at the hospital he had no time to look at views or to ride on the beach. Performing operations on wounded horses left little time to think until that familiar smell of sea, occasionally wafting through the smell of horse dung and chemicals, set up an itching in his brain.

A big chestnut gelding with bullets in his neck was led up to stand beside the operating table, tilted at a right angle to the floor. Corporal Forbes, with the dicky chest and a squeak in his breath, knew the drill and quickly strapped the nearest legs to the board while the soporific horse stood, already in a dream. The outer legs were roped by another two men. Captain King, wearing a surgical apron, opened the bottle of chloroform again and soaked a wad of cotton, which he packed into the bottom of a leather nosebag. Forbes strapped it on to the horse's head. It sighed heavily and its eyes rolled backwards. The men held their ropes as Forbes pulled the lever that slowly turned the table so that the horse lay prone for the operation. The dose of chloroform provided a short period of time to perform the extraction. The bullets had torn into the muscle under the mane and were lodged deep in the flesh but had not hit the respiratory tract or the gullet. Not too difficult this time.

The horse lay as if comatose on its side for a moment and then came to, struggling against the ties that held it down. Maurice sprang back, shouting, 'Hold on to the legs!' The animal continued to struggle, gasping for breath. Its nostrils turned red, froth bubbled from its nose and then it collapsed, its eyes rolling. It lay inert on the table. 'Dammit and dammit,' he said, his fist white with clenching.

He wrote in his journal that evening:

The horse shouldn't have died on only two ounces of chloroform. Something must be radically wrong with this stuff. Another example of suspect chloroform? Or is chloroform itself suspect?

This was not the first that had died on the operating table from the effects of chloroform inhalation. The stuff supplied was occasionally faulty, a lethal concoction. In the hospital laboratory he was experimenting on new forms of anaesthesia. He noted in his journal:

I've learned something useful. Have a patient intolerant of chloroform: have tried 4 times on different brands. Gave him 2 oz. of diluted chloral hydrate through the jugular, pushed him down all by myself. Operated on his foot and up he got! No problems so far. Shall try more.

King was preparing a report on his use of chloral hydrate as an alternative anaesthetic for animals, but he doubted the Army Veterinary Service would even read it. He pored over the veterinary reports from other hospitals, hoping to learn something from the endless statistics that were sent out. Were they having the same problems with the chloroform? He ought to let them know about the idea of chloral hydrate somehow.

Horses arrived from the Front almost every day. The ones to enter the inspection paddock last always hobbled. From a short distance away he could tell which foot was lame: some were footsore in two or more feet while others might be affected in only one. Puncture wounds in the quick of the hoof were common enough and had always been filled with iodine and tar by the mobile veterinary unit at the Front. But time was needed for footy horses to convalesce away from the mud they usually stood in for nine months of the year. If not attended to quickly enough on the field, the horses were deemed inoperative and would be disposed of. King recognised that before septicaemia set in it was better to shoot those remounts, for their value as meat, rather than waste the government's investment. The French had a penchant for horseflesh, but the carcasses had to be passed as fit for human consumption. Decisions had to be made from time to time. And journalists circled statistics like vultures.

He had found it necessary to shoot several horses thus afflicted when he was in the mobile unit in 1916. Jed, his right-hand man, held the rope while he placed the Greener's cattle killer to the whorl of fur on the horse's brow. As he applied the shock Jed stood at the head, watching the horse's eyes, talking soothingly in his Irish horseman's voice, and weeping over every horse the captain had to destroy. One flick of the lever and the horse would be dead. Far more humane than the Boer War technique of striking down suffering horses with a pole-axe.

But any animals evacuated to one of the horse hospitals were expected to survive and to be returned to active service. They arrived from the Front with chalk marks on their flanks encoding the decision made by the veterinary officer on the spot, often in very difficult conditions – under fire, under pressure, under threat. It was such a man who had to select those horses likely to live and those that were not worth keeping. He'd been there himself, and that was why he felt that every horse that made it to Hospital no.1 should be given the chance. They killed a lot of them in Hospital no.2.

Maurice was on good terms with one of the most important men in the hospital. Josh Anstey was the sergeant shoey in his sub-division, a stocky, muscled man who had been a farrier in the Yorkshire Dales before the war, not one of the newly trained cold-shoers. He walked around with chaps over his breeches as if he got up into them in the morning. He'd followed the horses out here, his business ruined when the horses were taken from the countryside – a wife and five children back home.

Sergeant Anstey cussed every time he bent over a cupped hoof and found a BEF nail. 'Them ASC bastards should be court-martialled. If they 'ad to walk barefoot on't nails they chuck abaht when they open packing cases them'd think twice afore doin' it.'

But when he cradled the foot between his knees and unpacked iodine-soaked wadding placed in the hoof by a veterinary officer at the Front, and found Caltrops – the three-pointed iron stars, thrown down on purpose by the Germans on BEF transport links to injure the horses – he broke into a sweat. Knowing any such horse was practically a goner, he poured in more iodine, slathered on BIPP paste, reported to Captain King and then swore as if rats were gnawing his feet. If septicaemia followed, as it usually did, he and King had to make use of the cattle killer together. He once muttered, 'We mek the best o' a bad job, we do. Thar's all we can do for them, any road. But, it's a crying shame we can't yuse tha' on sum o' th' lads.'

Also sent to the hospital were horses lamed by kicks from others. Kept in crowded conditions on picket lines with very little to eat, tempers flared easily and horses often lashed out at one another, causing severe contusions, sometimes fractures. Those with broken bones had to be disposed of for their food value.

In "C" and "D" subdivisions, without specialist equipment, King had examined two hundred and seventy five horses and found 10% with periodic ophthalmia, leucomata, or cataract afflictions, the causes of blindness. In his journal he wrote:

To make matters worse, the antistreptococcus serum supply is outdated and not sterile. (Not, I hasten to add, the quartermaster's fault.)

He was called to the phone just after he'd finished examining the day's intake of horses – mange cases from the supply lines, but there were also some debility cases, emaciated and broken down with exhaustion. Better than yesterday's consignment, which had been riddled with bullets from the latest offensive.

A faraway voice he didn't know said, 'Lieutenant Hutton here. I wonder if you'd mind helping us out. There's a young lady here... been found riding a remount near the village of Le Boscin. Says she knows you. We don't know what to make of her. Could you come over and confirm a few things?'

'Who? What's her name?'

'Says her name's Forrester.' The man's voice crackled on, 'Are you able to get hold of transport, sir? '

'What, today?' King almost shouted. 'You can't be serious.'

'Yes, sir, confoundedly inconvenient, I'm sure. But we haven't the deuce of an idea what to do with her. Look, we'll send a driver for you. Dashed grateful if you could find the time.'

On the journey he remembered how when Miss Forrester hadn't come back he had realised he was concerned about her welfare. He had phoned the fellows at Abbeville to ascertain if the remounts had arrived in good fettle, but the bloody line had crackled and gone dead and he hadn't been able to make them hear his damned questions. Had he had any intimation as to where she was, he'd have told them to ship her back. Anyway, once he'd put the phone down he'd forgotten her, assuming she must have done a runner for home from Dover. He had wanted Miss Forrester (or someone very like her) at the depot to instruct the new horsewomen, because he felt that females there would bring more stability to the personnel. Now this had happened. But if she'd got windy and gone home you couldn't blame her. The shock of Corporal Fox dying at the station must have had an effect on her. He had to admit the corporal's body lying there on the road in the dark had given him quite a turn. He thought he'd made it clear to her that she was to come back. But how come she had misunderstood? Or had something gone badly wrong? A brief explanation to a CO would probably sort it all out.

She had been out there somehow near the lines – God help her with that infernal impetuosity. This young woman… she loved horses easily as much as he did.

'My God, what have you been up to?' burst out of him as he entered the room. She was sitting alone at the far end by the window and looked as if she had been given a strafing.

'Oh, Captain, I'm in such a frightful hole.'

'I imagine you are, Miss Forrester.' He pulled off his cap and slapped it against his thigh, ran his hand through his brown hair. He remembered seeing her the first time: he'd noticed how her eyes held his, how her complexion seemed accustomed to being outdoors but was still soft. She brought a capable pair of hands at a time when, God knows, he'd needed the help. As soon as he'd trained up some ASC men to do a half-decent job they were invariably transferred elsewhere. The men at the War Office didn't know what it was like mixing city men with frightened, unpredictable horses. Anyone would do if they knew one end of a horse from another without being endlessly supervised, but she had been a godsend at the time.

'What are you doing here?' she asked in amazement.

'They tried to phone me at the Pluckley depot to verify your identity, but I'd been transferred over here. So they found me eventually at the hospital.'

'Over here? But I thought…'

'I'd had enough of all their confounded paperwork, so I put in an application to get back here. They must have got thoroughly fed up with my requests and thought it easier to give in.'

'They'll probably send me back home now,' she said resignedly.

'They aren't exactly ready to let you go just like that, I'm afraid. The military police are tending towards believing you are a spy – French or German, they aren't sure – and up to all sorts of nefarious ends.'

'I keep telling them I'm not,' she rubbed her eyes. 'Nobody seems to listen though.'

'Maybe my previous knowledge of you will help.'

'I'm so terrifically glad to see you.' She looked him in the face, but quickly frowned, 'Of course, they might think I've been deceiving you, too.'

'What on earth have you been doing? Why didn't you come back from Dover?' He sank down on a wooden chair.

'It's such a long story. I had this idea… I know it must sound muddled now… but, in the end, I just wanted to save one of the horses I came across with.'

'But why did you come across? And how?'

'No one stopped me. No one even questioned me. Major Porteous at Base Remount instructed me to take them to Brigade HQ. I wasn't going to say, 'But I'm female'. And the brigadier who took delivery of Sunlight and Magician only wanted a horse worth dying on when the time came for him to lead the next cavalry charge. As it would be one of the last-ever cavalry charges, he said, he intended to be mounted on a courageous good-looker. His place in history or something... what a flea brain!'

'This is war. Haig wants the cavalry to back up the infantry when they've broken through. The cavalry can double the amount of land taken from the Boche when deployed at the right moment.'

'How can horses stand up against machine guns and shells?'

'Of course they can't. They don't have to very often – cavalry command is very complicated – but, look here, this is really off the point. Please carry on with what you were saying.'

'I got past all sorts of people. They're upset their security systems don't work, and what's worse I'm a girl.'

'That's it. I agree. But I think you'd do well to tell me everything.'

'All too stupid of me, I admit. But they are making such a fuss.'

'You are going to get hauled over the coals. Not much I can do about that, but at least let's try and minimise the damage done.' As his eyes took in her expression a slow realisation dawned on him: she was, dammit, relying on him. Relying on him to tell her what to do. Relying on him to get her out of this mess. He could see it in the steady gaze of her eyes. Dammit! He continued, 'They told me you might be a suffragette and

198

objecting to the war and are here to stir up trouble among the ranks and make a nuisance of yourself, protesting or something.'

'Oh, it's that awful? So much has happened... I can't tell you everything... I was only doing... my elder brother, you see... both of them, in fact...' She was leaning over the table, her head in her arms, unable to say any more, hiding her eyes for the tears that filled them and kept on gushing however hard she tried to stop them. 'I'm sorry...'

He waited a short while. He looked down at her shorn hair, at the skin of her scalp, the back of her neck. It looked very vulnerable. He stood up. 'Miss Forrester, if you can hear me... at the moment, I'm afraid I'm all you've got. Listen to me, please. I'm known as your 'officer friend' and I'll do my best to represent you, to defend you, to prevent them charging you with a criminal offence, not the least of which is being in possession without proper authorisation of a horse belonging to His Majesty's Army. But there may be charges, unless... unless you can give me a really plausible explanation. So please tell me the full story. All of it.'

Because, it was going through his head, Miss Forrester might as well undertake to beard the Secretary of State for War himself, surrounded by his staff at their desks in their offices with initials and numbers on the doors; or browbeat the whole Army Council sitting at Whitehall, with Parliament and the millions of fellows behind it. Hers would appear as the action of an enemy, of a fugitive from justice, of an anarchist defying the whole of the established order. Perpetrated by a man, the crime would be staggering enough, but by a woman it was enough to give the entire Military Police apoplexy. And how was he to get her out of this fix?

He was thinking of the first day she had arrived, how

he'd thrown her in at the deep end thinking she'd never get beyond the first night. He'd made it as difficult as he could for her, but she'd risen above every obstacle. She reminded him of the Connemara mare he used to show jump as a young lad at Clifden Show, who would jump whatever he pointed her at. His opinion of Miss Forrester was very high, and he spoke sternly so as to conceal his regard for her. She had to know she was going to be in for it, if she couldn't fully explain herself to investigators who were already buzzing all round this particular hole she'd blown through their systems. He realised that beneath his thick khaki tunic his heart was aching for her. It wasn't quite proper. Not at all the done thing for a fellow, an officer even, the son of a God-fearing man – to be alone with a female, like this.

He sat down again, spoke more quietly, leaning towards her, in case she couldn't hear him properly. 'Miss Forrester, I… I've only got half an hour with you. Half an hour is what they said. Tell me about this escapade from start to finish. I need to make notes of the order of events as you give them to me.' He groped through his pockets, flipped open an empty drawer, pushed it shut. 'There aren't even enough damned pens when you need one.'

'Would you like to borrow this?' Cass offered him the black mechanical pencil she always kept with her, the red tasselled end towards him, as if the point were sharp.

'Yes, thanks… just what I'm looking for.'

She sat back in the chair and hid her eyes in her cupped hand for a second. When she lowered it and looked at him he passed her a crumpled handkerchief; she dried her eyes and blew her nose and said, 'Right, I'm with you, now.'

She cleared her throat as if it were dusty and continued, 'To answer your question… there was no reason to go back. You see, they didn't realise I wasn't a man. They didn't guess. I wore a uniform, knew how to keep in line, how to stand to attention. I'd seen soldiers being drilled every day. Most of the remount service just look after horses and get drunk when off duty. It wasn't hard to get by. I didn't go to the *estaminet* with the others because I couldn't hold my drink the way they could. I kept myself to myself.

'And, once I'd arrived, you see, I couldn't explain my being there so I carried on looking after the Irish horses, exercising them. They left me in charge of them. One thing less for them to have to worry about.'

'You could have just got on a ferry and gone back to Pluckley.'

'And leave the horses? Yes, I should have. You're right. But I didn't have a pass for the return journey and I didn't know what was going to happen. One thing led to another. Curiosity got the better of me and I desperately wanted to be able to deliver the horses myself, as Corporal Fox would have done.'

'You went too far, you must admit it, pretending all that...' He broke off.

'But I was stupidly fond of those horses. They hadn't asked to go to war and I wanted to see that they got there safely and... it was important for me to know where they were going.'

'Yes, I can see you might well have become attached.'

'My father would have told me off about that. He said not to be sentimental about horses.' She explained how he made most of his living from buying and selling good horses. 'It was a family business. We were all involved from an early age. But then the Army requisitioned Silver and the dear farm horses. They took them away.'

'I have to stop you there... to stick with the matter in hand. Time is short, you see.'

'I had to do it – for the horses' sakes,' she blurted, on the verge of tears again.

'Tell me what happened.'

She described her journey to the chateau and added, her lip trembling as if she didn't want to voice things that she'd seen, 'Once I passed what looked like a heap of old sacks but it was really... you know what it was... it was a heap of bodies. The horrors and the smells of battle creep up in the course of a day's riding, don't they? But I suppose soldiers just get inured to it.'

He was pacing up and down the room. It was comforting to do so, better than sitting down with her.

'Yes,' he said. 'Things do creep up on one.'

'You seemed to be counting something just then as you walked,' she observed.

'The number of steps it takes to keep things square, if you must know. You're the first person to notice. Eight steps in each direction.'

Nerves, he was thinking, get damaged. And it happens to everyone after a time. No one can take more than a few months in the firing line. Unless they keep themselves almost permanently drunk – it's the endless waiting and being absolutely on the alert at the same time.

'But you aren't walking in a square.'

'No, but it counts all the same so long as the lines are exactly the right length. I like to hear the sound of footsteps: reminds me I'm still here, not a figment of my own imagination.

Have you not heard his silent steps?

   He comes, comes, ever comes.'

'Did you write that?'

'No. Rabindranath Tagore. An Indian poet.'

'Who is coming with silent steps?'

'I think it is Truth.'

'Oh, I see.'

He took out his pocket watch to look at the time. 'So, go on, tell me about what happened.'

She told him about arriving at the chateau, what had happened when the shells started falling, about trying to find her grandparents' village, being arrested by the Red Cap. 'Now I'm here,' she said. 'It's all too ridiculous for words. I don't know what they're going to do with me.'

'The problem is to explain your intentions,' he said. 'What you were planning to do is what they're worried about. And why the dickens you were wandering about. You seem to have slipped through the security cordons with apparent ease. Lucky you aren't in the Army, or they'd court-martial you, you know. Falsifying identity, misappropriation of Army remounts – these are offences and carry serious penalties. But they won't dare do anything to you. Although you're wearing uniform you are a civilian in khaki, and a woman to boot.

'Look, I'm going now to see the general and explain what you've said to me about your grandparents and how upset you are, how it has disturbed you. Then I'll phone through to Major Porteous at Abbeville and get a reference for you off him. Then I'm thinking of proposing that you come to work in the horse hospital under my command. I can't guarantee they will swallow that, but it would get them out of the hole they find themselves in. What would you say to that?'

'Oh! Would you? Thank you. Thank you.' Her hand crept towards him as if to touch him, but she pulled it back. It was very big of him to stick his neck out for her.

'I think they just might go along with it,' he spoke slowly, thinking it out. 'It would hush everything up for them. If you were to go back to England now it could be all over the papers and the British Army would never live it down. It would rock the offices in Whitehall even.'

'Oh, I don't know how to thank you enough.'

'No more Army uniform, though. You will get placed in the Women's Auxiliary Army Corps and wear their uniform. You will not need to pretend to be anyone other than Miss Forrester. I warn you, though, it's going to be very hard work for you. Some of the cases I have to operate on are gruesome – shrapnel and bullet wounds, some shocking cases of malnutrition. And we have to deal with hundreds of cases of mange, too. Nowadays horses are being badly affected by gas attacks. Very unpleasant. You can't be squeamish, but then I'm confident you wouldn't let it affect you. I expect your main job would be to dress some of the wounds as they heal. Our role is to patch them up as best we can and send them back.'

'Patch them up? Send them back?' She sighed.

'Maybe once the war is over we can ship some poor creatures home. Who knows?' He was hunting for adequate words. 'Meanwhile, you be on your best behaviour and I recommend you make an effort to look like who you really are... get yourself out of that infernal uniform. They really don't know what to do with you, and that uniform is a red rag to a bull. But they do know how to treat a young lady.'

'But I don't want to be treated like a lady. Not in the least. Now I've got this far, I'm not intending to make it easy for myself, you know.'

29

It was a warm and sunny day when she arrived, and the felt hat made her head sweaty. At the gateway a few soldiers stood around in rolled-up shirtsleeves. Cigarette smoke curled into the air. Touching their caps, they said 'Good morning' and watched her as the sentry at the gate inspected her papers and pointed out the way to the women's bunkhouse. She walked towards it, past paddocks filled with ill-nourished horses, ribs showing, hip bones jutting up like wrecked boats. The heavy uniform skirt impeded her forward momentum as it curled round her legs. The laced shoes, tighter than the boots she was used to, made her toes feel scrunched.

Inside the bunkhouse the odour of cheap perfume and talcum powder made her sneeze. She found the bed she'd been allocated halfway down the aisle. The clothes she was wearing had been given to her by the quartermaster at the Women's Army Auxiliary Corps.

In the mess later she met some of the other girls and listened to their conversation as she ate. Her neighbour, a girl with round brown eyes and curly brown hair fastened down with metal grips, asked her if she'd just arrived in France. Cass shook her head and said she'd been working with horses.

'Oh, don't you type?' asked the girl with surprised eyes.

'I've applied to work with the horses. I can't type.'

'Then I think you'd better learn overnight.'

'There must be some mistake,' said Cass in some consternation. She thought Captain King had arranged that she was to work with the horses, but obviously that was not the case.

Next morning, after Reveille, she found herself in the typing pool. Sitting in front of the typewriter, she wondered why on earth the letters weren't in order. Why did the keyboard start with a Q and not an A? Why did the letters have no apparent order? It was all double dutch to her. The room exploded with the sound of clickety-clack. She peered over the machine, trying to make use of two fingers of each hand at a time. The letters formed into words that slowly built up like a little line of wagons on a railway. The bell pinged when the train reached the end of the line and, watching the others next to her, she realised she had to strike a lever that sent her on to the next line. It jumped very satisfyingly. The other women had finished the page before she had written a couple of lines. As they typed she noticed they barely looked at their flying fingers. She felt a complete fool. The tall thin dragon of a woman who was known as the forewoman and who directed operations in the typing pool yanked the paper out of her typewriter and said that as she had made mistakes she would have to start afresh all over again. The dragon leaned down to almost shout into Cass's ear, 'Try concentrating. Everything has to be done in triplicate, so use carbon paper.'

The piles of reports for the veterinary CO grew and she learned new scientific words such as *leucomata*, *cellulitis* and *stomatitis*. Forms for this and that were sent out every day. Form A.F. W3182 was collated from the wards each day. Form A.F. W3089 described treatments. And every day the numbers of horses on each ward in each subdivision were brought in, to be collated, recorded twice more and sent off by messenger. Lists of supplies from the quartermaster had to be copied and dispatched. Then, there were forms that accompanied each animal sent back to the Front. Reams of paper and numbers turned into nightmare columns that threatened to topple on to her. She'd never get through what she had to do. At night she dreamed of huge letters falling from the dark sky in order to crush her, and she had to crane her neck to look up in order to dodge round the missiles as they landed. Her typing speeded up a little.

Through the office window, despite the Dragon, her eye strayed to half-watch the new arrivals from the station. Some days there seemed to be hundreds. Often their coats were rubbed and sore. These ones had also lost their manes, their skin raw and bleeding. She noticed some arrived with huge boots over their hooves, while others seemed to blunder along, half blinded, probably from the effects of gas poisoning like the men she had seen at Exeter station, their hands on the shoulders of the man in front.

Once, a thrill ran through her when an animal that looked like their own young workhorse, The Plough, plodded by. The shock of seeing him made her stand up. It was something about the way he carried his ears, the tips very dark and pointed. The muscles inside her face tightened. Her stomach flipped over. Was it he? Or was her imagination on overdrive?

From the way he limped she could tell that the horse was lame on the offside hind leg. He was all skin and jutting bones. His head swung low. Without thinking, she ran across to the window and peered through. Her breath misted the pane so she rubbed a blurry patch to see better. It surely did look like The Plough from the back end, too. Her heart lurched. She turned and made for the door. The Dragon called, 'Where do you think you're going, Forrester?'

'I'll be back in a minute,' she said. 'Please, just one minute. I've seen someone.' She unbolted the unused side door and ran out into the rain. She called his name, but he couldn't have heard her voice over the noise of hooves and neighing. She called again, but the horse had already gone past and was way up ahead. A corporal escorting the animals spoke sharply, 'Get back inside, Miss.'

Her stockings were spattered and her shoes were muddied by then, so she couldn't easily turn back indoors. By the door, where rain spilled from the gutter, she washed off the mud, and after rinsing her hands she returned to her desk, her hair and uniform dripping.

'Right, Forrester, now you are so wet you may as well go and clean out the ladies' latrines before you knock off.'

She was going to have to get herself out of the typing pool or she'd go crazy. She must find The Plough. She'd never be any use as a typist and surely they would be glad to get rid of her. The Dragon would be in the officers' mess, and asking her would have to wait till the next day.

But the next morning the Dragon summoned her across to her desk. 'Forrester, you're more trouble than you're worth on a typewriter. You're the sort more at home in a stable. You'll join Subdivision F, where they treat animals for mange and parasites. They're short at the moment.'

Trainloads of sick horses arrived almost daily at the hospital. As the days passed she felt like someone with a split personality. She worked from Reveille at 5.30am to 9pm with only a few short breaks for meals, which she took with the men. At night she slept in the bunkhouse with the typists, whose fingernails were manicured while her hands were calloused and ingrained with horses' scurf, dirt under the nails. She sank exhausted into bed every night.

'Don't come near me. Don't want to catch mange off you,' the girl in the next bed covered her face with her sheet.

'You don't half pong, Nurse Dobbin,' gasped her other companion, Violet. 'We don't so much hear you coming in the door as smell you.'

'Sorry about that.' She slumped onto her bed. 'But I know how to sort it out.'

'Do you think we've time before Lights Out?' The evening was still light and they liked to stroll round the building before having to turn in. 'Go and get washed first.'

'I had a wash in the yard.'

'Well, it hasn't really worked, you know, Nurse Dobbin. Try using some soap.'

'How's the Dragon been today?' asked Cass a few minutes later, opening up a new packet of Black Cat and offering it to Violet.

'Oh, she's been breathing fire all day. It's all right for you – working with the men.'

'Oh, the sergeant is just as bad, I can tell you.'

'Let's have the card. I'm collecting them. Are you coming to the dance in the NAAFI on Saturday?'

'Crikey, I haven't got anything to wear.'

'Hmmm, perhaps we could sort that out somehow… But the trickiest bit is going to be scrubbing you down properly.'

'If no one dances with me, will you, Vi?'

The ghoulish cavalcade of sick and emaciated horses seemed never-ending. Things were obviously going very badly at the Front: there were reports of a surprise German offensive at Aisne. And all through that afternoon they shuffled into the inspection paddock for the veterinary officers to look them over and make a snap judgement about which sub-division to send them to – infectious eye and skin disease cases needing to be kept separate from those needing emergency surgery or those with damage to legs or feet.

The first three subdivisions were already having to put three or four horses into stalls designed for two. Other horses were sent on to subdivisions down the line. Cass spent all afternoon leading sick horses to their new quarters. There surely wasn't room for so many. Her stomach felt like a lead weight. Her legs and arms worked automatically. She couldn't allow her tired mind to ask herself questions. And when might she find time to look for The Plough? Where had he ended up – if indeed it was him she had seen?

'Poor beggars. This is just as bad as Passchendaele last year,' she overheard one trooper say to another.

The queue of patients didn't peter out until the evening. She thought the buildings would burst. Next morning it was announced that, in view of the pressure of numbers, there was an order from on high to drive the relatively fit horses to Hospital no.6 at Rouen.

Captain King was to conduct two hundred horses and forty men. It was estimated it would take no more than two days to trail the horses to Rouen. Forage would follow the line in motor lorries, which would then return with all the staff. The men left behind would have to manage without them for that length of time. Because she was in Subdivision F, Cass's name was on the list to go to Rouen. Each rider would lead four horses and be in charge of organising harness, nose bags, dressings if required, and personal kit sufficient for the two-day ride. Every member of the team must know their horses and their case histories well enough to keep an eye on their condition and be able to report problems quickly.

Captain King and the other veterinary officers decided which horses should make the trip. There was a final inspection after tea, at Defaulter's Parade, when any horses deemed unfit were finally weeded out. The sergeant in Subdivision F grizzled 'Nothing like moving the old beggars about. Makes it look as if there's progress. To them the horses are just statistics.'

'At least this lot won't be re-infected by the new patients,' said one of the officers.

Reveille was at 3.30 the next morning. Cass hadn't slept much. Her limbs swung into action. Water and feed the horses, then attend to herself, saddle up, mount and get her five horses into the line-up. Parade before departure at 5.30am.

If it weren't for the dreadful condition of the horses you wouldn't know there was a war on, she thought. Everywhere there was a sense of the grass rising like dough in the sun. At first the horses seemed glad to be out of the hospital, with the smell of newly turned earth, of grass and leaves. Blackbirds sang from a copse full of white blossom, and larks poured their up-and-down song across the meadows. In the distance, a group of trees seemed to be processing along the horizon. Cass wondered if she was seeing things. Were the trees really moving? With the swallows twittering overhead she watched the group of trees inch further along. An optical illusion, she thought, or floaters in my eyes. I'm over-tired, she concluded.

The horse she was astride had been an artillery horse. He had a wide face with a white flash down it and a Roman nose. He was well drilled and placid. From somewhere he had found some energy because occasionally he snatched at leaves as they passed a hedgerow. She held the reins loosely so that the horse could move his neck and head naturally without impediment. The four horses she was leading were listless. One was recovering from an operation and was nothing but a bag of bones. The other three were pack animals that had been gassed but were sound in feet and legs. Would they have enough breath and stamina for at least two long days of this?

An order came down the line to halt and let the horses eat the grass beside the road for a few minutes. She dismounted and undid her horse's girth. There was a froth of sweat underneath. His neck was wet. She took off the bridle to let him eat without the bit in his mouth. She patted him but he took no notice, intent on the grass. She knew she ought to give this one a break and ride a different one. But the saddle was a wide fit, and putting on an ill-fitting saddle would be harmful for the convalescents. The horses weren't fit enough for any more exercise than this, and they had hours of travel to go. She decided not to remount and to walk herself.

Trooper Jeffries was leading the group of horses ahead of her. He lit up a cigarette, blew the smoke into the air with satisfaction and started humming. He called out to her, 'Nice day for a ride, innit, hey?'

'Yes, isn't it? How are yours? Mine are about done in.'

'Oh, these blighters are looking forward to seeing the fireworks again. The thought of it cheers them up no end.'

'I don't think they'll be a lot of use, do you?'

'Well, numbers are always useful. Sending horses back to the Front makes a good paragraph in the weekend paper. But then they'll have to send 'em back to us before long.'

'Back to front says it all.'

She sometimes worked alongside Reg Jeffries with mange dipping, leading horses up to the corral and persuading them down into the new-fangled dip. Once they'd slipped down the ramp and were swimming in the solution, she helped Reg push their heads under water. He told her he'd been almost shot to bits in a trench but a sergeant had saved him from drowning in the mud. After he recovered he wasn't considered fit for service at the Front, so he volunteered to work at the hospital because his father was a milkman and had kept two horses.

Their horses continued feasting on the fresh grass and dandelion leaves growing along the bank. When Cass glanced over her shoulder the tree shapes had moved a little closer and had broken free of the forested hillside. She could make out a pattern of camouflage moving along: military barges on a canal. The horses could be watered there.

'How are they doing?' said a voice she knew.

'Aw right for the time being, sir,' Jeffries stood to attention. 'We'll get known for making advances at short notice, we will. They'll be lining us up for the Front soon. We'd make great fodder for big guns.'

Captain King had dismounted and was walking down the last half of the line to inspect all the horses at the back. The ones at the front were considered in good enough fettle. It wasn't too late to send any laggards at the end back to the hospital.

'Are these ones managing all right?' he asked Cass.

She saluted. 'Half and half is how I'd describe them, sir.'

'And how's the leg of 65231? I operated on that one a few weeks ago. Shrapnel case. What does the dressing look like?'

She was beside him as they both bent down to peer at the bandaged leg. He was in his shirtsleeves and she saw the white skin of his arms. His shaven cheeks looked more creased than the last time she'd seen him. He must have been up most of the night, she supposed. Crouching under the horse's belly she saw the tip of his tongue stick out between his lips, a habit of his when concentrating. She noticed bags beneath his eyes under the shadow of his peaked cap.

He squatted down to look more closely at 65231, running his fingers down the length of the legs, while the corporal looked down and gave Cass a wink. The captain stood up again and the corporal pencilled what he said on the form. The horse widened its hind legs and pissed on the dusty ground. The stream of yellow water ran towards their feet.

'Needs keeping an eye on, that leg. But no heat or discharge as yet.'

Before he moved on, he paused. 'And you, Miss Forrester? Bearing up all right?'

'In the pink, sir,' she smiled at him. 'But I'm going to rest this old chap and walk for the afternoon.'

'Not recommended. Best stay mounted. This isn't a pleasant hack, you know. Led horses are an easy target: you cannot respond to a surprise attack.'

And he was already talking with Penfold, who was behind her in the line, a quiet and religious man with one working eye, having lost the other at the battle of Loos. Before the war he'd been a postman and she wondered if you could still be a postman with one eye – but why not if you could still see enough to read the addresses?

There was nothing for it: she'd have to mount the Bag of Bones. This one had been carrying her kit bag and rations so she'd swap them round and hope for the best. The others looked far too frail.

The painful plod continued all afternoon and into the evening, with stops for grazing and watering. By nightfall the horses were attached to picket lines and a line guard was set up to see them through the night. The following morning it was drizzling and the procession shuffled along the damp road. The clouds grew thicker and rain ran off the horses' backs. Another halt was called. Captain King rode past at a trot and she turned in her saddle. A horse was being manhandled out of the line. Barely able to stand, it seemed to be listing, head bowed. She thought it would topple over. What were they thinking of? She knew the veterinary officer would have to shoot it. Another old crock was hauled up beside it. The Captain put his hands on the first horse's hindquarters as it crumpled at the knees and sank to the ground. It struggled a moment and then lay still. He squatted down and leaned over its head. He seemed to be saying something in the horse's ear: she saw his lips moving. After a moment he twisted round and pulled out his pistol, placed the muzzle almost between its ears and fired. After the report he paused, jumped back, put the pistol back in his belt and walked away. The remaining sickly horse stood with its head bowed.

Among the creak of saddles and the jangle of bits Cass became aware of an animated conversation going on with a French farmer who had joined the group of soldiers. He took hold of the sickly horse as the line was ordered to move off. She looked at Jeffries and he shrugged in a Gallic sort of way.

Around midday on the third day they arrived at the outskirts of the city. In the rain the horses' shoes slipped on the wet cobbles and there came a call from man to man to dismount. The cobbled road was punishing the horses' weary legs and sore feet. One hundred and ninety eight exhausted horses tramped onto the old racecourse. There were mountains of boxes containing stores and supplies, spare boots, tools, arms, munitions, all the requirements to prosecute a war. Near to the convalescing horses stood a ziggurat of hay bales. All awaiting transportation by rail, motor lorry or horse-drawn wagon.

On the way back to the hospital she sat in the back of the lorry with the men, as tired as herself. They were singing *It's a long way to Tipperary...* but she was thinking to herself, He asked me if I'm bearing up, but the big question must be about him. Surgery, operations and even more operations. Does he never rest?

*

He came into the stables and said, 'Shall we give those two a try?' The horses he was pointing at were convalescing mange patients, and sea water was recommended for their skin. It wasn't far from the hospital to the seashore. Over the dunes and there it was, sparkling in late afternoon sun that was still hot. Their hooves pressed deep into the dry white sand and grains of it flew up behind them. Where the tide had reached, each hoof mark printed the beach with the grooved V sign of the frog. Lighter than mud but harder going than dry earth. At every wavelet the horses started sideways: unused to water that moved towards them of its own accord and made such living sounds as it slid back over the sand – the force of it, the undertow and the white spill of breaking foam was unfamiliar – the way it whispered on the beach, flung itself upward as if trying to grab at their fetlocks and then sank back.

Breathing heavily, ears pricked, the horses watched one another as much as that fretful sea.

After a while their courage grew a little. Their hooves made deeper pits in the sodden sand at the water's edge. They bent their heads to drink but snorted at the salty taste. Heads flung upwards, their lips opened, whiffling at the air. They wiped their nostrils on the fur of their legs, shook themselves as if to rid themselves of irritation. The air was filled with a mist of ozone. The sea seemed to be creeping up the beach from far, far away.

Pressed a little harder by their bareback riders, they waded in deeper and the waves began breaking under their bellies. The beach sloped smoothly. On the horizon appeared the pinpricks of supply ships. No artillery noises here. Only the wheeling of the gulls and their plangent crying as if war was in abeyance. The captain's mount plunged in deeper and started swimming, his legs pulling strongly, his neck held above the water, tail stretched flat on the surface. Cass's horse followed suit. After a minute the horses hauled themselves back to the shore where, dripping wet, ears flopping, they shook themselves so violently the laughing Captain nearly came off. They set off at a gallop up the beach and on to the hard sand.

At the far end of the beach he came up beside her, 'That was fun… did us all some good.'

'They did enjoy it, didn't they? The salt should harden up the skin.'

They rode along for a while in silence, side by side. 'What do you think of Rupert Brooke's poems?' he asked.

'Hmm… I think they're very accomplished but, to be honest, he's actually rather trite. I like something with a bit more oomph, myself, something I can believe in.'

'That's what I thought, too. But one hardly dares say so.'

'What poetry do you like to read?'

'Yeats,' he said. 'Not war poetry. What about you?'

'D.H. Lawrence,' she said. 'Not a popular choice at the moment though.'

'You know his poetry?'

'Only some bits. I like his novels, too. Like *Sons and Lovers*… have you read that?'

'No, but I will do, if you recommend it. One day perhaps.' They fell silent for a while. The horses were tired and they walked more slowly. As they neared the hospital he said, his voice like a rasp, 'Look, what I want to ask you… is… have you given any thought to what might be happening?'

'What might be happening?' she looked at him but his eyes were on his horse. Her hand trailed along the horse's wet rump, salt beginning to dry white on the grey fur. His tone of voice was incongruous with his uniform.

'Oh, forget it,' he said.

As far as I'm concerned, thought Cass as she took off the tack, this work isn't becoming any easier. I can't live with the idea that the horses in our care are being cured merely to go back. To go back to that terrible world. If the Plough had been recovering here he, too, will have to go back and we all know how much they will suffer again – in the lines, in the mud, with the bombardments. We all know they may not survive. They say the war is drawing to an end but there seems no let-up in the numbers of casualties.

We can't get them shipped home. And we can't keep them here. While the war persists horses continue to be needed. The military situation is always paramount. I can't live with myself. I can't sleep. When I close my eyes I just think of them having to go back into battle, the mud and the heavy loads, not enough feed, not enough water. It just goes on and on, without ceasing. Will it ever end? And what will happen to all these creatures when it is over?

Oh, Orion, come and find me, please. Save me from myself. Where are you, blast you, where are you?

She brushed the dried salt from their coats and when she had finished she sucked her little finger by mistake, the salt taste lingering in her mouth for hours.

PART THREE

30

For months Cass had imagined herself arriving home. Would it look much the same or would everything be unrecognisable? Her mother had written to her that Fernley had been killed in Belgium, just before the Armistice and she could not imagine how it would be at Pepperton without him.

Along the road from the village the russet cattle in the fields looked as though they were fashioned of earth or autumn leaves. Ploughed fields glowed as the rain clouds parted to let through beams of late sunshine. And now home lay up ahead – round the corner and here it was – the dear farmhouse, illuminated in that moment by the sun setting on the ridge, flashes of coppery light in the windows. Her own Pepperton. It seemed to have risen from the ground as if yeasted, its rough stones speckled with mica and quartz, the granite buildings merging into the fleck and dot of field, dry stone wall and moorland.

Later, before the Captain took his leave, she walked with him around the garden and out across the fields that were once full of horses but were now grazed by sheep. A grey light gleamed from the serpentine river which seemed to have drawn closer, for acres of the woodland had been cleared – probably felled, he suggested, to make trench or tunnel supports.

Behind the neglected stables she spotted Swan, waiting for an evening feed. Calling to her excitedly, Cass unhitched the twisted gate latch and rushed across the field. The old workhorse swung her head and stared at Cass, who had come to a halt. The horse had aged, her belly swung lower, her spine protruded slightly. After several seconds, Swan blew through her nose, whickered, and lumbered towards Cass. Stroking both sides of the horse's muzzle, Cass said, 'Swan, darling, I'm back now. And you know me, don't you, old girl? You haven't forgotten.' Swan lifted her head and blew in Cass's ear. Cass leaned her forehead against the horse's neck while kneading the sweet spot on her crest beneath her mane, as Leo used to do.

With no daily routine beyond helping round the house and caring for Swan and the war ponies Cass didn't know what to do with herself. She must find an occupation of some kind. But what? She desperately wanted to hear from Orion, but had no address for him. When he had been released from prison Father was beside himself that he had gone off, leaving no forwarding address. But surely he would come back soon. There was so much to tell him. Now the war was over, couldn't he and Father be reconciled? She was not certain about the potential for this just yet. Maybe he was right to stay away a little longer, at least until the celebrating had finished.

A letter for her arrived one morning. The envelope contained nothing but a photo of herself. She wondered why someone would send her this and no note. With a shock she realised it was the studio portrait taken years ago that she had given to Frank, for when she flipped it over she saw her own writing: *To Frank, Waiting for you. Truly yours, Cass.* The postmark on the envelope was Ashamstead and she imagined Frank's mother must have posted it to her. His personal effects would have been sent back to his parents and amongst his belongings they had found this photo of her. It was difficult to know if she should write to thank them, but it appeared that they preferred no communication. This act would conclude what they might call The Forrester Business.

The word *missing* gave room for hope but now even if his body were found it would never be returned home.

The shock of it was a sudden sharp jab. She covered her face with her hands and sobbed, her fingers oozing tears. Later, she tore up the photo into pieces and threw them in the fire.

Did his parents feel sorry at all, she wondered, that they had upset him so much just before he died?

Various letters needed writing – to relatives to tell them she was home; to Florence and to girls she had been at school with. And shouldn't she write to the Lethbridges to offer her condolences without referring to the photograph? She sat at her desk and started writing. After a few lines she stopped. The thought crossed her mind... why not write a book? It would keep her occupied and at home. It would inform lots of people what had happened, what she'd witnessed. She wouldn't have to tell everyone individually over and over again. She could just say 'Wait until my book comes out'. Just write it step by step as it happened, she told herself, and the events would speak for themselves.

But as her pen touched the paper, the lines blurred. The pen would not write in straight lines. The nib kept sliding off the word she wanted to write; the ink leaked, smearing and smudging the white sheet. Her lines ran down the page like rain on a window.

Soon her hand started to shake, and she could not hold it still. She tried to force her hand to write, gripping the forefinger and thumb with her other hand to make the pen move across the page, to press hard enough to make the requisite marks on the lines, but the writing was illegible.

Where to start? How to begin? The pictures in her mind refused to be turned into words. Horses were stuck in glutinous mud. A grey could make no progress as it tried to lift its feet, floundering in the mire. Had this really happened? She called to it and the horse heard and re-doubled its efforts. Only when it did manage to lift one knee high enough did she see how its foreleg had been blasted away. She had no gun with which to shoot it, and there was no one else to do it. You couldn't make this up, could you?

She flung the pen against the wall and it broke, scattering ink on to the wallpaper. She had no control over her limbs, her body juddered.

There were no words to describe what she had witnessed. It was there in her mind like a plate nailed into the curve of her skull and it kept reflecting back to her what it was she couldn't do without a firearm. She screamed in the night for someone to shoot that horse or hand her a pistol to stop it continually hauling itself through the mud of her mind, past the burnt-out wood it couldn't reach with its bleeding stumps – the stumps she couldn't see till she called to the horse and it tried that bit harder to get across, its shoulders hoisting the frayed rag of one knee and then the other, when she saw it had no hooves.

Smoke wafted out of the front door and across the lawn. She piled more and more of her papers onto the fire, and black scraps, still burning on one edge, flew up out of the chimney and into the sky, twirling and twisting in the hot smoke. A voice was calling her and when she turned round to see who it was, Sarah pulled her away and her father threw a bucket of water on to the flames. 'I think the chimney's on fire,' he cried. 'I'll ring the fire station and then she needs the doctor. What the hell's the matter with her?'

31

Every Sunday the chaplain informed the men that the war might be drawing to an end, and this had the effect of making every day and every hour grow more painful with hope. How would they know when it happened? Those going out on work detail would presumably be the first to hear about it, but how long would it take for the good news to spread?

Orion had grown accustomed to sitting in the quiet, the not-speaking, the sense of being alone with thoughts coming and going in his mind. Outside, sparrows chirped on the window sill, ring doves coo-ed from the roof. The jackdaws cawed as they spiralled above the buildings. Closing his eyes for a while took him out of the walls, until sudden utterances prickled in his ears: his father's fury and his mother's bewildered tones. Opening his eyes might bring him back to his surroundings but would not quieten their voices.

Late one grey November morning the prison hooter started up – the signal for prison guards to assemble, perhaps because someone had gone over the wall. But a bell began pealing, too. Cheers broke out in a general pandemonium. Other prisoners started ringing their emergency bells. It was the end of the War, an Armistice had been signed – but it was not to be the end of their sentence. The prison governor gathered them together and said the conscientious objectors would be left till last, no releases until all serving soldiers had returned and been demobbed.

Arthur had once asked Orion if he would like to think of joining a group of them who were planning to do the opposite of war: they would make peace and reconstruct people's houses for them and mend their roads. A number of Quaker conchies had been invited to join the work, together with others who had become Friends while inside. The Quaker Mission was in a village more or less in the middle of nowhere. Would he maybe consider going with him? Arthur said he'd suggested this because Orion was a country man, knew about agriculture and the land. He surmised that as Orion wasn't from a Quaker family there'd be little sympathy back home for refuseniks. Perhaps he also remembered that Orion had once said to the group he wanted an opportunity to prove himself after the war.

And Orion realised he liked the way Friends didn't question him about his motives or his beliefs and yet accepted him. At Pepperton he knew there were no horses needing schooling or breaking. Worse, he and Father would not shake down easily together. Best to go away until the tide of war had receded from memory. Arthur's proposal struck him as more than just a good idea. He would write to Mama when he was released and tell her about it when the details were made known.

He knew he couldn't ask his father for help with the money for the ticket. Indeed, he would be aghast to think of Orion going to those faraway lands in the east where people were turning to Communism. He would never countenance the idea that owning property was a kind of theft. How would Orion explain he was going to work close to the borders of a country which his father thought of as lawless and godless? He had already given him enough shocks.

So it was not until the spring of 1919 that he and Arthur walked out of the prison gates and set off by train to London. Their release came earlier than others' because of their volunteering to join war relief work. The little world of the train compartment was a joy to him –

watching the landscape flow towards him and fall behind as the locomotive steamed away from the moors, later passing fields and copses, rivers and towns. A copy of Dostoyevsky's *Crime and Punishment* lay in his lap. When he looked up to think about what he had just read, he caught sight of his own face looking back at him from the window, frowning with his deep unease about the things he'd never said – and also by having so little money in his pocket when the cost of everything had gone through the roof. How was he going to explain to them back home that he was now on his way to help a potential enemy? He would write as soon as he had got to wherever it was he was going.

Across the Channel the train corridors were filled with people – soldiers returning home, refugees looking for a home, orphans whose home seemed to be the train or the platform. Cigarette smoke turned the air grey-blue. At each stop there was no way of knowing how long the train would stand or when it would depart. He longed to get out and stretch his legs, to walk up and down the platform as if he were a prisoner on exercise in a yard. The biscuits, hard-boiled eggs and tins of beans that he and Arthur had brought with them dwindled, ran out.

With the increasing weight of bodies the train seemed to struggle. Sometimes it clanked to a halt in the open country and let out a long sigh as if the locomotive was exhausted. People around him were talking, maybe arguing, he wasn't sure, but no one seemed to think it unusual that the train wasn't moving. Eventually they fell silent. Some people curled up and went to sleep, for others it was a chance to get out of the train and walk about in the dark, relieve themselves in the bushes.

Writing paper arrived in a consignment of goods that had got through to the mission. It was watermarked with the words *Basildon Bond* and Orion thought it beautiful.

May 1919

Dear, darling Cass,

I don't know how long it may take for a letter to reach you. My poor envelope, even though it has your name on it, can't negotiate tickets for itself, nor find a space among many weary travellers – refugees, migrant workmen or soldiers returning home to their families – but must lie in the sack and patiently wait until someone might pick it up and put it on the right train. If it's lucky, that is. If it's unlucky it might get burned along with all its fellows to keep some chilled mortal warm on some platform.

Not so very different perhaps from how I feel having arrived here – somewhere on the Polish border – after several days of travelling by every kind of train. I am lucky to be staying with a family on the edge of town. I share a room with the sons, Stefan who is aged about 14 and Jan who must be 16. Their mother, Anna, cooks us one hot meal a day usually. In the evening we have bread and cheese or a dish of yoghourt. My bed is a wooden board covered by an animal skin. There is a fire in the living room and the bedrooms have no doors so the heat enters all the rooms until the fire dies down. I do have a blanket from the mission and hope to get another.

It is a Quaker Mission where I am working. We are here to do reconstruction work after the war swept through. At the weekly meetings for villagers and Friends to discuss things the village elders say that the families here need horses, that they won't be able to help themselves until they can plough their land. Last night I learned that their horses had been taken away by soldiers, or were killed and eaten by whichever army was passing through at the time. 'A peasant isn't a peasant without a horse,' he said.

They need horses to pull timber. In fact, they need a veritable army of horses. Not the sick, emaciated creatures the

228

soldiers left behind but fit, healthy ones with energy enough to put in a day's work. Peasants understand the meaning of horse. And I understand how much work any horse could do in a day and it isn't going to be as much as is required. They'd be dead from exhaustion. How can it work out? A few horses will not be of much use… A large number is needed, but all the workhorses in Europe seem to have been victims of the war. Not just ours. So my task is to seek out new horses. Plus ça change, I hear you say!

But it's terrifically hard without news of you. I must keep my spirits up, hoping that one day I may get a letter from one of you. The mail is so often lost. I just hope it is not I who am lost to you. My thoughts are often with you all at Pepperton, remembering the river, the moors &c. One day I will turn up at the front door and surprise you.

32

Beside her face, Blackie's hooves were striking the ground; she saw dust and little stones flying up. She was being dragged along underneath him, her head bumping on the earth. Her clothing was flapping and spooking the pony. With her foot caught in the stirrup, one arm was being pulled this way and that. She still had hold of the reins in the other and was tugging the pony's head around so he could not set off at a gallop.

She must have briefly passed out, because the pony was standing still and Leo was beside her, disentangling her foot. 'Are you all right? Can you get up?' His face bent over her. She somehow squirmed to her feet. Her riding habit was ripped and when she tried to brush off the dirt she felt a flash of pain up her arm. The next second Leo was giving her a leg-up and vaulting on to their father's horse himself. 'Time to go home,' he said and he rode along beside her.

But now when both feet were held and her head was shaking involuntarily, Leo didn't come to her rescue. She wanted to cry out for him but there was some wadding in her mouth. After the shaking was over she was left alone in bed.

It came to her how she used to ride in the donkey cart. One day she had climbed out of the safety of the cart and sat astride the donkey instead. Seeing this, the boys hauled her up on the pony, Blackie, and then left her to it. Sarah found her crying with rage, as Blackie had simply dropped his head to graze on the lawn grass. After that, their father bought her a miniature side saddle and Sarah used to walk beside her while one of the boys instructed her. One afternoon a hunting horn must have sounded or a hound had yelped in the distance, because Blackie threw up his head and ran forwards. Cass, as she bumped up and down, turned round to wave to Sarah left behind on the lawn with her face ghost-white. Sarah... always watching over her.

Sarah, she thought, was like a muslin – the pattern dress that used to be made out of inexpensive material as the model for the finer version made of silk or lawn. When smoothed, you could see the warp and weft of her, easily dyed with onion skins or blackberries, but serviceable although not considered fashionable. Sarah stitched cuffs and sleeves, altered hems, repaired and altered calico and muslin dresses, turned collars on cambric shirts and put new elbows on tweed coats. Her skin snagged on silk and satin. She said the world out there was speeding up now that people drove motor cars, but she could only sew at the same old pace. She measured Cass for a new dress but by the time she'd finished it, adding in tucks and intricate smocking on the bodice, Cass had already grown out of it.

Sarah used to brush Cass's long hair a hundred times every night and wove it into one long plait. In the mornings she wound it round her head. Her mother wouldn't let her cut it short – even though Cass begged her to ask Sarah to chop it off at shoulder length.

And what had happened to Fernley? Where was he now? Who was watching over Sarah?

'You're such a cry-baby. They'll be giving you more Shocks if you don't stop that racket,' said a woman with green eyes. She sported a truly awful brown dress. Sarah would have had something catty to say about that. The woman's hair was all disarranged – she clearly hadn't bothered to brush it this morning. Why should she address Cass like this?

'I think...' wept Cass, 'I think I've lost my mind. I

231

can't think where everything I once had is gone. My brothers… where are they? Why don't they come here to fetch me?' She didn't know where the words came from. 'It's all lost… lost.'

'Yes,' said Miss Unbrushed Hair.

'Have you a pencil I could borrow?'

'Doesn't your husband know about you?'

'But I'm not married.'

'What a girl you are!'

The woman closed her eyes and started trilling:

O be joyful in the Lord, all ye lands:
Serve the Lord with gladness,
and come before his presence with a song.
Be ye sure that …

Cass said, 'But I only wanted a pencil for a few minutes and you won't let me have yours,' and pulled at the woman's arm. Nurse Bluebell hurried across and said it would be better if she had something to do. 'I know. What about helping out in the kitchen? Today you can do a bit of drying up and later you can move on to washing up.'

There had been a woman all in white she'd met when she was riding late one winter afternoon on her way home along the edge of the moors. The woman had long white hair and wore a white dress. She was standing at a fork in the path near the Quaker Burial Ground, singing. Silver had heard the sound from far off and was on guard, walking on tiptoes, ears pricked so hard they seemed about to meet. But Cass thought it the most beautiful song she'd ever heard:

Oh, my laddie…

When the singer saw Cass and Silver she stopped singing but remained motionless. She was almost luminous in the twilight of the winter woods.

'Hello,' called Cass. 'Sorry to have disturbed you,' she said as she approached, Silver stepping forwards tentatively.

'I rehearse here because the shape of the hills makes my voice resonate,' the woman said as if she'd guessed the question in Cass's mind. 'Like an auditorium.'

Cass looked round and saw above the trees how two steep hills opened out into an amphitheatre. 'And what are you singing? It's lovely.'

'A new song by Amy Gluck. '

And while she dried dishes Cass sang little snatches she didn't know she could remember. She dried each plate over and over again until Freda, who was washing the dishes, snapped, 'Stop your tuneless warble, will you? Get on with the drying, you stupid cow. Look, they're all stacking up. There isn't room left on the draining board.'

Cass looked at Freda's angry face and was so afraid she dropped her plate on the tiled floor, and that made Freda's expression change into something else. So Cass picked up another plate and dropped it on the floor, and another.

Air. She needed air, wind, weather – cold or wet she wouldn't mind. She couldn't stay inside a moment longer. For how long had she been cooped up? She pressed her nose to the window and looked out. Through the mesh of rain that spattered the glass in front of her eyes she saw only the wall of another building, as if they were in some kind of a shaft. Were they buried?

The dripping wetness made her think of Leo and Orion swimming in the river. The sun shone on the water and on their arms and chests. Leo's ribs seemed to open and close as he laughed. Orion's skin colour was whiter and it shone under the water. She never went in the water with them. She was different from them. It was not her place to play naked in the river. She thought she could be a brother to them but no amount of wishing would make it so. She was stuck inside her body and would have to make do with it. Nothing was to be the same after she realised that.

Someone spoke in her ear:

Have you not heard his silent steps?

He comes, comes, ever comes.

When she spun round there was only a blue tit on the window sill, pecking at the pane.

Sometimes she felt as if she were walking about inside a dream, in a world where people spoke the same words but the meanings were different. She couldn't speak this new language because she only knew the old one. If she were in a dream, did that not count... as living? Is dreaming life not as real as waking life? Was she awake when someone told her they would let her do some sewing now? It was said as if it were a privilege, but she had never done any sewing in her life before. Her fingers seemed fat and clumsy and without a thimble her forefinger was sore from pricks caused by pressing the needle through coarse fustian. She didn't even know what she was supposed to be making. Had she forgotten? Had anyone said? Would she be in trouble again and what would the punishment be?

She must be careful not to let her temper get the better of her and make her stab someone with the needle. She felt she was about to do just that. She stood up and let the fabric she was sewing drop to the ground. Rage mounted inside her from her feet, through her legs and into her stomach. Under her ribs it grew hot, mauve like the flame of a welding torch. She tore at the door but it was locked. The other women paused in their sewing and watched her with knowing eyes as she rattled the handle, beat on the panelling.

33

Caged, she was caged but they couldn't hold her... not the fiercest of them. They had to keep her shut away like this because she was too wild... she knew things jumped out at you from behind bushes or trees. They got you by the throat and no amount of dodging or back-tracking could help you escape. Everything was a shock.

It left you with only the sense of your sentient self, standing in a room you didn't recognise with a group of people who also knew not where they were, whose thoughts barely met before veering away from each other. Leo had said something like 'Words we speak try to link us together'; but often people don't connect. In the asylum she was aware most people's words couldn't make any connections and yet that was all they had between them. Too many meanings without any words.

She fell silent at last, went to look out of the window without weeping. They would think her out of her mind and send her back for Wrappings... the damp sheets they used to tuck you in grew so cold it flayed you to your very edges.

They used to say she was hallucinating when she spoke about the two Irish horses or the guard house with the Red Caps, and they took her for Shocks to get it out of her system. They put her in a robe and conducted her into a room with a red light like a bloodshot eye. They tied down her arms and legs as if she were a horse being operated on... she heard the tinkle of the buckles as the straps went through, the final pull across her body as they were tightened. She pulled at her hand to scratch her head but her arms weren't free and her ankles were held down tight. Her mouth opened to let out the feeling of scream that was burning through her throat, but they had bunged a wadge of thick stuff between her teeth. She had an urge to retch. A nurse plastered some paste across her brow and fastened electrodes to her head. The paste (like BIPP paste) would be sure to get into her hair.

When her head started shaking she forgot everything. Weeks had passed by the time she woke again and found herself already up and sitting by a window. One day she wasn't looking at a wall but at a field and in it was Blackie. He was down there and she must go to him at once. He mustn't be allowed to eat too much lush grass or he might get fat and the dreaded laminitis could make him lame, might kill him.

A steely resolve grew from inside her clenched hands: she had to get out into the outside air or it would drive her crazy. She needed to breathe: weather, rain, sun. Opening her palms to study the criss-cross of lines etched in there she suddenly knew what she must do – not speak ever again about what had happened, make them think they had cured her. That was the key.

'Doctor wants to see you today, Cassandra,' said the nurse who sometimes handed out the toilet paper outside the lavatory. 'You must go and wash properly and brush your hair.'

'Why me?'

'He's got some news for you, I expect.'

'News? What news? Am I going home? Or is it perhaps bad news?'

'I don't know, Cassandra. You'll have to go and find out. But he did ask to see you in particular.'

'Well, you're in for it – going to see the doctor in his office, I hear,' said Nurse Bluebell. 'You'd do well to wipe that look off your face before you go in to see him.'

Cass knocked at his door and waited for an answer.

She sat down on a chair by his desk. 'I understand you have gone silent all of a sudden, Cassandra,' said Dr Bates. 'What has changed to make you stop talking?'

'I have nothing to talk about.'

'An intelligent lady like yourself with an enquiring mind?'

'I am happy to listen now, Dr Bates. My mind is quite empty.'

'Listen to what?'

'Oh yes, I hear voices.'

'And what do they tell you?'

'What do voices generally tell you, Dr Bates?'

'I have never heard voices. I am not an inmate.'

'I never asked to be one.'

'What does hearing voices sound like to you?'

'It makes me think everyone here is not right in the head. At night someone or other is singing or weeping or calling out. And Shocks, you see, make everyone forget their past lives and nothing ever happens here to fill the space. It makes us all run round like chickens with broken necks. That and the paraldehyde. It leaves you emptied. And it can't be right for us to smell so bad, Dr Bates. Can I please stop taking it? See how I am, now that my mind is empty.'

'And how are the animals, Cassandra? Do they make you feel more at home, now?'

'The ponies – they don't like the smell. They don't like being near me. It makes me so sad when they don't like me.'

She had been wondering if she was imagining how the ponies moved away when she approached… it had to be the smell of paraldehyde, didn't it? Nurse Bluebell gave the patients a dose in a glass of milk before lights out… the milk was meant to mask the horrid taste but it didn't work. Paraldehyde made you drowsy and it meant that the nights were quiet apart from the chorus of snoring. But the smell was always on your breath... like an alcoholic's. Some of the ladies were used to it but she herself noticed it in others because, being outside with the smell of horse and stable, she was sometimes free of it. The animals knew she wasn't herself from the stink of her breath.

She was allowed outside now to see to their needs every day, to feed them and groom them. It was more real than sewing. Chickens, rabbits and pigs, all needing her care and attention, trapped as they were in the grounds of a madhouse. But you couldn't depend on lunatics to look after them properly, could you? Some of the almost-well ones were allowed out to assist her. But they were only less unwell for some of the time... pretending to be less mad in order to get here and then, when they arrived, they started talking, talking. They'd talk to the chickens, pick them up and stroke them in their arms, cuddle them so tightly the chickens squawked and fluttered in a panic. Cass had to prise the hens out of their arms sometimes or their bones would have been cracked. Once, a girl called Della chased them all out of their run and they flapped and half flew down the length of the pony paddock. But they couldn't fly away because their wings had been pinioned. Della had to be sent back inside.

Rabbits were known to be dangerous... you might yearn to pick them up and hold them close but they scratched and they would scream – in a human way. Such a sound could make pandemonium break out. And it was not good for rabbits to be dropped. So no rabbits were to be cuddled. Eva, who was to be avoided, was given the job of keeping the rabbits. She wouldn't let new people near them. New people were afraid of Eva. She was a broad-shouldered woman and very strong and wore her skirt wrapped round her legs like a man's breeches. She made use of a look in her eyes and even the rabbits followed her movements with their ears.

Cass looked for her mechanical pencil. She couldn't find it and thought maybe it was somewhere at home. Or had she lost it somewhere? – she remembered explosions, shells, but closed off the thoughts as fast as she could. Another lost thing... it must have gone the way of Leo. Using a lead pencil, she started writing out a list of what must be done and when. But the words wanted to escape from the page and they seemed to scurry round like ants. She stabbed the paper to keep them fixed. When it was finished it looked like this:

Reveille	6.00 am
Water	6.05 am
Feed	6.55 am
Dismiss	7.30 am
Houses	8.30 am
Sick parade	10.00 am
Defaulter parade	10.30 am
Grooming	11.00 am
Water	12.00 pm
Dismiss	12.30 pm
Houses	1.30 pm
Water	3.00 pm
Feed	3.30 pm
Dismiss	4.15 pm
Orderly duties	5.15 pm
Roll call	6.00 pm
Dismiss	6.05 pm

All staff had to tick off the jobs as they were done: collecting kitchen waste for the pigs twice a day; cleaning out the pigshed, the hen house, the rabbit house, the ponies' shed; making sure their water buckets were full and clean. In winter, ice had to be broken and the ponies and rabbits had to be fed hay – the right amount of hay, and only at specified times. All the animals were to be inspected every day to ensure there were no lice, no mites. Orderly duties entailed the scouring of buckets, the cleaning of grooming kit and wash cloths. No one must feed ponies or rabbits at other times or give them titbits, because the expectation would make them bite.

Ponies' coats were to be well groomed and Cass kept this job to herself, explaining that others couldn't be trusted to do it properly, or didn't know how to use a curry comb on their coats.

She was grooming the ponies one morning when Doctor's orderly came into the stable and called out – 'Forrester!' He shouted, 'Forrester. Doctor wants you now. Get your skates on.'

Such a nuisance that beastly man… full of his own importance… as if he isn't as mad as the rest of us. She wouldn't hurry for anyone, not when the grooming was so essential. She would jolly well finish what she had started. The orderly came right in to the stable and bellowed at her, 'There's a fucking visitor, you little stinker. Look sharp.'

34

As the door opened Orion saw a tall man of military bearing rise to his feet behind a polished desk. He wore a tweed suit, a watch chain dangling from his breast pocket like a warder's key chain. The orderly said, 'Your visitor, Doctor'.

The study was lined all round with oak panelling, above which the distempered walls were bare save for one painting of a seascape above the fireplace. In this formal room, Orion felt like a wild man, a foreigner who hailed from the deepest pine forest or from an isolated mountain valley.

Holding out his hand, the man in the tweed jacket said, 'My name is Dr Bates. How do you do, Mr Forrester?"

The doctor gestured at the chair in front of the desk. Orion said he preferred to stand, thank you very much. He had sat in a train for several days and had long ago lost the habit of chairs. 'I've been abroad for some time,' he explained. 'You probably know I was never a combatant.'

'Yes, I heard about you and your sort. Most men who are still living didn't get off so lightly. Not just gas in their lungs and legs blown off but minds that need to rest and forget. That's why we're still here.' The doctor sat himself down and regarded his visitor.

'I've come today to ask – does my sister still need to be a patient here, in your opinion?'

The doctor clasped his fingers together across his chest as if to protect himself. 'As you are her brother I will speak to you frankly about her. Over time she's become quite helpful to some of the other residents. She obviously knows about keeping livestock and is happy to work with patients who can't tell a cockerel from a hen. But she's still under observation: recurrences are always a threat.' Orion thought the doctor was looking at him as if he, too, might be a potential patient.

'What brought her here in the first place?' He had heard some of the story from Sarah and wondered what the doctor might say.

'Arson to begin with. But she was clearly delusional prior to that.'

'My sister – an arsonist? That's really not credible.'

'The fire merely brought things to a crisis. Let's say she could no longer function in her station in life.'

'But she was imagining things? What exactly?' asked Orion. These words had become unfamiliar to him: station in life? What on earth was that?

'She never talks about the episode any more. Our treatment does seem to have cleared away the obstacles for her. But, at one stage, she was claiming to have been at the Western Front and to have been in sole charge of cavalry horses.'

'I see.' Orion paused to think: it seemed improbable and his sister was quite a fantasist but you could never be sure with her. Anything was possible. What made the doctor so certain it wasn't true? She had been working with remounts. The doctor's eyes were on his face as if trying to penetrate his thoughts. 'So, Doctor, when might you consider discharging her from your hospital?'

'It hasn't been possible until now. You may not have realised she was suffering some of the effects of neurasthenic patients to begin with. She has been in a very bad state: stuttering, nightmares, contraction of the muscles of the legs – all of this has been cured. So, to answer your question… discharging her depends on what aftercare she can expect to receive. May I enquire if you're here to stay? I don't recommend leaving her alone

242

just yet… I am aware of what has befallen your parents. I am sorry.'

'If she can come home with me and needs me, then I will stay.'

'We have observed her closely over the last few months and so I think going home with you would be quite in order – provided that she is brought back if the delusions return. And you must prevent her from reading any fiction. And she mustn't be allowed to write – not fiction anyway. It clearly exacerbates her delusions.'

'Brought back? Here?'

'She may need further treatment. One can't be certain how she will react to normal life. And she hasn't been made aware of your tragedy.' The doctor's hands started straightening the papers on his desk.

Orion placed both hands on the desk. 'She hasn't been told? I see.' He glared at the doctor, 'So… she must assume she's been abandoned.'

The doctor hurried on, 'When did you last see her, Mr Forrester?'

'Before all this.' Orion sensed a dead weight tumbling through his body.

'Quite a long time, then.' Dr Bates looked at Orion as though sizing him up. Orion knew his appearance was likely to give surprise – the greatcoat that he was wearing, his beard. He was aware he must look uncivilised, unkempt. 'To be blunt with you, it occurred to me that her delusions may have had something to do with her feeling helpless and guilty about your choice of action, or rather inaction.'

'Dr Bates, I stand accused.' No point in rising to the bait. He refused to feel bowed. 'But did you know we had another brother who was killed before the war?'

'Yes, I know about him,' said the doctor. 'It was a shooting accident, wasn't it? Only a young lad. Tragic.' He hesitated a moment and continued, 'It's my job to ask difficult questions, Mr Forrester. There are things I need to know. You conchies need to realise how your families suffered for your objections.'

'Look, could I speak with my sister?' Orion broke in irritably, despite himself. 'I've come a long way to find her.'

'By all means. She'll be somewhere with the animals, I expect. Just one moment.' He went out of the room and came back a few moments later. Orion moved toward the window to look at the moors in the distance, the courtyard down below, the women in uniform who were walking briskly to and fro. 'I've sent someone to bring her up here.'

'Might she be told I'm here to meet her? I wouldn't want to give her a shock.'

'I think you may be a little surprised. She's fully recovered, in my opinion, but she might not be the woman you're expecting to see. Our treatment worked wonders although she needed a little more time than others. And of course she had no one at home.'

'I understand you were able to cure some shell-shocked patients within twenty four hours of arrival?'

'Yes, those with limb contractions and problems with speaking such as stammering or even mutism were all walking and talking normally within a day or two.'

'Great Scott! But how, in heaven's name?'

'We use a combination of deep massage on the affected limbs and electrical therapy to induce seizures and rid the body of illusion and fear. The same as we and the French were using on the rank and file suffering from shell-shock during the war to get them back to their posts as soon as possible.'

'But was Cass diagnosed as neurasthenic?'

'Look, Mr Forrester, between ourselves… I've never been totally convinced by Miss Forrester's original diagnosis. She is simply a classic hysteric in my view in her desire for solitude, her compulsive acts. Some people might put it down to her rather mannish habits – riding astride, wearing breeches. But I don't hold with those old-fashioned ideas. She's an independent-minded woman and heaven knows there are plenty of role models about these days. What she was exhibiting was a form of regression. Your late brother seemed to have some problems himself, didn't he? She's obviously inherited some weakness, something of that.'

'But the fact of losing a brother might well make her susceptible to mental or emotional breakdown, I should think. Did she really need electrical treatment for that?'

'She has actually needed more of that treatment than others. She was suffering serious delusions that she adhered to tenaciously. But I'd say the cure has been successful even in her case.' He paused, then added, 'So far as it goes, while under our protection.'

Orion felt exasperated by the man's apparent wish to make sure he went through the motions of guarding his patient, and his blithe manner in discussing her personal history as if she were an object of research. A rush of anger left him feeling limp. How could they have sent her here? Then left her here? It was monstrous. More than monstrous.

In the silence there came a gentle knock. When Dr Bates called 'Enter', Orion hardly recognised the slight figure who slipped through the door. Her gaze latched on to his face. He saw she looked pale as if she had been incarcerated for some years, demolishing the strength of her personality and leaving her body diminished. Orion said, 'Cass!' but she stood still, as if not recognising him, although spellbound perhaps by the use of her first name.

Orion glared at Dr Bates. 'What on earth have you done to her?' The doctor was watching Cass.

She seemed to sway as if hovering on the edge of a

cliff. She looked at one man and then the other. 'Cassandra, your brother has come to visit you. I would think you remember him, don't you?' said the doctor.

She stood quite still in the middle of the room and Orion rushed towards her, thinking she was about to fall. Her face was thin, haggard. 'Cass, Cass. I'm so glad to see you. I can't tell you…' He thought she looked so fragile he was afraid to touch her. He was afraid of her.

'Where the blazes have you been?' Her face turned from blankness to fury.

Orion couldn't answer. His throat felt constricted and no words would come. He wanted to laugh but tears spurted from behind his eyes.

'Can't you speak? Or are you a ghost?'

'I… I've come to take you home, Sis.'

'About bloody time, too. I've had enough of this place.'

Orion looked round at Dr Bates, who had sat down in his chair and was leaning over his desk, filling out a form. He scribbled it off and said, 'If you'd just sign here, Mr Forrester…'

'You're discharging her, are you?'

'I think her next prescription has to be a return to normality. As far as is possible for her.'

35

So many people had died, she had rather taken Orion's absence for granted. A No-Man's-Land lay between them. The not-knowing if he were alive or dead had hollowed out a trench inside her. She'd never imagined that his ghost would come at last and fetch her away.

In the taxi neither spoke for a while. The speed made her queasy… whizzing round bends, trees whirling by, house after house. The bumping startled her. Her eyes were not used to such distances. Through his jacket her fingers probed the boniness of his arms. She squeezed his hand, stroked his work-knotted fingers, looked into his eyes, saw aspects of him she remembered so well: the flecks in his pupils, a mole on his neck. 'It is you, isn't it?' she said. He nodded. 'And you won't leave me again, will you?' He shook his head. She felt very tired but wouldn't close her eyes. Her head lolled against his shoulder. He felt real and solid enough. Not at all ghostly. She calculated Dora would be taking charge of Blackie now she was gone.

She imagined her father coming to the door… it'd be jolly to surprise him. Mama would be outside somewhere, might materialise from the garden when she heard their car drawing up by the door.

'Why didn't you come earlier?' she blurted into Orion's ear.

'I wasn't here.'

'Where were you?' she asked through gritted teeth. 'Where have you been?'

They were passing through Ashamstead and the people walking about in the streets confused her. She said nothing. As they moved out into open country again she asked, 'Did you know I'd gone mad?'

'Only when I came home. Finally. I wanted to make it up with Father, with you all. I should have come back earlier. I'm sorry you've been left so long in that place.'

The motor car turned into the Pepperton driveway. The little windowpanes of the house looked white as lined notepaper. Grass was growing on the steps.

'But where have you been all this time?' she turned to look at him.

He said, 'I was with the Friends...' and stopped. He peered through the window up at the house as if expecting someone. It made her look there, too. The taxi driver opened the door and Cass jumped out. 'I've been longing to see the horses we saved. They were there in that field.'

'There are no horses here any more, darling Sis.' Orion spoke gently. 'Don't you remember most of them went to the war?'

'Yes, I know. Me, of all people. I remember that, of course I do. How could I forget?' She knew she sounded petulant but really it was very annoying of him to speak to her like that, as if she were simple. 'I don't mean those – but the ones the Captain and I brought back here afterwards... we bought them from the Army and we rode them all the way here. We set them loose in that field and – oh, you should have seen them, Orion – they rolled over and over in the grass with happiness... no more artillery, no more shelling, no more impossible loads. Where do you suppose they might be?'

'I haven't seen any.' Orion opened the front door and ushered her inside.

'Papa will know. I can't wait to see him. Where can he be? Oh, he must have missed me, poor darling. Where is he, do you think?' The hall smelled of emptiness – no bounding labrador, no tobacco smoke, no boots, no flowers. Dust in the air, dust in the grate.

'There's something I must tell you.'

'Tell me?' Her heart seemed to be twisting round. Why were there no flowers in the hall? She wanted to change out of the awful dress she was wearing.

'Cass, listen. Sit down a moment, will you? Let me explain, now we're here.'

'Yes?' She felt sure he was going to say they were only here for a while. A flying visit and then he was going to take her back. Panic started pumping through her body.

'I couldn't tell you in the taxi. Look, this is going to be a shock... did you hear about the influenza?' He steered her towards a window-seat.

'Oh, what is it, what is it?'

He sat down next to her. 'Father, Mama... they've passed away.'

'Passed away? Do you mean they are dead?'

'Yes, Cass, I do. They died peacefully... in their sleep, here at home. Sarah was with them.'

'But how? How can that be?'

'Spanish influenza has killed thousands, I'm told. Father got it and then Mama came down with it later... after she nursed him.'

Cass rose and sat down in a different chair, the one her father used to sit in to lace up his boots. There was a long silence while she rocked backwards and forwards in the chair, clutching the seat. After a while, she murmured, 'Both of them? Both dead?'

'They were very ill, you see, Sis.'

'I wish I'd been here. For them to die alone without any of us. How awful.'

Her face creased, crumpled. She felt winded. She put her hands up to cover her face and leaned forwards. Orion went to the chair and knelt in front of her, grasping her to him and they sat swaying together. Her grief was desiccated, no tears. Her throat was too constricted to speak. She pulled her head up, almost pushing him away from her: he could not comfort her. 'How long ago?' she croaked.

'A few months ago.' That little push made him feel she would never forgive him. She was all he had left in the world and she wouldn't forgive him for abandoning her. He stood up and took himself further away from her.

'No one told me anything. They said I get things wrong, that I forget what I'm told, get everything muddled. But no one told me that. Never! Never!'

'They were maybe afraid of giving you another shock in case you had a setback.'

'Setback? They were giving me the shocks. I prefer to be given the truth, Orion. Everybody has had too many shocks. So many people have died. Too many.'

'Let's just hope what the church says is true... and that they're together now.'

She suddenly thought of Sarah. Where was she? Jumping to her feet, she ran from the room, calling, 'Sarah! Sarah!'

She saw her figure through the kitchen window in the back garden and ran out to seize her damp, cold hands, just as they always were. 'Oh, you're all right. Thank heavens for that. I dreamed and dreamed of being with you again, Sarah darling.' Cass hugged her with all her strength.

'They were expecting you back all the time, you see, Miss Cass,' she sniffed, her eyes looking bloodshot.

'But didn't Father realise he only had to come and fetch me away?'

'They said you were much too poorly. Even for visits. I've missed you so much, I can't tell you.'

'Oh, poor Father. He must have been waiting and fretting. I hope to God that didn't weaken him. Do you think that was it, Sarah?'

'He caught the influenza. Soldiers brought it back from the war, they said. He had it really bad. He keeled over one day and went to bed but never got any better. People were falling like flies. I think his heart wasn't strong either.'

'His heart was weak? Perhaps because we'd all gone away? But then Mama fell ill – or did she die of loneliness? People can, can't they? Oh, what will I do, Sarah? What will I do now?' and the scream in her throat made it hurt as if she were holding down the urge to vomit.

There was a time when she'd thought all men were like her father. When he touched her, the roughness of his hands snagged on her skin. His touch was sometimes like a bird's wing, a glance of a touch on her hair as he passed her. With those hands he'd pulled old hens' necks, slipped a bit into a horse's mouth, punched holes in the ice so that the sheep could drink, prised a stone from a horse's foot, held the plough on course and steady, swung an axe, fixed a post and hung a gate, pulled lambs from out of ewes, pinched out their clogged noses to let them breathe their first breath. By the end of the day the lines of his hands were deep channels, where soil marked little tributaries. At dinner times his hands were scrubbed pink even in the creases of his knuckles. Once he cupped a moth that sparkled like salt in his hands to show her, and then released it into the night where the half-moons of his nails glowed.

Her mother was not someone who would have coped with being old and less physically capable than she had been. She would have found it infuriating. You could be thankful, Cass thought, she had been spared all that. But it wasn't how things should have been. If even one of them had been at home it might have been different. She must have felt completely alone. Poor, poor Mama, falling sick and being without her daughter or her son.

Cass slept in her own bedroom but it no longer felt

like a haven. She closed the door and was alone in her old room with the familiar view from the window, the patterned curtains and the red carpet with the green and gold paisley design, and she visualised her mother watching over her father as he grew weaker, and then feeling ill with the same thing herself, knowing she would be left alone with it. She could feel in her body the gap they left behind. She had not been able to say goodbye, and that made her sense their restless presence in the house. She must get down to the church to see for herself where they were buried. But now she could hardly move for tiredness.

When her parents had last seen her she was being escorted to hospital – for a bit of rest, someone had said. There had been a fire, smoke. A policeman said she had caused it. The family doctor had given her a sleeping draught. She couldn't remember anything after that except being left there. So much had happened before that. Events during the war years: the desperate journey along the Front with Sunlight, the arrest, the horse hospital, the shell-shocked horses, the horrible wounds she had tended, the misery of the frightened animals enduring the war of mankind's making. Then, after the long ride from Southampton to her home among the moors and fields, there was Captain King saying he must return at once to Ireland. To an Irish woman he had promised to marry. To a woman she was not sure that he loved. But he had promised... how did she know about that? Had he said as much? Not very likely.

Humiliation Hospital was what she called it... where they patch you up to send you back into the fray. She had lain on the bed struggling like the horses strapped down on the operating table. Chloroform had subdued them or sometimes killed them while the veterinary surgeon removed shrapnel or bullets from their limbs. They strapped her down too and attached the cups to her head… for a few seconds she trembled, and then her head, though it was held down too, was banging on the bed. Her skull was shaken and shaken, darkness poured in through her eyes. When she came to, her memory had been erased. She had nothing inside her any longer… she was a husk… hollowed out, an automaton lying in her bed while people brought her food. Later, she was told to get out of the bed and go and have a bath. She had to struggle to remember things like how to turn on the taps or the need to bring a towel, to check the temperature of the bath before she got into it. Was this what they called losing your mind?

After that, she began to remember normal things, like a hollow feeling in your stomach needs food, or a parched throat needs drink. Later, she liked to be with the animals on the hospital farm because they did not ask anything of her. She had groomed the two old ponies every day till each one's tail and mane shone like spun silk. It was the ponies which had helped her come back to herself.

She reflected that you can't beat out an iron bar to bring a horse into submission. You can't put the horseshoe into a furnace and then dunk it in cold water to make it love you. You can't bind a horse with shoes or take it anywhere it doesn't agree to go because you hammer nails into its feet. Didn't Fernley sometimes say you could see a horse's past in the inside of its hoof? You can't attach electrodes to a woman's head and apply electric shocks to make her forget what she loves. Love, she thought, is not in the brain: it lives in your skin and your bones, and also the vulnerable soles of your feet.

On her return from France, it somehow slipped her mind that she had been ordered by the frail old general never to say anything. So she had told people her stories about the brigadier and the horses, what he'd said to her, how she found herself wandering around behind the front line, how the pompous military policeman had thought she was a spy. She talked about swimming the recovering horses in the Channel, about the hundreds of horses who had to undergo dipping for mange, operations for bullet and shell injuries, and about Magician galloping off into the mud, perhaps drowning in it, and Sunlight whom she'd never seen again. These thoughts made her weep in the sitting room, or even at the dining table when she couldn't force a mouthful down her throat.

The one saving grace for her in all this had been returning home with the ponies that she and Captain King had rescued, the look on her parents' faces when she rode through the gate and up the drive. The house had looked more dilapidated than when she had left. Of course it would, though. That was natural – her father had lost his living when the horses were taken away. Now most families wanted a motor car, not a horse, even if there were any horses to be bought. She had wanted to persuade him to go back to the market, find some youngsters they could train up together. People, after all, did still want horses for hunting and sport. But the stuffing had been knocked out of him. Perhaps he had been assuming she was not capable without a brother to help her.

But then her dreams had taken her over, and the sleepless nights walking up and down her room, sometimes outside and into the fields. Some nights she would walk in the moonlight, the landscape colourless but glowing, where creatures and stones jumped out at her as if they were waiting for her. She was running on a scent along paths beneath trees or sheep tracks on the moors like a fox, watchful and listening, surprised by the glint of moonlight on a moving leaf, a whitened stone. The leaves seemed like ears listening to her. Her thoughts grew into brambles and they scored her legs, tore at her clothing, manacled her. That was how *they* caught up with her, shut her inside and wouldn't let her into the outside. She needed rest, they said, rest from running about like a wild creature. Was it that policeman who said that in his opinion, she was a ruddy liability?

36

Every afternoon Orion led his sister along paths they had known when they were young – into the woods or across the marshy fields to look for hares, snipe, badgers. They stumbled on places he'd almost forgotten, but when they arrived a kernel of their past would be lying in wait: a track, now almost overgrown, through the woods to their old hide-out; a copse where the roe deer barked at intruders; the meadow where the hares grazed, their slender ears on the alert. He exclaimed in delight and she would smile at him and he would think she was remembering too. Like re-learning the nouns and verbs of a shared language they'd stopped speaking. Often a thrush would sing from a beech tree and he wondered if it were the same one he recalled, or perhaps a descendant of that bird.

In the woods many trees had been cut down and carted away. The government said they would replace the trees they had used for the war but he knew it would take generations for them to grow to the size he remembered. Yet his father must have made some money out of them to help keep the farm going when the horse business was finished.

It was May, and everywhere spindles of leaves were unwinding. Each bee-filled tree buzzed as though it were a generator, swallows gurgling in the sky like springs of water. After the years that he'd spent behind bars and then in a ravaged countryside, the abundance of new leaf and life left him giddy. He wanted to leap and jump, do cartwheels. But he felt too heavy in his body to try that now. Lost the knack of it. Sometimes he ran through the beech woods that had survived, skimming past the trees, jumping fallen branches. Once his leg gave way beneath him as he landed. He was felled to the ground, feeling that something in the joint had snapped. He lay clutching his knee, afraid to get up and test it at first. But when he did, after several minutes, he found that it didn't hurt too much after all and he could limp home.

When he walked into the hallway he saw the sitting room door was ajar. Late afternoon sunlight shone on the paintwork and caught his eye. He heard the chink of glasses, the stopper of the decanter being removed. He expected his father's voice to call out to him, having heard the front door open and close, a mackintosh being taken off. Orion called back, 'Yes, a whisky. Thanks.' He stepped into the room and its emptiness was a shock. He glanced around and saw how light quivered on the carpet, wind blowing the clouds across the sun. On the sideboard the cut-glass decanters stood empty.

Whenever he came back to the house this emptiness made his eyes water, his throat constricted as if he might be sick – for each time it struck him anew how his parents were both here and elsewhere. Perhaps it would help to start clearing away their things, give shoes and coats away, go through their wardrobe and tell Sarah to keep any frocks or other items of clothing for herself. But until he could bring himself to do that, it was as if those who remained were all waiting for them to come back. And he didn't think his sister was ready for such finality.

After that first day at home Cass seemed to go blank, even further away from him. At times he caught himself wondering if he had done the right thing, bringing her back home. If only she would talk. Supposing the medical people were right and Cass was given to delusions? But it was, he hoped, probably her way of dealing with their parents' deaths. The shock of it had driven her back inside herself. Why had she not been told? It was inhuman of them. Or just plain cowardly.

Orion tried not to dwell on the letters he should have posted. He had assumed his family no longer wanted to know him. Had he been too quick to jump to conclusions? Leo had once said that words are not the only means to connect us. But they do make a useful start.

During their walks together, he began to notice how sometimes Cass seemed to engineer their route so that they passed a particular group of nondescript ponies. She watched them as they stepped forwards, pulling at the tough moorland grass. A pigeon whacking its wings as it clattered out of a tree, a cow starting to bellow would make the horses nervously lift their heads. Once, she walked towards them, her hand stretched out to touch them, but the horses moved off, shaking their heads as if bothered by flies. And she had come away, looking crestfallen but saying nothing.

Apart from that, it was as if she had no will of her own: she did whatever he suggested. It frightened him to see her like that. As if somebody else was in possession of her body: someone with caution in their veins, someone scorched by truths he would never reach. She seemed lifeless, not the sister he remembered, not the Cass with determination so flinty she could sometimes cut you.

He imagined seeing her from officialdom's point of view. Those stories she had come back with: what if they were true? She had certainly worked at the Remount Depot at Pluckley, albeit she had left rather mysteriously. Then her fiancé had been reported missing. Had she perhaps been driven mad by grief and gone to France to look for him? Not unheard of. The military police would have caught up with her, and her deceptions and fabrications might well have been grounds for their suspicions. She spoke French very well and had more than a smattering of German, and she might have appeared capable of being a spy. He figured that if anyone wanted to keep her quiet it would be the War Office. They could claim she was a danger to herself and to others. On paper she could easily be made to look like an hysteric, given to wild accounts, all serving to link her present troubles to her unstable family: he, the brother who was a conscientious objector, another brother who did not communicate and was shot when he wandered out of line. Was this what they considered 'mad'?

He had other preoccupations: they stuck in his throat like fishbones. How, he wondered, can I tell her that really we can no longer afford to keep this place going? How can I ask her to move house? However poor we are, I must make my home with her. I won't ever let her go back, so I must care for her and find a way to earn our living. She is not to go back to that torture chamber. But she loves this place so much – what am I to do? Coming home after what she had been through and losing both parents… you can't expect someone to lose their home as well. Would a new dog cheer her up perhaps? And certainly a decent pony. He must ask around.

How was he to earn enough for them both to live on? No one would employ a man who had been a conchie. It felt to him as though something inside him had become worn out, even his knee joints were not to be always relied upon to carry his weight.

The house had turned into a different version of itself: the shapes and sizes of windows, walls, floors seemed distorted, as if the lens of his eyes had warped. Yet the shapes and textures of the land had stayed the same. The paths he had been so familiar with felt like an extension of his own limbs, like the lines in the palm of his hand. They helped him cope – as best he could. He must not break down in front of her. He must not. Even when he saw how the woods he once knew had been cut down and taken away.

As Cass' physical strength came back bit by bit, their walks extended further away from the vicinity of the house. They talked about birdcalls, reminding each other of the songs that neither had heard for so long they'd forgotten some of the names of the birds. He tried to mimic the blackbird's song in words, just as he and Leo used to do. He exclaimed out loud at flowers and butterflies – little things along the paths that meant they found bits of themselves they had lost, immersed as they had been in the graveyard of politics for so long.

Once, it was she who commented that butterfly orchids were coming up in their usual place. And later she pointed out twayblade and sundew in the damp edges of the bog. He showed her droplets of water caught in the tiny hairs of a stem. Another time, they walked beside the river as far as the island, from where no trees had been taken. The wooden bridge was still intact, though rickety and in need of repair.

They took the steep path up to the moors; watched a kestrel hover in the wind; heard the *chink-chink* calls of the stonechats; spotted two hares zig-zagging down the slope and across some marshland; looked at the view laid out before them with the winding river below like a page from a map of their past. They knew the names of the farms and the people who lived there, remembered hunting adventures and waved a finger at places where they recalled jumping a great hedge, or where Mr So-and-So had once fallen off, or where the hounds had given magnificent chase after the barely workable line of a fox. The right words, he noticed, seemed to draw more memories from out of the shadows. Bit by bit, they were retrieving the language of their childhood, their mother tongue.

37

Cass was on the alert, afraid that if she slipped up Orion might send her back to Dr Bates. She'd heard the doctor mention the words set-backs, recurrences. It made the earth's surface more fragile to her. The sun shining on the water, the rain falling on the surface were only part of a veneer that might break through into another reality at any moment. Perhaps it was her own nature which she mistrusted.

She couldn't help wondering if the shocks could have altered the position of her heart. She thought perhaps it had moved and that she could no longer face people directly – not even her own brother. She did not know which emotion to use: they seemed to be stuck, not flowing naturally as they once did. She could not even grope her own way forwards... she was afraid of each and every sensation because it shocked her so... easier to follow her brother's lead.

Sometimes she wasn't sure what she was looking at: once, at the end of an unlit passageway the darkness stirred and quickened as Mama, adjusting the long string of pearls she often wore, came in from the back garden and walked towards her. She could materialise anywhere in the house: near the curtains and upholstery with French designs that she had treasured; in front of the fusty oak dresser where she had stored the glass and china vases she used for flowers from the garden; in the cloakroom where her old tweed coat hung above her lace-up boots. Cass could still smell her mother's scent inside that coat and when she felt through the pockets she found garden twine, scissors, a few of last year's conkers that had lost their sheen. But the smell of earth, tobacco and horse that used to trail after her father was always so horribly absent.

If only she had never gone away, had stayed at home to care for them both while they worried about possible invasion, blackouts and zeppelins; about stretching the rations; about holding the farm together without the income from horses. They would have worried also about her, and about Orion, even when they believed he was in the wrong.

When pressed, Sarah explained that at some point during Cass's absence from home, the remaining ponies had been put out to graze on the moors. Not Swan, of course. Her father had judged it better they should forage for themselves and not be allowed to eat grass all day and get fat. Cass knew he considered meadow grass dangerous for ponies. She sometimes spotted the little group in the boggy valley where they had taken to grazing: it was easy to pick out the grey mare like a beacon in the landscape, the Welsh cobs, the Connemara gelding the colour of granite, and the Dartmoor pony. She decided that she would gather them back to the farm for the winter, when it would be kind to give them hay and shelter – and they would be company for Swan.

Better not let Orion know about where she went every morning: it could be construed that she'd started wandering again. So at breakfast she would appear looking as if she had some purpose for the day. She clipped back her hair with two tortoise-shell combs or coiled it into a bun, applied lipstick and scent, wore a necklace. During daylight hours it was easier to do what other people asked of her. She wouldn't tell anyone about swimming in the river every day at daybreak, nor how on moonlit nights she would get up and walk to the island, where she could write. She would have liked to use Leo's mechanical pencil, but she couldn't find it anywhere.

Not that she could see what she wrote until later,

when she would murmur her wayward lines to herself as she wrote them out legibly in straight lines, only to stuff them into a drawer. Under cover of the darkness she saw all the way into her heart. The lines came to her in fragments and she wanted to fashion them into a whole, but finding out how to do that would be her quest:

Skies open and close,
a lid over my head
lets a ray of sun fall
across my face.

I swallow the glimmers
and it lets me see they look
through me by day.

Inside the house, the atmosphere seemed to her to be full of lumps, some days being more gristly than others. It made her feel confined when Orion was in one of his silent moods – sometimes for hours on end. You could not know what he was thinking, and the silence seemed like a widening space between them. On one such day the irritation followed her outside. From behind him she could tell, just from the position of his head, that he had assumed that faraway look. And when he chewed his cheek in that habit of his, it meant he was ruminating.

It sprang from her, 'Why are you always raking through the past?' she asked him. 'Leave it alone, can't you, to rot into the ground?'

'But I haven't said anything.' He walked on, without turning to look at her.

She came up beside him. 'You don't need to. I know. You're going over and over things, aren't you?'

'The past doesn't leave us,' he said. 'It hasn't gone away.'

'True. But one has to let new things happen, don't you think? Or we'd be stuck.'

'But it's where the future grows from.'

'Oh, you and your philosophy!'

'But it's about you – you shouldn't be grieving for Frank any more. You shouldn't.'

'And what makes you think I might be?' She was astonished. He had never seen the photograph she had torn up and burned. When had that been? She couldn't recall exactly.

'I don't know... I'm just assuming. He...he was your fiancé, after all.'

'Well, he wasn't. It was called off. It was sad he went missing after that.'

Orion continued, sheepishly because he was entering difficult terrain, 'But his parents forced him into it. Things might have turned out differently, if he hadn't been killed.' He was pressing his hands together so hard that he shook.

'Lots of people died, Orion. You don't need to feel sorry about me.' She took a step towards him, tried to insert her hand into his grip and asked, 'What on earth makes you mention this now?'

'Because...' He looked down at his hands but didn't continue.

She waited before saying, 'Because what?' She felt exasperated. 'What?'

'You couldn't have married him. Not him.' He kicked a stone away.

She felt as if they were wading out into muddy water. She asked, 'What on earth have you not been telling me?'

He cleared his throat and said, 'It was he who shot Leo.'

'Frank shot Leo?' She stifled a snort. 'Oh, I don't believe that!' Who was it who was supposed to be delusional?

'Yes. He did.'

'And how do you know, Orion?'

'I was there. I saw it happen.'

'It was an accident, I thought.' Panic was rising up from her feet, making her feel boneless.

'Yes, it was – but Frank still did it. He swung his gun round and fired too low.'

'Leo hit his head on a rock. Frank didn't shoot him deliberately.'

'No, but he was an awful shot. And if Leo hadn't been shot he wouldn't have fallen and smashed his skull on the rock.'

'Why, for God's sake, Orion… have you never said?'

'Father said not to at the time. He said it was an accident and Frank mustn't be blamed, because Leo wandered off when he shouldn't. Father said Frank's life could be blighted.'

'So Father knew, did he?' She was trying to work out which was the bigger surprise. 'So you did talk about it, then. But why bring it up now?'

'I've never had a chance to explain to you. I should have done but we were both away, if you remember. I tried to write you a letter about it. I supposed… but you never received it…'

'No, I never heard from you after your release. Nothing at all.'

'I wrote some letters…' He didn't seem able to say anything more. He looked up at the sky and she heard his feelings in the silence. She came up to him, touched his arm.

'…but I didn't send them.'

'You wrote letters and didn't post them?'

He pulled back, teeth tight against his bottom lip, eyes closed. 'I can't explain. I think I thought you wouldn't want to know me any more. I couldn't come back till I had done something worthy of you all.' His lips quivered as if he might be about to weep. In a shaky voice he said, 'Cass, I didn't know whether you had all given up on me. And when I saw the devastation everywhere I wasn't so certain I'd made the right choice back then. But I also knew I'd never forgive myself...' The words felt so naked she wanted to cover him. Her anger with him now felt like that of a child tugging at her mother's skirt when something was refused. She had not understood her brother because she had assumed too much that she knew him.

'...for what?'

'About Frank. I just haven't ever been able to let it go. It still haunts me, I suppose.'

His hesitating voice unbalanced her, as if she had knocked back a tot of neat spirits. 'Yes, I can imagine,' she said finally. She was thinking through the implications, and visualised tense family Christmas dinners, putting flowers on Leo's grave on his birthday or on the anniversary of his death. She shivered, 'Not a recipe for family harmony.' She put her arm on her brother's, and they moved along the path side by side.

'I thought it best to say nothing, after I heard he was missing. But then I thought you might still be in mourning and knowing the truth might help.'

'It's always better to know the truth. If indeed it is... Can you really be certain anyway? A line of guns: it could have been anybody.'

'I was sure.'

'But would you have just let me go ahead and marry him... without telling me?'

'No. Not that.' He stood quite still. He folded his arms over his head and closed his eyes with a heavy exhalation. 'Actually, Cass, I didn't know what to do.'

'Anyway, it was all hypothetical anyway. His parents wouldn't let him marry me so it wasn't going to happen. And I know deep down it wouldn't have worked out. He didn't love me enough to go against their wishes. Nor I him, for that matter. No need to worry that you've ruined my life.' She nudged him, kissing his cheek. 'And of course I wouldn't have given up on you.'

A shaft of light opened on a ridge up ahead. A line of hawthorn trees on the slopes turned red-gold in the sun as if the tips of the twigs were bleeding.

One morning she was out walking alone when she heard a drumming on the peaty turf. Turning to look round, she saw pricked ears appear on the crest of the hill. Led by the grey mare, the herd of war veterans was streaming over the heather and rough grass. Nearing her, they slowed, blowing and panting, panting and blowing. Their manes had grown long and the tips looked singed by rain and sun. Their forelocks dangled over their eyes. She stood still, her heart singing, while they came toward her – sniffing, sniffing – as though they remembered her just this once. She spoke to them quietly and they drew closer to catch the quietness in her voice perhaps. She could smell their sweet grassy breath, saw the wet mud on their rumps where they had rolled. Their ears strained forwards, then swivelled backwards, and pointed forwards once more. When her hand stretched towards them, they stepped sideways, and with one mind they backed away, snorting, before breaking into a trot, then a canter that beat on the turf – away towards the tor. When she looked back she could see their silhouettes on the horizon. Their freedom gladdened her heart.

Their presence out there on the moor was her truth. She had to be sure that her memories were her own and not invented ones, or told to her by other people. She had to think her life through, cross-reference as if checking an alibi to see if things fitted. The existence of the ponies was a trig point from which she could begin to see a way forward. One step at a time though. Because at any moment she could take a wrong path that led nowhere. A sheep's path. Someone else's wrong turn. She might arrive at a point and find she had forgotten everything, even her age. Like playing a game of hide and seek, she thought, when no one finds you and you realise they have stopped looking and are doing something different.

Snippets of what had happened started to come back to her more often. But they needed checking too, somehow. She and the Captain – he insisted she called him Maurice, but she found it difficult – had bought some of the horses which were otherwise destined to be horsemeat. They'd looked over the horses labelled with a C for Cast and chosen five of these rejects between them. At the auction, they had outbid the butchers who were on the lookout for the many bargains. He paid for the horses' passage. Humans weren't allowed to travel in the hold with the horses, and she'd worried about what their condition would be like when they arrived.

The crossing that had brought her and Maurice King back to England was crammed with too many wounded men on board. She remembered the shock of the ferry hooting as it turned into the port, the shudder as they docked at the quay. She had leaned a little groggily over the rail to watch the thick hawsers being wound round the capstan, the passengers waving at those who had come to meet them. She'd made her way uncertainly down the gangway into the tumult and in among hundreds of happy and tearful reunions.

Captain King had grabbed her hand so as not to lose her. She gripped his hand back. It seemed to fit nicely and she liked it there. That feeling of her hand in his was something she remembered. Or had that been in a dream? How could you tell the difference? She had been a bit breathless because of the crowd pressing in, but he held on tight as he led her to where their horses were being unloaded: the grey mare she'd chosen who had had ophthalmia but was expected to recover, the two Welsh cobs he'd once removed bullets from, the Dartmoor pony she'd taken a shine to, and the Connemara he had chosen for its kind eye. He had muttered about a lad from Connemara who had been killed: was his name Jed or Gerard? She was already looking forward to showing her father the horses, though she couldn't imagine how they were going to get them all the way home.

However, Maurice seemed to have thought of everything. She left it to him, but when they got the horses to the railway station they were told that all the freight trains were full. There was nothing for it but to ride and lead them all the way.

The days were short and the evenings long. The miles riding home when so much didn't happen between the two of them. The explanations he hadn't given. She'd thought her heart might break inside her ribs, spill its contents all over the road. What had happened? It was all so long ago.

What had he said to her that evening as they sat by the fire at an inn, the night before they arrived at Pepperton? Something about having to scoot back to Belfast, to get himself decommissioned, or they might not release him from military service. Being an officer in the British Army meant he could get caught up in the coming struggle. Serious trouble was brewing between Republicans and Nationalists in Ireland and the situation was volatile: hayricks in his father's parish had been burned, officers were resigning from the Royal Irish Constabulary, chaos was about to break loose. He had to return urgently to see his family, to dig up some guns he had buried for his father and to set the record straight with someone... but he would come back as soon as he could. 'I'll be free then to say what I want' were the words she remembered.

But wasn't it all just wishful thinking? Wasn't it the Shocks that had made her muddled? And perhaps what he wanted to say was nothing much at all. Maybe she'd read too much into that – she dimly recalled his once mentioning an almost-fiancée in Ireland? Was that the bit about setting the record straight? She remembered how he had talked very fast and she had listened at the time but maybe hadn't taken it in properly. Anyway, the past was over and done with now. Leave it to rot.

He'd stepped towards her and taken one of her hands in both of his. He turned it over and kissed the palm, then closed her fingers over the place. He clasped her hand and placed it under his arm so that his elbow held it against his body, his other hand moved the curls from her neck and he bent and kissed her ear. She heard the sound of his lips parting inside the channels of her brain and she wanted to face his face, and her free hand reached up towards his cheek. Her eyes rested on his for a moment. She looked sideways, felt herself blush, leaving her hand where it was, tight under his arm. 'You know I would never get used to you without your peaked cap,' she laughed as she slipped her hand back. 'We can't do just what we want, can we?' she had said to herself or to him – she didn't know which. Had he taken that silly remark about his cap as rejection?

What did that gesture of his signify? It had more than made up for what he wouldn't yet say. But how could he have done that, if it hadn't meant anything? Was he cruel or simply wanton? She hadn't believed so. The trouble was, he hadn't said anything at all afterwards. That fateful moment of silence, which had seemed so short and unimportant, had stretched into the months and years that had followed.

But she had never let on. She was proud of that.

The next morning she rose early as usual before anyone else was awake. Carrying a duffel bag containing a towel and some spare underwear, she took the path through the woods to the river by the island, where the current curled back on itself against the bank. The water was cold, and dark as treacle. It had rained during the night and in the middle of the river the current was wild, impossible to swim against, but its forward momentum created an eddy along the bank that flowed gently backwards.

She undressed, folded her breeches and blouse and stepped into the water. The cold flowed over her skin and sank deep into her flesh as it swept up her limbs, taking her breath away. She lowered herself into the patch of calm, slipped under the water as if it were an eiderdown, swam upstream a little way, felt the familiar tug of twisting currents and touched the edge of her fear. Back on the bank, she felt heat creep through her – from her toes, over her legs and up her torso, through her neck and shoulders and into her face. Her arms and hands were tingling. She had been one person and now she was another. Drawn to the risk of being pulled under and coming through once more.

She ate an early breakfast on her own. On the stairs she met her brother, who said, 'Oh, there you are. I wanted to tell you, Dickon has a litter of pups. I said we might take a squint sometime? If you like?'

'Rather! Oh, do give him a tinkle and we could whizz right round.'

When she went upstairs to brush out her hair and tidy herself, she found on her desk a small bundle of unopened letters addressed to herself. For some reason, they hadn't been left on the hall table where the post was usually put. The envelopes bore no stamps and their corners were dog-eared and battered, as if they had been squashed in a case. Her heart skipped a beat.

She took out her paper-knife and slit open one of them at random. On the first sheet of paper she read:

When you receive this letter please ask Father to read it and tell him that I trust one day we can be reconciled. I hope that Father may feel that, in the end, I did pull my weight.
Your loving brother,
Orion

Unfolding the sheets of tightly folded notepaper, she wondered if she'd ever decipher her brother's writing, cramming the pages. He had had so much to tell her. So much that their father and mother would never know about him.

PART FOUR

38

Cass pulled the damask tablecloth straight, smoothing out the wrinkles with the palm of her hand. The smell of soapflakes and starch made her nose tickle as if she were about to sneeze, eyes smarting at the whiteness of the shiny fabric. She'd found this cloth in the cupboard where someone had folded it away after last using it in that era Before The War – in that other world she used to inhabit, when she was the girl she occasionally dreamed she had been. That was when Mama, with Sarah's help of course, made events such as this happen. That was when they were all together and happy, before the dark trenches of separation and misunderstanding began to flood and collapse around them.

Orion didn't know where his wedding breakfast was to be held. It was to be a surprise for him, having it on the island – their island, the place that had grown into them as children. Over the past week, old Mr Guthrie had brought planking across the bridge to make a table. That morning she had plonked the canteen of silver into the back of the car and now Mr G was carrying the cutlery, plates, bottles of wine and dishes of food. Pip the labrador ran back and forth, tongue lolling, tail thrashing with anticipation.

Cass arranged the cutlery in the correct order as Sarah had taught her: fork on left side, large knife outside smaller knife on right side. She laid out the twenty places around the table, filled vases with water from the river, and set pink and white sweet peas from the garden in the centre.

The pony's harness was to be decorated with paper

flowers and fitted with bells. Orion would be driving his new bride from the church in the old style, and everyone would be there at the island to greet them.

Under the canopy of trees the light was dim. But the sun at midday would pour into the clearing in the middle. High time her brother was married, she reflected, but it couldn't have happened before now. A pity their own parents would not see it. But it would never have happened if the bride's father had been alive and capable of putting an end to the whole idea – Miss Eveline Lethbridge, Frank's younger sister, marrying not only into the enemy's family but marrying the enemy himself and soon to be called Mrs Orion Forrester!

Mr G's son, Lenny, was on hand to make sure the gramophone was kept wound up and to change the Amy Gluck records – the *Song of the Nightingale* which was still so popular with Charles Kellogg's whistling imitation of a nightingale, and *My Bonnie Laddie* which Cass had first heard being sung by the woman in white. If the music petered out it wouldn't matter because by then the party would be in full swing and the river would add its vivace gushings and divertimento gurglings.

After the groom had carried his bride across the bridge and everyone had finished exclaiming, they sat down to eat, the trees conducting shadows across the glade. Pip sat under the table, on the alert for falling scraps.

Cass was sitting next to the best man, Arthur, who had been in prison during the war with her brother, toiled with him on the so-called Conchies' Path across the moors, and taken him to work at the Quaker Mission. On her right hand side was Sarah. She looked down the table and there was Colonel Westwood, whose sons had both been killed in the war. Opposite was another conscientious objector, Harry, who had also gone abroad to do reconstruction work. When he returned he had helped renovate the old wing of the farmhouse for Orion and Cass to move into, so that the main house could be let out. Her old friend, Florence, was next to him and with her hair neatly bobbed she looked rather different from their days at the Remount Depot: very elegant in her grey and violet low-waisted dress and purple silk stockings. She kept glancing down the table at Cass. There also was Dickon, who had survived the war as a shoey, and whose huge hands were stroking the petals of a sweet pea in front of him.

Such a mix, she thought, could never have happened like this Before The War. To her, it looked as if she were seeing them all from under water, in slow motion. She felt that the air they were breathing was green – air that was full of the sound of the leaves fluttering above their heads, the trees enclosing them on the island.

Everyone seemed to her to be on the point of realising some intangible thing that could only be reached by crossing the bridge and stepping into an altogether different world. Would they say things to one another they didn't normally say? Might Propriety itself be cast aside?

Cass had fashioned little boats out of small bundles of wooden pegs tied together with string, with sails of coloured tissue paper. The guests were given one each to launch from a shoal that jutted out into the river. The men laughed as they balanced precariously with their champagne glasses on the slippery round stones. There was much applause as all the boats sailed off. They charged down the current, swirling round in the eddies, some of them tipping over and others staying upright in a backwater until Harry got a stick and pushed them out into mid current again.

Shadows shilly-shallied on the tablecloth and over people's skin and hair. Lenny re-wound the gramophone from time to time, and saxophone and song drifted downstream. A mist was beginning to rise off the river but nobody seemed particularly bothered, though wraps were pulled over a few arms. Cass was listening to conversations up and down the table. She and Sarah were used to being quiet together. She said nothing about it, but the sense of missing their parents, Fernley and Leo made her feel as if a new organ had grown within her, especially on such an occasion.

It was delightful to watch her brother and Harry talking so animatedly. She saw the little gestures between him and Eveline, how she looked at him with her mouth full, how he covered her hand briefly with his own.

Later, they cut the cake, decorated with sugared pink and red rose buds from the garden. Afterwards, when everyone had got up and was milling about, exploring the island and gazing at the river, Orion found Cass, put his arms round her and spoke into her ear. 'A marvellous day, Sis. You have thought of everything.'

'I hope we have. Sarah made lots of lists. Good old Eveline, letting you carry her like that.'

'Now look, when we come back we want no fuss made of us. No fuss at all. And when you're away at university this is still your home. Your writing is your priority and we will do nothing to disturb you. That's a promise.'

Someone squeezed Cass's shoulder, 'I haven't yet congratulated you on your scholarship at Oxford. A degree in History? We must go riding together again. It will be such fun,' said Florence. She was now studying Archaeology at Girton as she had planned. 'And I love your book of poetry, dear Cass. Your stay in hospital proved to have a silver lining perhaps. You have written so movingly about it: I felt I was there.'

'They never wanted me to write, you know. Said it would be very bad indeed for me.'

'Do you suppose our better understanding of mental

278

health will make treatment more humane?'

'Only a very few good doctors can make a difference to individual patients. How can someone who thinks they are one thing be persuaded that they are really another?'

'And tell me something else. Has anyone persuaded you out of your single state, Cass?' Florence always asked Cass the kind of questions nobody else would.

'I don't think I'd make much of a wife, Flo. Men are safe from me. Anyway, I haven't much chance to meet anyone. There are so few available.'

'I'm still sorry about your loss. This day might have been yours.'

'Oh, fiddlesticks. I'm hardly the only one, am I? And it was only ever an engagement in name. He was about to go to war and asked me because I was a decent rider. And I agreed because I felt sorry for him. It must have been nice to have someone thinking of you back home, a photo of a sweetheart to look at, letters. It was a long time ago.'

'Has there been no one else, Cass?'

'But why are you asking me about marriage? I thought you didn't agree with it?'

'I don't mean marriage necessarily. A lover perhaps?' Florence drawled the word as if she were exhaling cigarette smoke. 'You're very alluring, you know, you'll meet someone at Oxford: one of the brainy types.'

'I think I'll only look at a man if he resembles a horse. Don't worry about me. I'm quite content. I only go for four legs.'

'Talking of which… I have been campaigning against diving horses in America. Have you heard about it? They get a horse to plunge down from a high dive, maybe forty or more feet up, into a pool of water. There's a stunt rider strapped on. They're making a lot of money out of it.'

'Horse diving? I've never heard of it. A rider, you say?'

'Yes, a woman called Sonora. She lost her eyesight in a diving accident but carries on doing it blind. The practice has caused an outcry, I can tell you, Cass.'

'That makes our stunts look rather tame.'

'I've been writing protest letters to everybody I can think of. We must get the awful show stopped somehow.'

'I'll do whatever I can to help.'

Sarah came up and said, 'Excuse me, but may I have a quick word?'

'I'll just go find another drop of bubbly, if there's any left,' said Florence, who wobbled back towards the dinner table.

Sarah said, 'Someone's arrived. Says he knows you.'

'Didn't you ask him to come another time?'

'I did, but he said it was urgent.'

'Urgent? But who would come now?'

'He wouldn't give his name. Said you knew him. He's waiting by the bridge.' Sarah gestured with her eyes.

Cass peered at the bridge and saw a tall man standing there. Her heart sank a little. There had been so many of them: veterans from the trenches who had returned home to unemployment and destitution and had taken to the road and, once there, became attached to their unemployed freedom. Cass had always tried to give them something: a bowl of soup, a loaf of bread, a little money. But she had completely run out of her father's old clothes to give away, and what they often wanted most was a coat or a warm jersey. Having to sleep rough after all they had been through in the trenches was such a terrible disgrace, in her mind. Sometimes they brought things to sell that she didn't really want – old tools, cutlery, aprons, knick-knacks – or wanted work that there wasn't enough money to pay for. Some of the old regulars still turned up from time to time, sometimes wearing her father's old clothes. Mr Guthrie had been one of these men: he had arrived on their doorstep and had made good. It felt inauspicious to turn such a man away from a wedding party.

When Cass didn't reply, Sarah said, 'Perhaps I'd better fetch your brother to deal with him.'

'No, don't bother Orion. I'll see to him.'

She couldn't see the man's face against the sunlight. But, as she approached, he said, 'Cass?' His voice sounded as if he was afraid of being wrong.

She was about to ask how he knew her name when he spoke it again and she half recognised his voice. But she couldn't remember his face. He'd called her 'Cass'. It was strangely unconventional. Not quite proper. Maybe he was an old school friend of Orion's. Or more likely someone from prison days. His eyes shone black under the brow of the hat that he wore. He took it off.

At first she couldn't answer, for the surprise of hearing her name. Looking at the gaunt face and thinning hair she said, 'I know you from somewhere, do I?'

'Of course, you must, Cass.'

'Sorry, but you'll have to tell me. I haven't been myself.' She was holding Pip's collar so that he wouldn't jump up at the man. She didn't know why but her heart was tapping the inside of her ribs as if it had swollen.

'I'm not in uniform any longer, so you mightn't...' His voice was coming to her from a distance. 'Cass, I had to find you.'

'Maybe Orion knows...' Bewildered by her forgetfulness, she called to Orion who was threading his way towards them. Sarah must have told him after all.

'Look, who are you? Have we met before?' Orion asked.

'I... I thought you'd... My name is Maurice King... I knew Cass... Miss Forrester, during the war. We... ah, we tended the horses together...'

His voice sounded like an echo, a rhyme she once knew but had forgotten.

She heard her own voice go husky in her throat, 'Oh, Maurice… why have you come?'

'I was hoping you'd still be here, Cass.'

'Well, it's a case of better late than never, I suppose.' She couldn't think how to react. What was he expecting? Why arrive now?

'Dash it! Am I too late?'

'Too late?' she asked, 'Too late for what?'

'For your wedding.'

'Oh, it's not me getting married. It's my brother. But you weren't exactly on the guest list.'

'So I might still be in with a chance?'

'In with a chance?' She was puzzled. He was looking at her in a strange way, rather like Pip who went weak and floppy when expecting dinner.

'I have something of yours I should have returned to you long ago,' he said, and held out the ebony mechanical pencil she thought she must have left behind in the chaos at the chateau.

He handed it to her with the red tasselled end towards her, as if the point were a knife. The sight of Leo's pencil made her heart skip. When she took hold of it, the feel of the barrel fitted her fingers like a part of herself she had lost and then found.

'You lent it to me once and I forgot to return it.'

'Did I? Oh, my brothers will be so relieved it has turned up,' she said, unable to look at him for the tears she didn't want him to notice. She couldn't see the pencil properly through the blur but it grew warm as her hand and her heart slipped into place. Her thumb and forefinger automatically twisted the barrel and a lead appeared and retreated.

'I bought some new leads for you and cleaned up the propelling mechanism, which had got a bit stuck. I'm sorry… I should have given it to you long ago… but…'

'Where on earth have you been?' she finally blurted.

'I was in prison for a while, I'm afraid.'

'Prison? How come?' Not another one, she thought. It's too bad of him. Poor Colonel Westwood: he must think this place is an ex-convict's rest home.

'It's a long story. There's been civil war in Ireland.'

'Yes, I read about that. But it's difficult for us over here to follow what's going on or to understand.' She hadn't been putting two and two together. She felt a fool. 'Do you think it's over?'

'A lull before a storm perhaps. I… I was court-martialled and jailed… for refusing to fight against my countrymen, basically.'

'You've come to the right place then.' She waved her hand across her face to stifle a giggle.

'The ponies? The Connemara mare? You kept them?'

She had forgotten how he breathed between phrases as if he weighed each one carefully before uttering. 'Yes, they're fine. Getting on a bit now.' She grasped his sleeve and tugged him across the bridge onto the island. 'Now remind me, please, what was that Rabindranath Tagore poem you once quoted to me… do you remember?'

'Have you not heard his silent steps?

He comes, comes, ever comes.

Was that the one you had in mind?'

'Yes, yes,' she said, 'That's it. But you've taken far too long about it. Are you not engaged yourself?' She let go of him and ran her forefinger along her collarbone. 'Sorry, I'm forgetting myself – how about a glass of champagne?' He nodded and followed her as she threaded her way between the trees.

'There now,' she said, while he stood regarding her, his gaze running over her hair, her face. It made her feel self-conscious. He must have noticed, because he said, 'I do indeed feel like a glass of champagne,' and he tipped back his head to knock the whole lot back. A whitethroat started singing in a tree nearby and he glanced up to look.

She felt there seemed to be too much to say, to know how to say any word of it. She felt a little giddy. Was it his closeness or was it the thought of a whole glass of champagne? Her heart was knocking a rhythm in her ears, thud, thud. Surely he could hear it?

'No,' he said at last, 'that engagement wasn't meant to be. I went back to break it off.'

'You can't believe... you can't even begin to understand what your being here means to me,' she said, trying to sound business-like. She was watching his every move. She realised that people might be looking at them. Florence would recognise him and rush across to speak to him at any moment. The other guests might be curious about his appearance. She decided she wasn't going to let herself worry.

'I think perhaps that I might...' he started, but his breath was slow, as if he might choke on his words. He wasn't looking at her now, as if he wanted to keep back what it was she might see in his eyes. Like the time on the beach with the horses.

'But you really can't,' she said briskly. 'Look, first we must show my brother the pencil and you must tell him how you came to have it. I want you to meet some people and tell them what you know happened to me. You're not in the Army any longer, are you? They all think I'm a lunatic, you see. They pretend they don't, but deep down they do. All of them. I shall have to introduce you to everyone, if you can bear it. Please, would you mind telling them that I have been telling the truth, that I'm not deluded, really I'm not, and never have been.' Her hand fluttered to her neck again. She flicked her gaze away, '... before you disappear again.'

'That might take some doing,' he blinked and bit his lip. His features creased as if they were stifling the urge to laugh, or to cry, she wasn't sure which. She couldn't catch his eye.

'One more thing, perhaps I should warn you... have you noticed that certain places let you see more clearly into the truth of things? Well, this is one of them. There's a tradition about this island: once you've set foot here things have a habit of coming out in the open.'

She heard the clatter of plates and cutlery, raucous laughter rising through the leafy twigs.

He picked up one of her hands in both of his, turned it over and said 'I can't...' and stopped. He looked down at her palm and continued, 'I'd been hoping against all hope that maybe you hadn't lost the only thing I left you.'

Her intake of breath was a shudder. She ought to be attending to the guests, circulating a bit. Lenny seemed to have stopped winding up the gramophone. 'Just so that you know, in case it's a surprise. That seems to be a general rule here, anyway.'

'A sort of touchstone.' He closed her fingers and weighed her hand briefly in his before giving it back. 'Does it work only on the island?'

'No, it's just the fact that one has been here. It sets things in motion. Whatever they might be. It's always been like this. For us. That's why I keep coming back.'

'And my clumsy steps led me to your island. I have been too silent. But I'm here ...'

Research

The Imperial War Museum allowed me to access their archive material and to make use of their extensive library. Their staff helped me to find books, including finding material on conscientious objectors. The Friends' House Library in Euston gave me access to their archive material and their library. The Army Medical Museum near Aldershot allowed me to use their library. Dartmoor Prison Museum displayed letters from conscientious objectors.

Books that helped me:

An Officer's Manual of the Western Front 1914-18, Conway Books 2008

Arthur, Max (ed) *Forgotten Voices of the Great War* Ebury Press 2003

Barbusse, Henri, *Under Fire* (translated from the French *Le Feu* 1916) Penguin Classics 2003

Bell, Julian (ed) *We did not fight* Cobden-Sanderson 1935

Bourke, Joanna, *An Intimate History of Killing* Perseus Books 1999

Brooke, Walter, (Brigadier) *Gladeye The War Horse* Collins 1939

Burgess, Alan, *The Lovely Sergeant* The Companion Book Club 1963

Coleman, Emily Holmes *The Shutter of Snow* (first pub. 1930) Dalkey Archive Press 1997

Cooper, Jilly, *Animals in War* Corgi 1984

Dakers, Caroline, *The Countryside at War 1914-18* Constable and Co. 1987

Ellsworth-Jones, Will, *We will not Fight* Aurum Press 2008

Galtrey, Sidney, *The Horse and the War* General Books 2010

Graves, Robert, *Goodbye to all That* (first pub. 1929) Penguin Classics 2000

Hislop, Ian (ed), *The Wipers Times* Little Books Ltd 2006

Holmes, Richard *Tommy* Harper Perennial 2005

Lawrence, Dorothy, *Sapper Dorothy* Leonaur Books 2010

McIntyre, Ben, *A Foreign Field* Harper Collins 2002

Manning, Frederic, *Her Privates We* (first pub. 1929) re-printed Serpent's Tail 1999

Wheelwright, Julie, *Amazons and Military Maids* Pandora Press 1989

Articles consulted:

'Diary of a World War One Veterinary Officer' Canvetjournal

'British Cavalry on the Western Front' by David Kenyon

'Evolution, regression, and shell-shock: emotion and instinct in theories of war neuroses, 1914-1918' by Tracey Loughran

'Story of Romsey Remount Depot' IWM archives.

Websites consulted:

Army Medical Services Museum *www.ams-museum.org.uk*

Imperial War Museum *www.iwm.org.uk*

Peace Pledge Union *www.ppu.org.uk*

RSPCA *www.rspca.org.uk*

Blue Cross *www.bluecross.org.uk*

References: